Queendom of Chaos

This book is a work of fiction. Any references to historical events, real people, or real places are used fictitiously. Other names, characters, places, and events are products of the author's imagination, and any resemblance to actual events, places, or persons, living or dead, is entirely coincidental.

ISBN: 979-8-9858109-0-5 | ebook

ISBN: 979-8-9858109-1-2 | Paperback

ISBN: 979-8-9858109-2-9 | Hardcover

Library of Congress Control Number: 2022903540

Developmental edit by Dr. Plot Twist

Copyedit by Kimberly Cannon

Proofread by Judy Zweifel

Cover by Hannah Sternjakob

First printing, 2022

www.meganaldridge.com

Queendom of Chaos

MEGAN ALDRIDGE

To my husband

my heart is yours forever

I can do all things through Christ who strengthens me

— PHILIPPIANS 4:13

CONTENT WARNING

This book is intended for adults and includes elements of violence, racism, adult language, and sexual situations.

MORTA
ECATE
FORE
Ma
Forest's Edg
MONTES
MOUNTAINS
PHAS RIVER
PEDRO LAK

TAEGAIA
LAKE FOLTI
The Grower Land
BLESSED IRIS
KE
GANA
Bhazi
THE GARDEN
Lady of the Golden Blade
BHAZI LAKE
EMPIRE OF THE MOTHER
Vastraht
The Temple of Demeter
R
Lemos
THE OLY-MOUNTAINS
ITE SEA

PROLOGUE

Water crawled inch by inch, pulling itself onto the bridge and slithering through the village streets. The swell turned violent, slamming people down in its path. It barreled into homes, clutching anything within its reach and dragging it out to the streets. Dwellings crumbled as people sprinted for higher ground. Too few reached the hill's peak as water devoured the tops of fir trees.

"No!" the young girl gasped.

Her mother laughed. "It's all right, little one. I can stop reading if you're too scared."

The girl curled up to her mother. "No, it's okay." She scooched even closer, placing her mother's arm around her. "Ready."

The girl's mother smiled before returning to the book:

Villagers plunged their arms into the merciless river,

reaching for the hands of people rushing by that grabbed for anything outside the raging waters. Women screamed as loved ones disappeared beneath the surface, dragged away by the current and swallowed whole.

The three goddesses laughed at the little humans scurrying about and screaming as the river washed so many of them away. Amphitrite adjusted her crown of seashells and jewels and clanked her glass with Demeter's. "This was an inspired idea."

"Truly," Demeter replied, sweeping her golden tresses from her shoulder. "I can't believe it took us so long to finally do this. It's even more fun than I thought it would be." She beamed and turned to face her sister. "What do you think, Hecate?"

Hecate scoffed. "I think you both waited too long. These humans are softer than the old ones. I'm not sure they'll be able to handle it." Hecate put on her best pouty face, though it could never work as well as Demeter's baby cheeks and wide eyes. Hecate's narrowed brows and stern face worked better for intimidation than anything else, so she returned to her usual annoyed look.

"Nonsense," Amphitrite said. "These will work just fine for us. I'm having fun already." Hecate rolled her eyes, and Amphitrite continued. "Oh, lighten up, dear sister. Enjoy the show. It's about to happen!"

The three goddesses huddled together, peering down from Olympus over the balcony ledge. They waited impatiently as the wave built higher, blotting out the sun and obstructing their view of everything below. The deafening crash of the wave thundered around them as it submerged the villages. When the water receded, a smile crept onto each goddess's face. Their plan had worked—the only remnant of the villages being a large hollow in the earth.

Demeter sprang up from the bench, almost knocking over the bottle of wine on the railing. "We did it!"

The goddesses joined hands and jumped together, rejoicing in their triumph. When they finally calmed down, they picked up their glasses and went over the plan again.

"How long should we give them?" Demeter asked.

Amphitrite replied, "Let's give them some time to adjust. They've had a great upset. We don't want to frighten them further."

The two goddesses nodded in agreement. Amphitrite was always best at making important decisions.

Hecate spoke. "One more round, then we will greet them in their new home, far from this world." She winked at her sisters. "Our little secret." Hecate grabbed the bottle and poured them each another glass as they giggled to themselves.

Once the goddesses had finished off their drinks, it was time for the next step. They joined hands and set off for the far side of the universe. Sparks rained behind the goddesses as they soared through space. Just before their arrival, they unbound their hands so each could make an entrance into the new world.

Amphitrite, goddess of the seas, plunged deep into the ocean. She grabbed on to a dolphin, riding it to shore on a wave fifty feet high. Her jewels and skin glistened in the water.

The humans stopped their frantic scrambling to marvel at her arrival. When she stepped foot onto the sand, she kissed the dolphin, thanking him, and he swam back to sea. Amphitrite gazed upon the humans she and her sisters had brought to this new world. The crowd stared back from a distance, not daring to come closer to the power that exuded from such a being. Some dropped to their knees as they recognized the sea goddess.

Before a word could be spoken, the ground quaked, and the crowd screamed out in terror. They dispersed, until they realized they had nowhere to go. They grabbed whatever was near—a tree, a rock, even a loved one—until the ground settled. A stalk shot out of the soil, reaching one hundred feet into the air, adorned on top with the goddess of harvest herself, Demeter. The stalk bowed to lower the goddess beside her sister, who welcomed her with a simple nod. When Demeter stepped off her stalk, it sprung back up and turned into roses, showering the humans in white petals. The crowd stared bewildered at the goddesses. But the sisters did not look back. Instead, they looked to the skies.

Day instantly turned to night, and a large violet moon rose in the sky. The air became thin, and a chill descended on the crowd, a collective shiver sent up their spines. As the beam from the moon kissed the beach, Hecate—goddess of the night, moon, and magic—rode it down to complete the trinity sisterhood. Once her toes met the sand, daylight returned, and the humans exhaled a breath of relief.

Side by side, the goddesses walked toward the cowering humans. Three brave souls stepped forward. The largest of them spoke.

"What is the meaning of this? Where are our homes?" He motioned to the empty land around him that had once contained the flourishing villages they had built by hand.

"And what have you done with our land? And the skies?" the second man said.

A young woman chimed in, "We never settled on a beach. And the sun is not blue. The clouds are not pink."

The crowd nodded their agreement with the three but didn't dare speak a word as the goddesses looked among them.

Amphitrite lifted her hand. "We have made you a new home, a new world."

The first man spoke again, "A new what?" He stepped toward the goddesses; his hands balled into tight fists.

"Oh hush," Hecate said. "What was so great about the old one? This one is going to be much more fun."

"How's that?" the man asked.

"Because this one is all about us," Demeter said with a smug look on her face.

The crowd murmured among themselves. The young woman stepped forward, crossing her arms. "How is this world about you, Demeter?"

Demeter laughed. "Because the only goddesses you'll be worshipping are us."

A voice from the crowd broke through. "Never!"

Several humans chanted in agreement, though most only cowered.

The goddesses did not waver, but the skies turned dark, the ground shook, and the waters rose. Children screamed, and mothers comforted them with anticipation of the end. Just as quickly as the threat of death loomed over them, it retreated.

The large man yelled out to the goddesses, "You cannot win our affections with your threats!"

The goddesses paused, turning away from the humans and discussing the matter among themselves.

"Perhaps they will not give in to fear," Amphitrite said.

"We don't want their fear; we want their love, their adoration," Hecate said.

"Then maybe that man is right. If we want love and adoration, then that is what we must give. Agreed?" Demeter said.

The three goddesses nodded and turned back to address the crowd. "We apologize for frightening you and your children. All we wanted was your love. We do not consider ourselves goddesses of hate. For our indiscretion, we each have a gift for you all, for this new world."

The young woman called out, "That's it? An apology and a gift fix what you've done here?"

The crowd nodded their agreement.

The sisters stood stunned. They'd done everything right. Why wouldn't these humans accept their new lives and praise them for it?

Hecate rolled her eyes and stepped forward in a huff. "Enough!" She held up her hands, waves of blue energy flowing and dancing around her arms. Many of the humans cowered and fell back with a gasp. In one quick motion, Hecate cast her arms out wide and sent the energy from her being into the sky. It exploded in a flash of light, and flecks of blue dust rained over the humans and the land. Hecate turned on her heel and walked back to her sisters, who stared at her with brows raised. With a quick smile, she turned back to them to watch her work in action.

The humans' faces softened before they each knelt before the goddesses.

Demeter whispered out of the corner of her mouth, "You did it."

Amphitrite smiled and looked toward the other goddesses. "Let's finish what we started, my sisters."

Demeter stepped toward the crowd and extended her hand. The young woman, who had spoken earlier, hesitated a moment, then joined hands with the goddess.

"For this land, I give everlasting prosperity and life. And for your bravery to speak for the people, I grant you command over the land. A queen among men. Your family shall be granted the same favor, your lineage shall bear this responsibility for all of time."

The woman bowed to Demeter. "I accept this honor, Demeter. We shall worship you as our truest goddess in our new home. Thank you."

Hecate stepped forward, offering her hand to the second brave man. "For your world, I grant magic, woven with the fertility of the land. You will be granted favor as well, and your family under the same conditions, with rule over all magic entails."

The man bowed, accepting his new role, and naming Hecate his family's truest goddess.

Amphitrite offered her hand to the large man. "I will grant you and your family the same stature and responsibilities in this new world. You will have command in the sea."

The man wrinkled his brow.

"I am granting you this." Amphitrite guided the man to the edge of the water, laid her hands on his shoulders, and motioned for him to step in. Once his feet hit the water, his legs turned to fins. He was a merman—a king of the sea. He bowed to Amphitrite. "Thank you, Amphitrite, truest goddess to our home of the sea."

The goddesses turned back to speak to the crowd. "Find the others on the far side of this world and tell them what has happened here," Amphitrite said. "Use these gifts to build new homes." The humans shouted their thanks to the goddesses, whose hearts filled with love and joy they had long been searching for.

The goddesses left their new world to return home to Olympus, keeping their little secret all to themselves and never returning.

But any time one of them felt a twinge of loneliness in their heart, they looked across the universe to that small world they'd created, where those humans had kept their promises and built temples honoring only them.

The young girl snored as her mother closed the book, kissed her on the forehead, and quietly walked out of the room.

CHAPTER ONE

Frogs hopped along the edge of the lake. Their splashes blended with the chirping crickets, nearly drowning out the hiss and whistle of the passing locomotive. Even after nightfall, the heat from the southern summer left beads of sweat under Sam's shirt.

He swatted at the mosquito that pricked his neck, then went back to reading the letter in his hand while he waited for Annabelle, hoping she'd been able to sneak out to meet him safely. The thought of her walking the streets alone after dark worried him, but the women's boarding house stood much too far away on days he was set up at the market.

Sam's brows rose at the words in front of him, a laugh escaping his lips.

"What's so funny?"

The delicate voice bade Sam to spin around. Annabelle stood directly in front of him, showing off her breathtaking smile. Her face glistening in the moonlight emptied his head from all other thoughts. He could manage no more than to stare at her sparkling blue eyes and freckles—like stars in the sky.

"Belli!" Sam jumped up to embrace her. "Nothing. I just got this interesting letter."

"Oh?" A giggling Annabelle kissed Sam's cheek. "What's that, now?"

"Remember Jimmy? He worked down at the docks but moved north to follow that Du Bois fella?"

Annabelle nodded.

"Well, he sent me this." Sam handed the paper to Annabelle. "Read on the back page."

Annabelle tilted the letter to read in the moonlight. "I met her, the woman of my dreams. I know I've only been gone a few weeks, but this is true love. Mary is—"

"After that," Sam insisted.

Squinting at the paper, Annabelle continued, "Professor Du Bois has officially formed the group, calling us the Niagara Movement. The mission is equal rights for us Black folk. I know you lost hope in that after what happened to your family, but this time, it feels different. I think this may be the start of a better future.

"You need to come up here, Sam. Big things are happening, and we can finally get you a lady. Mary has a sister . . ." The rest she read in silence. "Oh, Sam. This is wonderful!" She threw her hands around his neck. "Do you think it's true?"

Sam shrugged. "Jimmy's no sucker, except for being fooled in thinking I don't already have a beautiful lady." He twirled Annabelle around as if to show her off, then turned to speak to no one but the lake. "Isn't she stunning?"

Pretty as a peach, his mama would say.

Annabelle laughed. "Ain't that the point? We would've been doing something wrong if someone knew about us." Her tone shifted more serious. "But really, Sam, maybe we don't have to run away. If things are changing—"

"Things ain't changing that fast. Don't be duped into thinking anything will happen in the South. Folks around here don't care about movements for people like me. They'll be the last in this country to do what's right."

Annabelle sighed. "You're right. I was just hoping . . ."

"I know, my sweet Belli." The urge to comfort her took over —he grabbed her by the waist and pulled her close. Looping her arms through his, she settled into his chest.

Sam swayed side to side, carrying Annabelle with him. A smile snuck across his face as he imagined them in the middle of a dance hall, moving with the slow melody of a piano and violin. In his mind, they didn't have to hide—they were free to listen to the local musicians and enjoy a few drinks before heading home together. Annabelle would insist on him doing a real dance, and he'd object like always. *My feet don't pick up the music right,* he'd say.

She had tried to teach him to dance for so long; it was almost embarrassing how he couldn't get it down. The thought made Sam let out a breath of laughter.

Another splash pulled him back to reality, the dream slipping between his fingers. He held Annabelle tighter. A droplet of sweat trailed down between his shoulder blades, collecting in a pool. He didn't mind the damp spot growing on his lower back. As long as Annabelle was in his arms, he'd put up with a little extra perspiration.

Sam closed his eyes to take in the smell of the surrounding woods, letting the sharp scent of pines envelop him. After a few breaths, the fragrance turned sweet. Sam swept Annabelle's pearly tresses to one side so he could nuzzle his head on her shoulder. The scent changed from pines to soap, and he welcomed it. He could never afford such a luxury.

When the dance ended, Sam smiled as Annabelle kicked off her boots and removed her stockings to dip her feet into the lake. She hiked up her skirt to keep it out of the water, taking care to keep it below her knees. The moonlight bounced off of her pale feet.

Laughing to himself, Sam joined her in the water and watched his dark brown feet disappear in the lake alongside hers, slipping his arm around her shoulders and holding her hand. His toes waded, side to side, under the surface, and he was thankful for the small bit of relief from the heat. Sam wouldn't miss anything about Charleston, except their lake.

A slight tilt of his head allowed Sam to take in Annabelle's half smile as she stared out at the water. "What are you thinking about, Belli?" Sam playfully nudged Annabelle as he planted tiny kisses on the nape of her neck.

The gesture elicited a giggle as Annabelle leaned into his nibbles. "I can't believe we're leaving tomorrow—we finally won't have to hide. Not everyone will be thrilled with it, but at least away from here, we'll have a chance." Annabelle squeezed Sam's hands tight and sighed. "With the way I grew up, I never thought I would find happi—"

A flash momentarily blinded Sam as white consumed everything around him. All at once, everything went black, and agony surged through his body. A ringing started in the distance, intensifying to the point where Sam was sure his ears would explode. He cried out as another flash of white sparked in his eyes.

The pain was gone.

When he could see again, Annabelle stood a few paces from where they had been sitting. With all color absent from her cheeks, she stared at him expressionless.

A shiver from the abnormal chill in the humid southern air took over, and his feet were completely dry. The look on Annabelle's face twisted his stomach as he stared at his hands. Horrified by the blood painting his arms, he refused to look down again.

Annabelle ran to Sam and collapsed onto her knees in front of him. "Sam, oh deary me, you're all right! I thought you were gone." Tears streamed down Annabelle's face.

An explanation for the terrors refused to come to mind. He sprinted to the water, desperately trying to scrub the blood from his hands. A quick look at his body settled his nerves; he wasn't bleeding from anywhere. The sobs cutting through the air grabbed his attention, and he looked back to Annabelle. "What do you mean? I'm right here. I'm fine."

Annabelle opened her mouth, but only air came out. Shaking it off, she tried again, the words coming out in quavers, "There was a giant flash of light, and you disappeared."

The world went silent as Sam searched for the right words. Any words. "What?"

Erratic breaths consumed Annabelle, and she gripped her stomach while falling to her side, seemingly unable to hold herself up.

Oh no, Belli, not again. Sam rushed to her side. "It's okay; I'm right here. Everything's all right." He put his hand on her trembling back, then reached for her hands. "Shh." Once Annabelle met his eyes, he took deep breaths, waiting for her to copy him. "Just look at me, Belli. Only me."

Annabelle squeezed Sam's hands tight. "I can't breathe. I can't breathe." Her eyes welled with fear as she choked out the words.

One thing always helped Annabelle when she became overwhelmed. "I can do all things . . ."

Annabelle looked up at Sam with crumpled brows. He squeezed her hands and nodded with encouragement.

With a shaky voice, she finished the verse, ". . . through Christ who strengthens me." The two repeated the mantra three more times before Sam went silent, letting the sounds of the night take over.

Several minutes passed before Annabelle matched Sam's slow breaths. She peered up into his eyes, managing to stop the tears, and calmed.

After a few more moments of staring at one another, and sure Annabelle had gotten through the worst of it, Sam spoke. "What happened?"

Annabelle stumbled over her words, "I don't know. I was sitting against you with your arms around me, then there was a flash, and you were gone. I didn't know what to do. I started to run for help, but then there was another flash, and you were there again, right where you were before."

That didn't make a lick of sense. All he could remember was pain. He couldn't possibly have disappeared, right? He pushed the thought from his mind and placed his hand gently on Annabelle's cheek, his thumb brushing at her freckles. A single tear fell from Annabelle's eye, and Sam gently kissed it away. He didn't know what happened, couldn't possibly begin to understand it, but that wasn't what Annabelle needed to hear. "I'm fine now. We're okay." Sam helped Annabelle to her feet and wrapped his arms around her, stroking her back until she settled against him, her breathing back to normal.

"Maybe we should have the doctor take a look at you," Annabelle said.

"What for?" Hiding the fear would be easier if he understood what had happened. "I'm not hurt, and no good can come from us going into town together. We've made it this far without getting caught; we just need to make it one more night. The doc can't do anything for me. I'm fine." Sam gazed back at the lake. "Let's just sit here a while longer. It's the last time we're going to see this place. Let's enjoy it." At that moment, he wanted nothing more than to forget everything that had happened, to go back to holding his love by the water.

"You're right."

The pair sat back down at the lake's edge, Annabelle against Sam's chest. The sounds of the night cloaked them once more while Annabelle stroked her fingers along Sam's forearms. A welcomed touch.

A fiery sting shot through his arm, and he bit his lip to stifle a scream as he recoiled.

Annabelle bolted upright. "What's wrong?"

After pulling back his sleeve, he stared in disbelief.

"What is it, Sam?" The tremble in her voice worsened.

Sam shook his head as he lowered his arm to Annabelle. Emblazoned on his forearm, where there should have only been scars from tending to the crops, was a luminescent mark in the shape of three roses, almost glowing against his dark brown skin.

Annabelle gasped and put her hands over her mouth.

The struggle with whether to focus on the anomaly itself or the unbearable pain battled in his mind. Keeping his composure seemed impossible as he gripped his arm. *God, what is happening?*

Before he could think what to do next, Annabelle grabbed Sam's hand and pulled him toward the lake. Sam resisted, but she kept pulling. It puzzled him to think what she was doing until she submerged his arm in the water. A rush of pain, followed by a wave of relief, washed over him.

After all they'd been through, he should have known better than to doubt the brilliant woman in front of him. Shaking the water from his arm, Sam grabbed her by the waist.

Color rushed to her cheeks when he kissed her forehead.

"I love you," Sam said.

"I love you, too."

The words always made his heart smile, no matter how many times he'd heard them. "Maybe we should call it a night. Tomorrow is a pretty important day. We both need the sleep."

"Are we really going to just ignore this?" She pointed to Sam's arm.

A shrug was all he could muster. "Let's talk on the way?"

The sigh confirmed her frustration. "Yeah."

They laced their fingers together and strolled back to town.

As they left the lake, Sam tried to ignore the hooded figure watching them from the tree line.

Annabelle continued her deep breathing as they walked down the alleyways toward her home. She'd grown accustomed to strolling the dim roads while walking with Sam and used the same path traveling alone in the dark. Being spotted alone on the streets in the middle of the night without a proper explanation of where she was going couldn't happen—she would look like a lady of the night.

Their relationship had been a secret ever since they'd met ten years before. If they were caught together, it would mean death for them both. But Annabelle had stopped thinking about that long ago, or the thought would've consumed her every waking moment. Every morning and night, she thanked God for the man next to her—she couldn't imagine her life without him.

Annabelle leaned into Sam as they rounded the next corner. Even though it was easily the hottest day of the year, Annabelle ignored the heat in favor of Sam's arms.

The events of the evening raced through her mind, but it wasn't safe to talk yet. To avoid suspicions, at the heart of the town, Annabelle released Sam and walked several paces ahead. One more street to go before they could breathe. Before they could make a sound.

Darting up the street, Sam offered his hand in assistance. Only a few more steps and they'd be safe behind the gate and under the steel staircase attached to the apartment building.

As Annabelle pulled her leg through the gap, she tripped on a lid that had rolled away from its trash bin, falling into Sam's arms. Covering her lips stifled the slight squeal. Sam raised his eyebrows to Annabelle, asking if she was all right, and she nodded back to him.

The slow creak of metal cut through the air, and the pair turned around in horror as two bins tipped over in the alleyway. The cans made a deafening clatter in the silent night, and Sam and Annabelle had no choice but to run for cover against the nearest building wall.

Several windows thrust open above them, the groans of upset men turning Annabelle's stomach upside down. Deep breaths and prayers kept her calm as she looked to Sam, whose smile and big, round eyes reassured her as always.

A woman's voice emerged. "What is it, Harold?"

"Just an animal digging through the garbage again. Go back to bed."

Once the windows closed, Sam grabbed Annabelle's hand and pulled her around the corner. They ran until they knew they were safe and let out sighs of relief. Though they had done the routine for years, it was no less of a risk each time.

Sam spoke first, "I know how worried you are about all of this, but nothing has changed. This mark on my arm . . . we can't dig any further."

Annabelle bit at her lip. "It's not normal, Sam. Something here ain't right. People don't just disappear and then get burning marks on their arms. And where did all that blood come from?"

"I ain't saying it's normal. What I'm saying is we have to let it go. Besides this mark on my arm, I feel totally fine."

Annabelle narrowed her eyes, and she could have sworn she saw the slightest twitch on Sam's face.

"I promise, Belli. But we can't go to anyone in town. There is no one we can trust."

"What about Helen? She's always been nice to me. Her

mother was a nurse; perhaps she can . . ." The downturn of Sam's eyes made her stop.

"I know you mean well, but Helen doesn't like me. Any time I see her around, she pretends like I ain't even there."

"But she's always been so kind to the school children and me."

"Well, you aren't Black. I'm telling you, you're barking up the wrong tree with that one." Sam awkwardly shifted, pinching the bridge of his nose, and let out a sigh. "Look, we leave tomorrow, and then we can leave this behind too, as if it never happened. Please, can we just forget about this?"

Annabelle stared at her feet. Not having any answers gutted her. "What matters to me is that you're all right. I trust you."

Sam kissed her forehead. "Thank you."

In all the commotion, Annabelle hadn't realized how close they were to the boarding house.

She had requested the only private room when she moved in, as a means to accommodate her students without disturbing the rest of the girls, but not having to sneak by other girls in the hallway or tiptoe past their rooms made the meetings with Sam easier. Though she knew better than to ever have him inside.

Annabelle turned to Sam, who still held her hand, and reached up to kiss him goodnight. She was tall for a woman, nearly a head above the others, and with the help of her boots, only had a few inches between her and Sam's lips.

"Goodnight, my love." Annabelle smiled before she snuck another kiss, unable to resist the feel of his full lips against her own.

"Goodnight, Belli. I will meet you here before sunrise, as planned. I can't wait. I love you."

"I love you." Annabelle turned and walked back toward her room, leaving Sam to walk home alone in the dark.

AFTER TAKING ANNABELLE HOME, Sam sat on his lumpy, hay-stuffed bed, examining the scar etched into his forearm. *Where did this come from?*

He got up from his bed and paced the room, trying to think of any explanation as to why Annabelle had been so scared, why he had a scar, and why, for some reason, he couldn't remember any of it. Arm still throbbing from the burn, Sam grabbed some water to help cool it off again. It took only two large steps to get from one side of the room to the other.

When he leaned over the pail, a hooded figure reflected on the surface. Overcome with shock, Sam fell backward, hitting the pail and sending it into a spin. The water dripped into a puddle next to him.

"Who are you? Get out of my house!"

The cloaked figure removed his hood, revealing a short man with slicked-back brown hair. "Please, there is no need to be afraid. I am a friend."

Sam slowly stood, clenching his jaw and curling his fists. "I'm not going to say it again: leave my house!"

"Then who is going to tell you what that scar on your arm means?"

Sam's hand instantly went to his arm, wondering how this man could possibly know anything about the scar. "I don't care about the scar. It was a fluke, a flash of lightning. Now get out!" His theory didn't hold any water, but it was all he had.

"I cannot leave—I made a promise to you. I am here to help Annabelle."

At the mention of Annabelle's name, Sam swung. This had to be a trick. He threw his right arm straight for the man's face, but his hand went through him. "What the . . .? This is the Devil's work!" He swung again. This time, Sam slipped on the puddle of water, and his entire body went through the man.

"As I said, I am a friend. I am not here to harm you, but I cannot stay long. Projecting myself to your world is difficult, and I fear she will soon find me." The man kept glancing over his shoulder nervously, but Sam only saw the empty wall behind him. "I come with a warning."

Sam barely heard the man speak, trying to figure out how he had just gone through a . . . man . . . ghost . . . projection? Powerless to make the man go away on his own, he had no choice but to listen. "Who are you?"

The figure smiled. "I am your friend, Keres."

THE HOT NIGHT air gave no mercy as Annabelle hummed to herself, navigating back through the streets with expertise, but she enjoyed the song of the crickets as she neared Sam's home. Seeing the streets of Charleston for the last time made her a bit sentimental. After all, it was the only home she'd ever known. She had never imagined missing anything about South Carolina. It was the place her parents had abandoned her as a baby, where she had to figure out the whole world on her own. Well, until she met Sam.

That day at the orphanage, she had peered out the window

as Sam arrived. There was something special about him; his gentleness drew her in. Though Sam was quite strong and large for a child, he spoke with such tenderness—his soulful brown eyes gave him away.

Excitement pushed her toward Sam's house, though she expected him to be asleep by now. When she'd arrived home, a delivery of the newest addition to the Oz story, *The Marvelous Land of Oz,* sat on her doorstep. It had been a year since its release, and she'd spent all that time trying to acquire a new copy, but she didn't have the money to spare. Though now, it meant more than just reliving her and Sam's favorite world—she would give this copy to the students at the schoolhouse as a parting gift.

But first, she wanted to bring it to Sam. Of all the wondrous books they'd read together, they held *The Wonderful Wizard of Oz* most dear, discovering it Sam's last year before he'd aged out of the orphanage. Oz had become an escape for them.

Sam read more than anyone she had ever met. It was part of what made him such a wonderful poet. In case inspiration struck, he carried a little notebook with him everywhere he went, and she considered herself blessed when she noticed a sketch of herself inside the front cover. She loved being his muse—that's what he'd called her. It made her feel like the most loved woman in the world. His crooked smile every time he became entranced in another poem made her giggle.

The front door stood as a reminder of how close she dared to get to Sam's house. After she dropped off the book and gave Sam the morning to read it, she would take it to the schoolhouse on their way out of the city.

As she bent down to lean the book against the door, the light from inside caught her eye. Curiosity overcame her, and she peeked in to see what had kept Sam up so late.

A cloaked man she'd never seen before stood in the center of the room, much shorter than Sam, with perfectly groomed brown hair and deep olive skin.

Sam always had his window open, and she could hear everything they were saying.

"KERES? I don't know any Keres." Sam's blood heated.

"I need you to believe me, to remember. You cannot run away with Annabelle. The Dark Queen is searching for you. She figured out a way around the spell. She is going to kill you."

Someone burst through the front door.

"Sam, what's happening?"

Sam balled his fists and wrinkled his brows. "Annabelle? What are you doing here?" He released his knuckles.

"What am I doing here? What is *he* doing here?" Annabelle looked at the stranger, tilting her head and raising a brow. "Who are you?"

"I am Keres. But I do not have time to do this all again. Sam, you and Annabelle are in danger. You need to find the oracle; he can help you get back here. He can work miracles." Keres pointed to a spot on a map that appeared out of nowhere.

Before Sam or Annabelle could react, Keres charged at Sam, who instinctively stumbled back into the wall behind him. He went straight through Sam's chest, but when Sam turned around, Keres had already disappeared, taking the light with him.

Sam and Annabelle searched for a match. Once the candles near the bed and on the table were lit, Sam looked at Annabelle with only confusion. Annabelle sat on Sam's bed, and he knelt on the floor in front of her.

"What just happened? Are we going crazy?" Annabelle buried her head in her hands.

"No, my love. I have an idea." Sam rubbed at his chest. "I think maybe we were struck by lightning tonight, and it's making us see some impossible things. That is the only possible explanation." Something was wrong, but that was the last thing she needed to hear. His gut churned, unable to stomach lying to Annabelle.

"Are you feeling all right? Did it hurt when . . ."

"I feel fine; I'm just a bit on edge, is all."

Annabelle looked into Sam's eyes and grabbed his hands. They were both shaking. "What if he's right? What if we really are somehow in danger?"

"Don't believe a word that . . . thing said. It's not possible to travel to another world because this is the only world. There is no magic, or Dark Queen, or any danger. Going to some lake a hundred miles away in . . ." Sam looked at the map. ". . . Savannah, ain't gonna show us anything other than we listened to our imaginations. Let's get some sleep, and tomorrow we can leave this place, just like we've always wanted." Sam stood, pulling Annabelle with him. He held Annabelle in his arms until she stopped shaking.

"You're right. We don't need to worry about anything other than leaving and going west tomorrow."

"That's it, Belli. Tomorrow, we can start a new life."

Annabelle sniffled and gazed up at Sam. "Can I stay?"

Sam hesitated. In all the uproar, he hadn't let it sink in that Annabelle was in his home. She'd never been inside before—they were careful never to be caught like that. "We really shouldn't . . ."

"We're leaving before sunrise. Please, I'm scared."

Sam couldn't send her back out into the night feeling frightened. "All right." His bed he gave to Annabelle, and he lay on the floor beside her. Before blowing out the candle, he caught a hint of a shadow on the floor in the corner of the room.

Walking over to pick up the book, Sam smiled to himself as he read the cover, then turned to Annabelle. "You got it." He hadn't realized Annabelle had already fallen asleep, so he sat back down and opened the book.

A message from Annabelle to the children decorated the inside cover. The children held a special place in Annabelle's heart. It would be hard for her to leave them behind, and she'd picked the perfect parting gift for them. Sam turned to page one and began reading, falling asleep with the book still open on his chest.

As he always did, Sam awoke before sunrise. Final preparations needed to be done for their big day. Though he didn't want to admit it, Annabelle staying the night made him glad. He didn't want to scare her any more than she already was, but he wasn't sure he would have been able to sleep without her there, not with everything that had been going on.

All he wanted was to build her a home and give her the

family she'd never had. He'd written two poems about sitting on the front porch in their rocking chairs, watching their grandchildren play in the fields as they held hands, living a truly blessed life.

With Annabelle sleeping peacefully in his bed, Sam stared at her snowy waves strewn over her face in a way that made him chuckle to himself. Quick to get dressed and ready, Sam looked around the room to see what needed to be done.

He grabbed a rag from the table and soaked up the rest of the water on the floor, then finished packing his belongings for their journey. Sure he had nothing else to do, Sam walked over to the chair and opened his notebook to a clean sheet.

That's odd. The last page in his notebook, which should have been blank, displayed a string of tally marks. *One, two . . . twenty-nine.* Unsure of how they'd gotten there, Sam ignored the marks and instead searched for a blank piece of parchment from somewhere else in the house.

After several minutes of scouring, Sam found a stack of unused papers under an old notebook. He didn't yet know what to say, but he owed the old man something.

Dear Mr. Anderson . . .

When he was just fourteen, Sam started working for Mr. Anderson—the year he left the orphanage. Mr. Anderson let Sam stay in the shack on the far side of the field from the main house, as long as Sam agreed to help keep the farm running and stay out of trouble. And any food Sam had helped grow that didn't sell became Sam's to eat. Besides Annabelle, Sam only had respect for one person in this town, and that was dear old Mr. Anderson.

Everyone else had treated Sam as less than human for no

reason other than he was Black. It stung that Sam couldn't give him a proper goodbye, but this was the best he could do without putting him and Annabelle in danger. He hoped Mr. Anderson would understand.

Once Sam finished his letter, he reached for the book Annabelle had brought. Then he grabbed a basket and left the house to do his final errands on the farm.

LIFTING the world would have been easier than Annabelle trying to open her eyelids. Exhaustion had its hold on her, and it had no plans of releasing her anytime soon. After everything that had happened the night before, she had sweat throughout her sleep. But now it all felt like a distant dream—the kind where mind and body were disconnected and the only way to watch everything happening was behind hazy, broken glass—and that's how she wanted to keep those memories.

A quick scan of the room showed Sam had left. Annabelle made her way over to one of the two chairs at the table to wait for him. When she sat down, she saw a note with her name on it.

My Belli,

I have gone to get us some food. I will return shortly, and we can begin the first day of the rest of our lives together.

And thank you for the book. It was wonderful. It made me feel fourteen again, falling in love with your big blue eyes and reading about fantastic adventures. You are so thoughtful.

I noticed your inscription and have already returned it to the children at the schoolhouse.

Love always,

Sam

His thoughtfulness brought a smile to her face. The map Keres had pointed to the previous night beckoned her over. A large circle drawn near a lake had the words *oracle* and *miracle* written next to it. Just the sight of it put the fear back into Annabelle, so she took the map down, crumpled it, and tossed it away. As she paced the room, her mood lightened with the whistling tune of Sam walking toward the house.

The door creaked as Sam pushed it open and quietly walked in with a basket full of fruits and vegetables from the field. "Good morning. I hope I didn't wake you."

"No, I've been up for a bit now." Annabelle nodded at the basket of food. "That looks delicious. Thank you for getting those."

"Of course." Sam set the basket on the table and leaned in to give Annabelle a kiss on her forehead. "So, are you all packed to go? After breakfast, we need to go grab your things before everyone wakes and notices us leaving."

"Yes, I'm all packed. I'll just need a few minutes at home to freshen up." The thought of knowing how close they were to leaving excited Annabelle.

"You sure you want to do this? Last chance to back out." Sam chuckled.

"Of course I want to do this. You are the love of my life. And what about you? It's not like you're getting a princess out of this." Annabelle laughed, thinking about the book Sam had read just that morning. "I don't have much to offer. I don't even know how to be a proper wife or mother." Annabelle's smile faded at the thought of her childhood.

"Annabelle, you are incredible. I know you will be everything I ever need because you already are. You are going to be a wonderful mother to our future children. I wouldn't choose anyone else, ever." Annabelle felt better as she stared into Sam's deep brown eyes—those eyes that always comforted her and told her everything would be all right, even if she didn't know how yet. Sam's kiss on the tip of her nose brought a smile back to her face.

The scar on Sam's arm refused to let go of her attention. "You should keep that covered so it doesn't get infected." The only logical place to look was the single drawer in the room, and when she pulled it open, to her delight, Sam kept a few scraps of fabric and scissors in the drawer, perfect for wrapping his arm.

"Thank you."

Glad she had thought to cover the scar, Annabelle smiled at Sam. It would make it easier to ignore for a time.

They enjoyed the rest of their breakfast together, then snuck back out to collect the rest of Annabelle's things. As they stepped through the gate, Sam stayed silent, but Annabelle noticed his glance back at the main house and the way his eyes flicked away just as quickly. They had to make their way through the city swiftly; the sun would be rising in the next hour, which meant that many of the city folks would be up along with it.

The timing had to be just right—if they were on the roads out of town at night, well, that would be much too suspicious.

Even though they'd gone through the plan a hundred times before, now that they were actually going through with it, Annabelle's stomach wouldn't stop turning over, and she knew how red her face was from the burning in her cheeks.

"We have a bit of time left before we leave. Would you like to go to our lake one last time?" Annabelle looked at Sam in excitement but was surprised to see his brows low and lips drawn tight. "Sam?"

Sam looked into Annabelle's eyes. "I'm sorry, but there's one more thing I have to do before we can leave."

THE TWO UNMARKED headstones hid among the field of goldenrods. The light of dawn shone over them, creating a sense of peace with its deep purple clouds hiding the rising sun. Sam stood over the graves, grateful Annabelle was at his side.

He choked back tears as he laid a single yellow flower on each plot. Sam hadn't visited the site since they were buried thirteen years prior. He couldn't bear to relive the memories, so he'd hidden them deep inside. This was his last chance to say goodbye. He wasn't sure what to say or what to do.

"Would you like me to say a prayer?" Annabelle's voice was soft and gentle.

Sam turned to her with tears welling in his eyes. This beautiful, thoughtful woman had chosen him, and he couldn't be more thankful for her gesture. He nodded and turned back toward the graves.

"Jesus said to her, 'I am the resurrection and the life . . .'"

Sam listened as Annabelle spoke words of faith and life over them. The morning breeze calmed his heart. When she was finished, he asked for a moment to say his final goodbyes, and she obliged, making her way back to the road to wait for him. Sam knelt on the ground and kissed each headstone, finally giving in to the tears. He stood and backed away to follow Annabelle. Before the graves were fully out of sight, he let go.

"Goodbye, David. Goodbye, Mama."

SAM STAYED across the road as Annabelle scurried into her room. She hurriedly washed her face, pulled up her hair, slipped into her best dress, and grabbed her already packed bag. She had to appear the part of a traveling woman, in case anyone asked questions.

Everything needed to be in its proper place, and one last glimpse in the mirror showed Annabelle had done well in her presentation. She grabbed her sunhat that hung from the mirror and put it on, adjusting it just so. Satisfied with her reflection, she took a final glance around the room and walked out the door.

When Annabelle came out of the house, Sam grabbed her bag. Having gone over the plan dozens of times, she had no apprehensions he knew his part well. He would play the role of her employee—at least until they reached a safe distance away from South Carolina. Annabelle looked at Sam, who gave her a reassuring smile, and knew they were ready.

They used the main roads this time—the fastest way out of town—and began what Annabelle thought would be the hardest part of their journey. As neither of them had a good excuse for traveling, they had no choice but to walk several stations away to buy the tickets. If Tulsa, the first stop, fell short, they could head up north, where plenty of mining jobs existed. A whole exciting life waited for them outside of the Deep South.

When Charleston was almost out of sight, Sam and Annabelle turned to look back at the city they'd called home for so long, just as the sun stretched over the horizon. Annabelle knew the enormity of what they were about to do, and they instinctively reached for the other's hand. With one more breath, they turned toward the west, a limitless land in front of them—their chance at true happiness.

Sam took one step and collapsed.

CHAPTER TWO

"Sam!" Annabelle dropped to Sam's side, holding his face as her world spun. "Sam, look at me!"

Sam was rigid, his body locked up, and he groaned through gritted teeth. "My heart . . . help!" He could barely get the words out, gripping his chest tight as his face turned a shade of purplish red.

Annabelle's eyes teared up, her breath irregular. "I don't know what to do, Sam. I don't know what to do . . ."

A portly man ran up from behind Annabelle. With all the commotion they were causing, it was no wonder someone had taken notice. "Ma'am, are you okay?"

"Sir, please, I don't know what happened." Annabelle moved aside so the man could see Sam on the ground, holding his hand tight.

As soon as the man laid eyes on Sam, his brows narrowed, and a vein popped out of his forehead.

The man latched on to Annabelle's hand. "Come, child. We needn't waste our time on *him.*"

"No, stop!" With a bit of struggle, Annabelle pulled herself free and ran back to Sam, holding his hand in hers. "I can't leave him."

The man put the pieces together, turning red as his eyes bounced between Sam and Annabelle.

He spat at Sam's feet, then turned to Annabelle. "There's the wrath of God for you, whore." The way he whirled around reminded Annabelle of a children's spinning top wobbling back over the hill he'd come from.

The hilltop made for a better vantage point, and she scanned the area in desperation to spot a house other than the one the man had just walked into. She needed help, and he wasn't about to give any.

His was the only house she could get to in a time that mattered, and she was running out of options to get Sam back into town. With the hope of someone else willing to help, Annabelle sprinted for the door. She pounded on the wood, calling out for aid.

No answer.

As Annabelle turned back toward Sam, a whining sound came from behind the house. Annabelle poked her head around back, where two horses puttered about.

No, you can't. It's not right. . . . But Sam needs help, and that man was so horrible, just like all the others . . .

Before she knew what she was doing, Annabelle walked the horses over to Sam, who still screamed in pain on the dirt road. "Sam, I can't get you up all by myself. I need you to help me get you onto the horse."

Sam's breathing went from shallow to deep, and he bit down on his lip while lifting a hand toward her. Annabelle grabbed Sam's hand and pulled on his large body as hard as she could. Somehow, she managed to get Sam to his feet. Then she turned to the horse, and to her surprise, the horse knelt for Sam.

"Good horsey . . ." Sam leaned onto the steed as Annabelle pulled him as far over its back as she was able. When Sam was secure, the horse stood, and Annabelle mounted the other.

Although Annabelle had only been on a mare once before, she would figure it out for Sam. As she had seen plenty of men do before, Annabelle grabbed the ropes around the horses' necks, and after a few failed attempts to go the right direction, guided the horses to the only doctor in town that she knew.

The shame of guilt washed over her as the portly man shouted in the distance behind them, screaming at her about his horses, and she urged them to go just a little bit faster. *God, forgive me.*

As they steered through the streets, Sam stopped making noises, and Annabelle's heart stopped, thinking the worst. She sighed a heavy breath of relief when she saw him breathing and wiped the tears that had already formed in her eyes. He must have passed out from the pain and the exertion of getting onto the horse.

"Hold on, Sam, we're almost to the doctor." Annabelle continued her deep breathing, trying her hardest to push out the rest of the world, to not let it consume her. She kept her gaze forward, focused on her breath, and quietly repeated her verse, ". . . who strengthens me."

As soon as Annabelle could see the doctor's home, she leapt off her horse and ran to the door, pounding over and over, shouting in hopes that the doctor was home. The door cracked open.

"Ms. Monroe?" The doctor stared at Annabelle in tired confusion; she must have just woken him. "What is the meaning of this?"

"Please, sir. Sam collapsed and needs your help. He passed out from the pain."

"Let me see." When the doctor's eyes landed on Sam, they went wide, darting between Sam and Annabelle. As he put the pieces together, he backed into his home. "I can't. Now go away before someone thinks I'm helping you!" He slammed the door in her face.

"No, please!" Annabelle dropped to her knees and buried her face into her palms. She sobbed uncontrollably. It wasn't long before Annabelle and Sam had drawn a crowd into the streets. People whispered to each other and drew the same conclusion as the doctor. Annabelle tried to hold the tears back as she looked at the people ambling toward them and saw a familiar face.

"Helen!" Helen was another teacher who Annabelle had grown close to over the last year. Annabelle ran to her friend. "Helen, I need you." She motioned over to Sam. "No one will help him, and I don't know what's wrong." Helen drew a hand over her mouth at the sight of Sam on his horse.

Finally, someone who would help.

Helen grabbed Annabelle's hands and started to pull her away from Sam.

"No, stop, he needs help!"

"The only person you should be worried about right now is yourself. Come, before anyone else sees you with that negro."

Annabelle gasped at the ugly words. "How can you say that!" Annabelle pulled back hard to release herself from Helen's grip. "I'm not going anywhere with you—you disgust me!" Resisting the urge to slap Helen's shocked face, she turned and made her way back over to Sam.

The crowd heated, quickly closing the gap between themselves and Annabelle while shouting unspeakable evils at Sam. Some of the men picked up speed with balled fists and furrowed brows.

She hurriedly got back onto her horse and guided her and Sam back to the road leading out of Charleston.

This time, she didn't look back as she started the journey west, praying she could find someone to help them along the way.

HOUSE AFTER HOUSE, town after town, she received the same words as from the first doctor and the same looks from townspeople. More than once, she'd had to run out of town, away from villainous men shouting racial epithets.

It had been a full day, and yet Sam had still not awoken. As scared and alone as she felt, she had to fight for him. No one else would.

Don't give up, Annabelle. Just one more town. Someone will help us there.

With nothing else to occupy her mind, Annabelle turned her thoughts to the peculiar events of the previous night. Sam had disappeared right before her eyes. Then that strange man, Keres, had appeared, speaking about some oracle. Was she going mad? No, it couldn't have been real—it was all a bunch of fiddle-faddle. Or lightning, as Sam had suggested. Annabelle pushed the thoughts away and continued on.

Night cast its shadows, revealing a soft glow of candle lights that signaled the next town. She prayed she would find one good soul to help Sam. She only needed one.

Annabelle noted the run-down town with their broken shacks for homes. She wondered if anyone would even be capable of helping them here. Townspeople sat outside their homes, and Annabelle almost cried with joy. They were all Black.

"Help, I need help! Is there a doctor somewhere?"

People looked at Annabelle like the stranger she was, seeming curious about the Black man on the horse beside her. The townspeople whispered to each other, and Annabelle had the sinking feeling she'd gotten back home. But then, an old man stepped forward.

"Bring him inside. I can help." The voice hit Annabelle like melted butter on a freshly made biscuit. An old Black man in tattered clothes stood on a nearby porch. Something about his crooked grin and kind eyes told Annabelle he would be able to help.

Tears filled Annabelle's eyes as she followed the man to his house, Sam in tow. She only hoped it wasn't too late to help him. Annabelle yanked Sam from his horse, and his eyes shot open.

"AHHHH!"

She and the old man struggled to take Sam inside and put him onto the table.

"MAKE IT STOP! MAKE IT STOP!" He sweat profusely but was cold to the touch, and he wouldn't stop shivering.

Annabelle sat in a chair next to Sam, crying from the heartbreak of Sam's pain, as well as the generosity of this stranger. But mostly, she cried because she was powerless to help him.

"Hold him down. He needs morphine for the pain," the doctor spoke sternly to Annabelle, who did as he instructed. He gave the medicine to Sam and grabbed a bottle of chloroform to put him to sleep.

"What's wrong with him, doctor?" Annabelle prayed the old man had an answer.

"We will have to wait until he is awake again. I knocked him out to give the pain medicine time to work. When he wakes up, he should be feeling a little better. Until then, all we can do is wait."

So, Annabelle waited, and waited, and waited some more. She had never prayed so hard in her life as she did while sitting in that room. She prayed thanks for the generosity of the doctor, Duke, for taking them in. She prayed for forgiveness for not pushing Sam more to go to the doctor in town when they were at the lake. Perhaps without the pressure of all the onlookers, the doc would have helped Sam. Annabelle had known something was wrong but let it go because Sam had asked. And she prayed for forgiveness for the anger toward Sam. Nothing beyond protecting her had ever been his intent, and without meaning to, resentment had crept over her as she watched him sleep on the table.

She needed to set her mind elsewhere.

Annabelle took to tidying up to pass the time, folding and

refolding the few clothes into their bags, rearranging more than once, but none of it was enough of a distraction. She contemplated changing out of her dress but couldn't be away that long in case Sam woke up. Feeling utterly helpless as she sat in the chair watching Sam sleep, she stepped out onto the porch for some air.

The breeze was a welcome relief on her sweat-soaked skin. Annabelle made her way to the steps and sat down, hugging the railing to keep herself up from the exhaustion. She closed her eyes for what she told herself would only be a moment, but when she opened them again, a small crowd had gathered, all eyes on her, whispering among themselves. Annabelle slowly stood and walked around back to check on the horses, where she found a young boy petting them and feeding them hay.

"Hello," Annabelle said. The boy glanced up at Annabelle and quickly backed away from the horses. "I'm sorry, I didn't mean to frighten you. I just wanted to say thank you. You're so kind to think of them while I was away." The young boy hesitated, then gave Annabelle a shy grin before running back to his home. Annabelle smiled after the boy, then made her way back into Duke's and sat at Sam's side.

She stared at him until her eyes became too heavy to hold open.

A groan nearby woke Annabelle in an instant. She looked out the window at the sun beaming in. Somehow, she'd slept the entire night, but her body felt as though it had been just a few minutes. Sam groaned again, and Annabelle jumped to her feet, yelling for the doctor.

Duke hobbled in from the next room—the only other room in the small shack-like home. He grabbed Sam's hand and spoke gently. "Sam, my name is Doctor Abbott, but you can call me Duke. Annabelle brought you here on a horse after you collapsed. Do you remember that?"

Sam looked around the room, locking eyes with Annabelle, who gave him an encouraging smile. "I don't remember anything but pain. I could hardly breathe. It still hurts a little . . ." Sam turned his focus to the doctor. "What's wrong with me?"

"Well, now that you're awake, I can start on some tests. Let's start with trying to sit up."

Sam sat up with the help of both Annabelle and Duke. Duke ran test after test with Sam's body. He had him perform different exercises, listened to his chest, and poked and prodded all over his body, scribbling page after page onto a notebook with a frantic look in his eyes.

When the tests were complete and Sam had time to rest, Duke came back with his diagnosis.

Annabelle stood. "Well?"

"I'm afraid it's not good news, my dear."

Annabelle's heart sank.

"After listening to his body and giving the morphine time to do its work, I only know one thing: Sam's heart is failing, and other parts of his body are shutting down because of it. I'm sorry to say I have no idea why. I'm stumped."

Annabelle slowly sat, a million things running through her head. "So, how do we fix it?"

"I don't know what's causing it. I can't help him. The only thing that's worked is managing his pain, but the heart is no good. My prediction is he doesn't have much longer before his body shuts down completely."

Her world spun once more as the walls holding it up crumbled. His hand on her shoulder brought a sliver of comfort, but when she stared into his eyes for reassurance, she instead found the one look she couldn't bear—everything would not be all right. "Sam, I can't lose you. I don't know how to live without you."

Sam closed his eyes and shifted in his seat. Annabelle knew he was struggling with what to say. He clenched and released his fists before opening his mouth. "It's all right, Annabelle." Sam's voice quivered, and he tried to cover it with a cough, but Annabelle noticed.

She knew Sam well enough to know he was full of life, that this wasn't easy for him. Her mind raced, trying to find the right answers.

"No, we can't accept that." Annabelle looked to Duke. "What can I do for him?"

Duke sighed. "Darling, it would take a miracle."

Annabelle snapped upright. She ran around the room, packing up their bags. "Duke, help me get Sam on the horse."

"Annabelle, where are y'all going?"

"We're going to find the oracle."

CHAPTER THREE

The road behind them was nothing but dust kicked up by hooves. Annabelle adjusted her hat to keep its shadow on her neck. She wiped her forehead with her handkerchief, praying a gust of wind would grace them at any moment.

"Please, stop. I need to rest." Sam struggled to get the words out. He could no longer keep himself upright on his horse after days of traveling.

Annabelle had been pushing them to get to the oracle, barely giving them time to sleep or eat. She hated the wear she was putting on Sam, but she feared what would happen if they didn't rush.

"I think you're right. Let's sit here for a spell. But then we need to get you to someone who can help." The aches in her body begged her to stop, no matter how much she hated to admit it.

Pulling the horses to the side of the road, Annabelle helped

Sam down and leaned him against a boulder, then went to search for food and water.

With little provisions to be found, Annabelle raced back to Sam, not wanting to leave him alone longer than necessary.

Her legs cried out in pain from keeping upright on the horse, and her eyelids fought to stay open, but she couldn't give up on Sam. Not when there was still hope.

"Annabelle, why are you dragging us to some man we both know doesn't exist?" Sam reached for her hand.

"I can't just let you go. Not without turning over every stone, looking for every possible solution. Wouldn't you do the same for me?"

Sam sighed. "You know I would."

"Then you know why we have to go." Annabelle turned away so Sam couldn't see her tear up. If she looked at him, she knew she would cry all over again. "I can't lose you."

Sam paused. "You won't."

Annabelle wiped her nose with her handkerchief and looked out into the distance. She squinted in the bright sun but thought she could just make out the silhouette of a town.

"Looks like we're getting close to a town. We're running low on food—I can only find so many berries out here. We should keep moving and rest more there."

Sam nodded as he pushed himself up. Once Annabelle got him onto his horse, she swung herself back over on her own and steered the reins back toward the road.

They reached town sooner than she had anticipated, which was a relief. Sam could only push through for so long. What he needed now was somewhere to rest. Perhaps they could find a park with a nice tree for Sam to sleep against while Annabelle went into town to do some shopping. Annabelle kept her eyes peeled for roads with fewer travelers, but they all seemed to be full of townsfolk enjoying the beautiful day.

A fountain and trees in a small courtyard were only a few roads into town, and she decided that was as good a place as any for Sam to rest. She ignored the stares from onlookers as she helped Sam down off his horse and onto the ground. As his skin touched the grass, Sam smiled, and not more than a few seconds passed before he was snoring.

Annabelle giggled to herself as she tied the horses to the tree nearest Sam, doing her best to conceal their bags in a nearby bush. Lightheadedness threatened her with a gurgling gut. This wasn't her best idea, but it was all she could do. They needed food, and Sam needed rest. Nowhere would be safe to do that, so she took a moment and prayed he would be protected until her return.

As she reached into the purse, her gut sank as she pulled out several coins. If she didn't play it carefully, they wouldn't have enough to get them a train ticket once Sam was healed. She stuffed the coins into her pocket and caught her reflection in a nearby window.

Dirty.

It was the only word that came to her as she stared at herself. Dust and mud caked her everywhere—her face, her dress, and especially her shoes. Annabelle did her best to wipe off what she could, adjusting her hat one last time before walking toward the shops.

She received lots of stares on the first road, but once she turned the corner, people stopped recognizing her as the woman that rode in with a Black man, and they paid her no attention.

Clear skies called to her in the open streets, free from all the electric lines. Charleston had been one of the first cities to get them, but this town wasn't yet cluttered with a sky full of wires. Though it seemed like the town had everything it needed, there were far fewer shops.

She dragged her hand along the rough brick walls, careful not to hurt her fingers. When the wall ended, Annabelle looked up to the next building. She stopped cold in her tracks.

Peering through the front window of a schoolhouse, Annabelle watched a young woman teaching her students. Annabelle's heart wrenched, thinking about the children she'd left behind. Though she had to get away for her and Sam's safety, it didn't make leaving the school children any easier. She'd left them without warning, and it was something that continued to weigh heavy on her heart.

Across the street from the school, Annabelle spotted a food stand.

Delicious assortments of fruits and cheeses called to her as she filled a basket. Unsure how much longer they'd be on the road, she made sure to grab enough for the next three days.

She paid the man and thanked him for the food, then set back toward Sam. All she needed to do was put the food into her bag and fill their canteens with water, and they'd be ready to go.

As she rounded the corner back toward Sam, a nearby gathering caught her eye. Curiosity took over, and Annabelle made her way to the crowd. As she wiggled her way in to see the cause of the commotion, laughter erupted from the spectators. Two men sat across a table from each other, playing a game of cards. She covered her mouth as she caught herself joining in on the laughter.

One man sat in nothing but his drawers, while the other sported a grin from ear to ear, fully clothed. The undressed man was heavy set with body hair running wild, his mustache and head hair the only ones in place. An older man—quite a sight out here on the streets. His eyes narrowed at the man across from him as he threw another coin onto the pile in the center of the table. He set down his cards and half smiled at his opponent, sure he'd won this round.

The other man grabbed his chin. While he stared at his cards, he ran his hands through his blond hair. He appeared to be about half the age of the man in his drawers. It seemed certain he'd lost. As the man began to place his cards down, a smirk crossed his face, and the crowd gasped. The younger man had won.

Confusion took over the older man's face.

His opponent taunted him. "You seem to be forgetting how this works, good sir." He gestured to the man's drawers.

The old man turned red over his entire body. He balled his fists and slammed them on the table. "The hell if I do!"

Amused by the absurdity of what was going on, the younger man only laughed. "You knew the rules when we started."

The old man stood up forcefully. The innermost of the crowd stepped back in anticipation, but the young man didn't even flinch.

"Are you done, then?" The younger man smirked.

The old man rattled, a vein popping out of his forehead. Annabelle thought he was going to charge the blond man, but instead, he bent down and picked up his jacket, reached inside, and pulled out a handful of coins. He threw them on the table and gathered the rest of his clothes before marching off in the opposite direction.

The crowd dispersed, and Annabelle watched the man chuckle to himself as he collected his winnings. Another man stuck around and said something to the younger man, who just laughed again. He pocketed the coins and turned toward Annabelle. The two locked eyes, and the man smiled at her. She returned the gesture, but before she could turn back to where she was headed, the man's eyes went wide, and he ran past her.

Annabelle spun around to see the crowd had found a new form of entertainment. Her stomach dropped as she raced to Sam, who had positioned himself behind the horses, using them as a shield. A few members of the crowd pulled their fellow townsfolk back to leave Sam alone, but most of the crowd wanted in on the fun.

Annabelle forced her way through the crowd, praying the right words would come to her when she needed to use them. Before she could get close enough to Sam, the thud of a body being knocked to the ground reached her.

"Sam!" Annabelle kept pushing her way forward, catching only glimpses of the scuffle. Another man went down, and the crowd moved as one to circle around the fight. Annabelle called out again. "Sam! Sam!"

"Annabelle?" Sam's voice cut through the crowd. She could see him now—still behind the horses and not in on the fight.

Annabelle moved to her left to reach Sam, but the man in front of her stepped back hard in his enthusiasm and knocked her to the ground. Her basket went flying, and fruit toppled everywhere, getting trampled by oblivious onlookers.

With the crowd tightening in all the action, Annabelle struggled to push herself off the ground. She winced as the shuffle of bodies tossed her back and forth on the ground. The air became harder to breathe with dust kicking up into her face, her lungs begging for a gap in the crowd. Hoping to find a way through, she turned her head to look at the skirmish as a boot kicked her in the back of the head.

Annabelle fell limp on the spot. Black spots filled her vision. Her hands reached up for assistance to pull her to safety, but none came. She closed her eyes and started to pray.

"Annabelle! Annabelle!" The voice sounded distant.

Annabelle opened her mouth to scream, but nothing came out. The sounds of the fight grew louder—punches and cheers echoing in her head. She looked for Sam's feet to see if he was still all right, but she couldn't focus on anything. She moved her hand along the back of her head, trying to ease the pain. Something wet oozed over her fingers. She brought her hands around and could barely make out the sight of blood dripping from her fingers.

A pair of hands wrapped around her and hoisted her up over someone's shoulder. Whoever held her walked away from the crowd to the far side of the park.

No. Stop. I can't leave Sam. The man ignored her. *Please, stop!* Why wasn't he listening to her? She tried again but realized the words weren't leaving her lips. She was being kidnapped, and she couldn't even scream. *Sam! Help!*

The man slowed down and dropped Annabelle from his shoulder, leaning her against a tree and holding something out to her. Initially, she pushed it away, but he insisted. Annabelle grabbed it and held it close to her face.

A canteen of water.

She crinkled her brows and looked up at the man. It was the companion of the man who had won the card game. He gestured to the canteen, and she drank. The cool water refreshed her as she felt the man's hands on her head.

"Don't!" she screamed as she recoiled.

"I'm not going to hurt you. I just want to see the wound."

Annabelle hesitated before nodding—wincing at the motion —finally able to meet the man's gaze as her vision began to clear up. He focused on the wound with his dark, deep-set eyes.

He had a full beard, speckled black and gray to perfectly match his hair. The man had a stern look about him but gently cleaned out the wound. Wrinkles began to take hold of the man's brow and eyes. She imagined he must be in his early forties.

"How bad is it?" Annabelle couldn't handle delaying the journey due to her own injury.

"You'll be fine. There's not much blood." He used water to scrub the blood out of her hair. "How does it feel?"

Annabelle pressed her hand to the wound. The throbbing had already died down, and her vision was back to normal. "Much better. Thank you."

The man grunted in reply and offered a hand to Annabelle. She grabbed it tight as he helped her to her feet.

As soon as she was up, Annabelle turned to where she had left Sam.

"He's fine," the man said.

"Excuse me?"

"Your husband. A couple guys got into it with each other after my brother decided to throw the first punch." The man looked a bit embarrassed.

"Why'd he do that?" Annabelle looked back at the man.

"Well, I assume because your husband called out for help."

Annabelle smiled to herself, hearing someone refer to Sam as her husband. "I need to get to him." She walked toward Sam and the horses.

"Yes, ma'am." The man followed after her.

She could hardly contain herself as Sam came back into view. "Sam!"

"Belli!" Sam leaned against the card winner and nearly collapsed trying to reach Annabelle.

She threw her arms around him and let the tears flow freely. "I'm so sorry. I tried to stop them, but I—"

"Belli, it's okay. We're all right now. A few people helped me, and no one got hurt." Sam looked at Annabelle's hair, still holding a faint tinge of red. "What happened?"

"I got knocked down, but this man helped me." She gestured toward the man who had finally caught up with her. The man who had helped Sam appeared to be about ten years younger than his companion. "You're his brother?"

The blond man tilted his head downward. "Yes, ma'am. I couldn't see you once everything started."

"Thank you so much for helping him. Sam isn't quite himself right now."

The man extended his hand. "It's my pleasure, miss."

She took his hand. "Please, Annabelle."

"All right, then, Annabelle. My name's Ace. This here's my brother, Elroy." Ace looked between Sam and Annabelle. "What are y'all doin' out here, anyway? Can't you sleep at your own house instead of here on the ground?"

Sam kept a tight lip, so Annabelle answered, "No, we aren't from here. Sam is quite sick, and we're looking for someone who can help."

"Ah. No doctors in your town?"

Annabelle shook her head. "None who can help."

Ace's eyes widened. She could hear the question burning in his mind.

"Something's wrong with his heart. We heard a healer out this way may be able to help."

"A healer? What kind?"

"Oh, well . . . Umm, we've heard him be called an 'oracle' by some." Her cheeks burned red. She was suddenly aware of how ridiculous this must all sound.

The two men exchanged a look. "Wow, an oracle. That way?" Ace pointed in the direction they were heading.

Annabelle nodded. "Yes. Out near Savannah."

Ace smiled and nudged Annabelle on the shoulder. "Well, ain't this just the biggest coincidence. We're headed that way ourselves, aren't we, Elroy?"

Elroy nodded, staring at his brother.

"Ah!" Sam slipped from Annabelle's arm, landing hard on the ground.

"Sam!" Annabelle scurried to his side. "What do you need?"

Sam gripped his chest, his skin turning a deep purple and a vein forming in his neck.

Tears fell from Annabelle's cheeks. "I don't know what to do!"

Ace knelt beside Sam, unbuttoning Sam's shirt around his

neck, then grabbed out a handkerchief and poured some water on it.

Once Annabelle realized what Ace was doing, she grabbed the hankie from his hands and laid it on Sam's forehead. "Shh, Sam. It's going to be all right."

"I'll go find help," Elroy called as he ran back toward town. In the distance, pounding echoed through the air.

Sam squeezed Annabelle's hands, his breaths turning back to their normal pace and the hissing of pain dimming. "I think I'm all right, now."

"Are you sure?" Ace cocked his head sideways as he examined Sam. "You look awful."

"It looks worse than it is. I'm fine now. Let's just go."

His side glance at the onlookers was far less inconspicuous than he probably thought.

Elroy sprinted back to the group. "You're right. No help here. You need to get him to Savannah."

"You know, we could all go together," Ace jumped in. "If y'all wouldn't mind the company." He beamed at Sam and Annabelle.

Annabelle didn't know what to say. On the one hand, these men were complete strangers. On the other, they had helped Sam and Annabelle—twice—and the journey was exhausting. Annabelle looked at Sam, who gave her a nod. The decision was hers.

"I think we'd quite like the company . . . if you're offering." Annabelle felt a sense of relief as she said the words.

"Indeed, we are. Now, Sam, let's get you on that horse and to that wizard you need so much." Ace beamed.

"Oracle." Annabelle laughed. "And thank you for your help. I can't tell you how relieved we are to have met you."

Annabelle gathered what food she could salvage from the ground and loaded up the horses. Elroy gave her a hand to get onto her horse while Ace helped Sam to his. The four rode out of town toward the sunset.

THE ATTENTION the group got from strangers in towns irritated Sam to no end. He'd grown used to the stares and hate from almost anyone he came across, but that didn't make it any easier being the odd one out of the group. The glares seared into the back of his neck through every town they passed. Ace and Elroy didn't seem to notice, but Annabelle did. What he couldn't stand more than anything was the look of pity on her face every time someone shouted profanities his way or followed him a bit too long with their eyes. She didn't mean anything by it, but it didn't take away from the fact that he just needed to be treated like everyone else . . . which was never going to happen.

Sam grabbed the reins tighter and kept his gaze forward, gritting his teeth. This town seemed especially behind the times, even for the South.

"What's all this?" Ace asked.

Annabelle leaned forward on her horse and answered, in just above a whisper, "It looks like they haven't taken anything down from the election earlier this year. I'm not sure why."

Ace stopped to read one of the signs in a shop window. "Who's Roose-avult?"

Annabelle turned to Sam, brows raised and eyes squinted. Sam shrugged.

"You don't know who Theodore Roosevelt is?" Annabelle said.

"No. Should I?" Ace stared up at her with his big eyes.

Sam scratched his head. "Uh . . . yeah. He's the president of our country." A moment of reflection filled him with questions. "Where did y'all say you were from again?"

Ignoring the question, Ace turned back and began walking again. "Oh, *that* Roosevelt. Sure, we know him."

Elroy backhanded Ace on the arm.

Bubbles gurgled in Sam's stomach. It didn't sit right with him, that someone wouldn't know their own president, but he lost his train of thought as a man ran toward them with a baseball bat.

"What are y'all doing letting his kind on a horse?" The man spat as he spoke, revealing only two teeth in his mouth. "What are you doing associating with a ni—"

"Enough!" Annabelle screamed, cutting the man off before he could complete his insult.

"We mean no harm; we are just passing through."

"Shut yer mouth, girly!"

Ace put his hands up. "Excuse me, sir, but that is no way to talk to a lady. Our friend here is sick." He gestured toward Sam. "We're trying to get him some help."

The man with the bat glared at Ace. "He's your friend?" He knocked the bat repeatedly in his palm.

The weaker Sam's body became, the worse the cough. Control, even speaking, evaded him.

"Yes, you see? He's very sick. Now, if you could just step aside—"

"Why should I?" the man almost shouted.

Elroy let out a loud sigh. "Because the sooner you move, the sooner we can be out of your town."

Ace crossed his arms and leaned back while Elroy balled his fists. Sam prepared himself for the worst.

The man grumbled. "I s'pose yer right." He begrudgingly stepped aside, glaring at Sam as the group made their way past him and out of town.

Sam looked down at the brothers. Perhaps having these two around wouldn't be the worst thing.

IT WAS JUST past sunset when the group found somewhere to camp for the night, hidden from the road. After tying up the horses and laying out the blankets, Ace built a fire, and Elroy went to look for some food.

Alone, on a comfortable blanket, the two embraced each other while taking in the priceless moment. For the first time, they lived as an official couple, publicly. Such a feat surely warranted a kiss, even if just a light peck on the cheek.

Sam looked at Annabelle and smiled, then glanced down at her dress. "You don't have anything else to wear for this long travel? We're far enough from Charleston if you want to change into something more . . . comfortable." Sam waggled his eyebrows at Annabelle.

Annabelle huffed. "I'm a teacher, Sam. Not everyone has

working clothes like you." She stuck her tongue out at Sam, who laughed.

"Hey, you know I love you in a fancy dress. It was just an interesting choice to stick with, is all I'm saying."

Annabelle probably looked ridiculous but didn't care. This was the dress she had saved for the day she would marry Sam. Little had she known that would never be allowed. So, she did the next best thing and wore it the day they ran away together. She'd needed to look her best that day. Though now, the white dress was stained more of a brown shade from the constant kick-up of the dirt road. "I need to wash this."

"I saw a small pond just over that hill. Want me to come with you while you wash it?" Sam winked at Annabelle.

Annabelle blushed, hoping Ace hadn't overheard. "No, I'll be all right. You boys should get to know each other, anyway." Annabelle stood, grabbed her bag, and headed for the pond.

SAM SAT in silence with Ace. He shifted himself against the log, stifling the cry of pain that coursed its way through his body. Clenched fists kept the shaking under control, and Sam wiped the sweat from his forehead with the back of his hand.

Life wasn't going at all like he thought it would when he left Charleston. He never expected to be making the trip with two strange white men. A trip with a destination they had never planned—because he was dying. Sam closed his eyes, willing anything to take his mind off of his doomed fate. Anytime he thought about it was a punch to the gut, like he was hearing it all again for the first time. The burden wasn't getting any easier.

Sam opened his eyes and gazed up at the stars. *Why is this happening to me?*

"So, how long have you and Annabelle been together?" Ace gave Sam a wink as he threw more wood on the crackling fire.

"Well, there's a complicated story." Sam smiled back. "We first met when I was nine, she was eight. We were kept separate at the orphanage, but there was one spot we would play that no one ever checked. We instantly became best friends. She's always been so kind-hearted and smart. She was my everything." Sam gazed up at the sky. "When I'm gone, I'm not sure what she'll do."

"Hey, don't talk like that. We're gonna get you to where you need to be. You'll be just fine." Ace flashed his winning grin. "You know, Elroy won't say anything, but he has someone back home that makes him feel the way Annabelle does you. That's what we're doing out here. Trying to get back home."

"How did you get separated from your family?"

"Now *there's* a complicated story. But that's too long for tonight. Besides, I think Elroy is coming with the food."

Elroy approached with a couple of squirrels in his hands. Sam became nervous, thinking about having to cook and eat the animals. He hadn't eaten an animal in almost twelve years. Something about it didn't sit right with him. Sam was about to say something when he saw Annabelle coming back wearing her gray dress and cloak, her wet dress in one hand and some apples and berries clutched in her arm. She knew him so well.

"Sam, look what I found near the pond!" Annabelle skipped back to the group.

Sam couldn't help but think of how beautiful she looked in

the moonlight with her pearly waves tracing her figure down to her slender waist. She was breathtaking.

Annabelle handed him the food and turned to the nearest tree to hang her dress to dry. Sam and Annabelle ate the fruit as Elroy cut and cooked the squirrels.

THE GROUP SAT around the fire eating in awkward silence. Ace and Elroy were pleasant enough company, but Annabelle still wasn't sure why they wanted to stick around with her and Sam.

"So," Ace said, "what do you two do for fun?" He looked at them with food all over his face.

Annabelle giggled. "Umm, well, Sam is a writer. He's really good. One day he's gonna be published."

"Is that so?" Ace asked. "I'd love to hear one of your stories."

"Maybe later." Sam would never share his stories with anyone other than Annabelle. They were too special.

"I'm a terrible writer. Can't focus long enough to finish a story." Ace laughed, wiping his mouth clean. As he shifted in his seat, a loud rip sang out. Ace stood. "Oh foot, it seems I've ripped my pants. Not again. . . . See, Elroy? I told you, you didn't fix them."

Elroy rolled his eyes. "I never touched your pants. And did you really think the tape would hold forever?"

"Well, yeah," Ace said. "Only a fool could mess that up."

"Probably why it didn't work," Elroy mumbled under his breath.

Ace put down his food and picked up his bag. "I'm sure there's more tape in here somewhere."

Annabelle cut in, "You can't be serious. That will never hold."

"Oh, yeah? What makes you the expert?" Ace teased.

Annabelle got up and grabbed her bag. After digging around, she held up a travel sewing kit.

"Ah, so you are an expert. You don't think my trick was clever?" Ace beamed at Annabelle.

She shook her head. "Come here. I'll fix that for you."

Ace bounced over to her. "Thanks!" He stood in front of Annabelle and started to remove his pants.

Annabelle's face went hot. "No! I can do it while they're on."

"Okay, then." With a shrug, Ace stuck out his leg for Annabelle to examine.

Annabelle went into her own world as she steadied her hand and pulled the needle through the fabric again and again. It wasn't long before she was tying off the end. "There, good as new."

Ace examined her handiwork and smiled. "You're a genius! This is great. Thanks, little lady." He reached out and ruffled up Annabelle's hair.

Annabelle chuckled at the gesture—perhaps out of pure embarrassment at the notion—and smoothed her hair back into place.

Ace took a seat next to Annabelle, who was putting her sewing items back in their proper place. "You never answered me, Annabelle."

"Huh?" Annabelle placed her bag beside her and grabbed Sam's hand.

"About what you do for fun."

"Oh! Well, I sew—"

"No, what do you do for you?"

Annabelle bit her lip and looked at Sam, who smiled back at her. "I—I guess I sing."

"What!" Ace shouted in excitement. "Me too!"

Annabelle blushed. "That's nice."

"What do you sing?"

"I, um—"

"Ace, leave her alone," Elroy said. "You're prodding too much."

"Oh shush, killjoy. She sings!"

Annabelle shrugged. "I don't know."

Ace stood. "Well, I can't be around another singer and just leave it be." He opened his mouth and turned his eyes to the sky. "Mmm ah . . ." The rise and fall of his voice filled the sky with song.

Annabelle smiled, feeling the same way about music. If she didn't have such stage fright, she could be a part-time singer. When tutoring in music, Annabelle felt her most comfortable. Children didn't judge.

Sam nudged Annabelle from behind. "Go on," he whispered into her ear. "I know you want to."

Hesitation halted the no on the tip of Annabelle's tongue, perhaps even transformed it into a yes. It would be easier to cling to insecurity, but she didn't have to. At least, not anymore. The new Annabelle could be anything, even brave.

Especially brave.

With a gentle squeeze of her love's hand, Annabelle found the courage to stand beside Ace and let her voice dance with his. United in song, the two delved further into the music until reality blended in with the melody.

Trees swished along with the gentle breeze, the fire cackled in delight, and Annabelle swayed and swayed, completely enveloped in the rhythm. One song became two, and then three. When Ace grabbed hold and twirled her around, laughter overcame the group. If not for Sam clapping, she would have remained lost in the moment and missed the beautiful sight.

For far too long, true happiness had not graced Sam's face—nor filled him with so much life.

Ace let go, and Annabelle went spinning toward Sam. She fell into his lap, the four roaring with laughter.

When they finally calmed down, and Annabelle had wiped the laughing tears from her eyes, she reached for a bit of squirrel.

"What's that?" Annabelle jerked her chin toward Elroy, who played with his finger.

He moved his hand to reveal a ring she hadn't noticed before.

"Wow, that's beautiful! Is it a pearl?"

Elroy nodded.

"Does your wife have a matching one?" Annabelle figured something so beautiful had to have a perfect match out there.

Elroy grunted. "Something like that."

Annabelle looked at Sam, who shrugged. If Elroy didn't want to talk, she wouldn't push it.

The rustle of grass behind her made the hairs on her neck stand on end. She hesitated before taking another bite.

A low-growling hiss emerged from behind the tree, and she saw the jaws just before they attacked.

With a grunt, Sam pushed Annabelle out of the way, the creature lunging for the squirrel carcass right next to her. It bit down on the bones but immediately spat it out, scanning the body up and down as it sniffed them. The bulk of the squirrel was nearly picked clean from Elroy's handiwork, so the creature shifted its gaze to Annabelle, who held a bit of flesh in her palm. It slowly twisted and crawled toward her, keeping the three men back with its massive tail.

Wha— What is that? Annabelle had never seen anything like it before. It wasn't a creature; it was some sort of beast. Its body looked like an alligator with its scales, talons, and tail, and even the head was shaped like an alligator's, but it did not walk low to the ground. It stood tall on all fours and had fur in random places. The beast had a black mane around its head and eyes that glowed red. If Annabelle didn't know better, she would say it was some sort of cross between an alligator and a lion.

The beast continued its crawl toward her, cutting her off from the rest of the group. She slowly backed away as her chest grew heavy and her feet tingled. She made it three steps before something bumped her. It was the tree. The horses freed themselves and ran back toward the road in a panic, the beast ignoring them completely.

Annabelle took a deep breath and counted to three before running to the open area beside her, but something pulled her back before her second step. She turned around to see what was holding her back—her dress clung to a low-hanging branch. Annabelle grabbed at the fabric, pulling as hard as she could. The creature came closer, but she couldn't pull herself free. She tried removing the gown, but it was pulled so tight around her ankles, she didn't have enough room to maneuver herself out of it. The beast's footsteps drew nearer, but she was out of ideas.

"No, no! Annabelle!" Sam tried and failed to get up, to get

between the beast and Annabelle. Sam's eyes widened in horror as the monster crept closer and closer to Annabelle. He gripped his chest, reeling on the ground to push himself up.

Annabelle put her hands together for a final prayer, and the beast coiled back to spring for her. She let out a scream, throwing her clenched hands up onto her forehead and covering her face, and the beast let out a wail. But Annabelle wasn't attacked. She peeked through one eye.

Elroy had grabbed his blade and ran at the creature from the side, impaling it before it could strike. The beast whipped around to face Elroy and made a low hiss, followed by a growl. Elroy let out a similar sound, and the creature stared into his eyes. Elroy made the sound again and lifted his hands toward the monster. The beast seemed to calm itself, curling around to lick its wound.

Annabelle stood shocked as the creature headed back through their camp, tossing up all of their belongings, then disappeared into the night. Elroy chased after it, and a few moments later, there was a loud shriek, followed by silence. Elroy emerged from the trees covered in black sludge.

Sam stumbled over to Annabelle, who still leaned against the tree with her hands together. Annabelle stared blankly into the distance and fell into Sam's arms.

"Oh, Belli, I thought I lost you. I thought . . ." Sam cried into Annabelle's shoulder. "I'm sorry, I'm so sorry. I should have done more. I should have protected you."

Annabelle stared at Sam. "Now you know why I have to find the oracle. Even if he's not real."

"I know. We'll go to the ends of the earth if we have to. I'm not giving up." Sam composed himself. "I'm sorry."

Ace walked over to Sam and Annabelle. "Are you all right?" Ace put a hand on Sam's shoulder. "We need to get out of here and find another place to sleep tonight. Elroy has already started packing our things. Let's go."

Annabelle turned to Elroy. "What was that thing? I've never seen anything like it."

Elroy shrugged. "It's gone now."

Annabelle approached Elroy. "You were amazing. Thank you."

Elroy shrugged again and continued his work in silence.

Sam and Annabelle joined Elroy in packing up the destroyed camp—the beast had done its damage. It had gone over Sam's bag and scattered his belongings all over the ground.

Annabelle helped Sam pick everything up. Luckily, everything was intact, except for his jacket, which was shredded down the back and one arm, but she could sew that up later good as new. They stuffed it into the bottom of his bag and gathered the rest of his things, ready for this awful night to end. She picked up her belongings, disappointed to see her sunhat torn to bits. It was unsalvageable, so she left it on the ground.

Sam leaned in and whispered in Annabelle's ear. "Have you ever seen anything like that creature before?"

Annabelle shook her head. "Have you?"

"No. Never. I just . . . I don't know what to think about all of this."

"I know. I feel the same way." She peered over her shoulder. "Whatever it was, it's gone now. Let's just keep moving ahead."

Sam pulled Annabelle close and kissed her cheek, her heart fluttering. She squeezed his hand and went back to gathering their effects.

Once camp was packed up, the group walked back to the road. Ace put Sam's arm around his shoulder to help them move along quicker. Annabelle let out a sigh of relief when she saw the horses walking in circles at the end of their path. She ran up and hugged them. The shame of stealing the horses had been eating at her, and she didn't think she could also bear the guilt of losing them. The group grabbed the horses and searched for a place to rest for the night, even if none of them would sleep.

ANNABELLE AWOKE the next day to find the men had already packed up camp and had started loading up the horses. She croaked as she turned over and attempted to get up. The weight of the attack, the ever-looming danger, and Sam's predicament all pushed her back to the ground. After a quick morning prayer, she was able to hoist herself to her feet.

Sam stood near his horse, who seemed to be in tune with whatever Sam needed, always doing his best to help Sam get on and off with as little pain as possible.

Sam's eyes stayed glued to Annabelle, she figured because of the night they'd had before. Strong arms wrapped around her the entire night, and though she felt safe with him there to protect her, sleep neglected to give the feel of rest and refresh. Annabelle got onto her horse, and the group began the day's travel.

She could have sworn the sun was moving closer with the intense heat that morning. Though she had already taken off her cloak and pulled back her hair, she wished to roll up her sleeves as the brothers did without fear of being branded an improper woman. Instead, she would have to settle for soaking a piece of fabric in cool water every time they passed some and wrapping it around her neck. Elroy had volunteered to do this for her, so she wouldn't have to get too close to the water. A sweet gesture she appreciated.

Because of the heat, they had to make more frequent stops than in days before, which greatly frustrated Annabelle—she needed to get Sam to help as fast as possible. She decided to turn her attention toward anything besides the heat.

Looking at Sam on his horse, she became thankful he had strength enough to ride. With everything that had happened over the last week, they counted themselves lucky with the friends they had made. Sam and Annabelle had begun to trust Elroy and Ace, especially after the incident with the mysterious beast.

Annabelle watched the two men, a bit jealous of their relationship. She loved what she had with Sam and wouldn't trade that for anything, but she always dreamed of having a sister.

Sam had a talent for always knowing how Annabelle was feeling, and when he flashed his eyes at the brothers, she knew he had once again figured out what was going on in her mind. Sometimes, she thought he knew her better than she knew herself. Sam blew a kiss to Annabelle, and she blew one right back.

Ace looked back at the sweethearts and cracked a smile. "What are you two thinking about on this beautiful day?"

Sam laughed. "How did you two get separated from your

family? Belli and I know what it's like to live without family, and we can't imagine being separated like that."

Ace and Elroy exchanged glances, and Elroy nodded to his brother. "We aren't from . . . around here. Where we live, the town's leader didn't like us speaking out against her heinous crimes. We awoke one night with bags over our heads and feeling rather woozy." Ace ran his fingers through his scruffy blond hair. "She had gotten someone to take us all the way out here and beat us while we were all tied up. Elroy was barely breathing. It took weeks for us to recover. As soon as we were able to walk, we started the trek out this way, hoping to find someone to help us get home. We don't have any money or personal items besides what we've been able to scrounge up. That's why we need help. A couple of days into our journey, and we met you fine folk." Ace gave Annabelle a smile.

Elroy turned and coughed, looking as if he were wiping away tears.

Annabelle gave Ace a knowing look. "Sam and I have dealt with people like that before. . . . How can a person be so horrible as to separate somebody from their own family and home?"

"Well, Annabelle, when someone has evil in their heart, they are capable of more than we could ever think."

Annabelle shook her head, and a somberness hovered over the group.

The foursome pulled over to take another rest and search for water. Once their canteens were full and legs rested, everyone stood to journey again. Ace turned to Annabelle. "So, what's your story?"

Annabelle bit at her bottom lip as she thought about where

to start. "Well, I don't really know the actual start to my story. I never knew my mother or father—I was brought to the orphanage when I was still a baby." Annabelle paused, trying to steady her voice.

As well as she knew her own story, it didn't hurt any less having to say it out loud; pain crawled over her every time she thought about it. She calmed herself and began again. "I was wrapped in a little blue blanket with my name stitched on it. There was a photo of a man and woman pinned on my blanket, and the back of it said, *To our Annabelle, we love you to the stars.* The blanket was lost in a fire started by one of the boys at the orphanage. Luckily, I always have my photograph tucked into my dress, so I still have it." Annabelle grabbed for the picture of her mother and father to show Ace.

Before she could reach it, a gunshot rang out, and Ace screamed.

CHAPTER FOUR

Ace collapsed into the ditch, a trail of blood and Elroy running after him. Annabelle turned to Sam, who frantically yelled at her to run.

A distant ringing echoed in her ears, and everything around her seemed to slow down. Sam waved his arms at her, motioning for her to get on her horse. The ringing intensified, and her legs became molasses, slowly dripping to the ground. She scanned her surroundings. The brothers were nowhere to be seen, and Sam stumbled toward her waving his arms in big circles, pointing away from the fast-approaching cloud of men on horseback.

Just as everything had slowed, the next moments happened so quickly, Annabelle was powerless to do anything. A man leapt from his horse and tackled Sam to the ground, tying his hands behind his back.

She tried to call out to him, but another rider hauled her onto the back of a horse, carrying her off before she could even finish yelling Sam's name. Terror filled her as the last thing she saw before the blindfold pulled over her eyes was Sam being hit in the head with the butt of a rifle.

Annabelle's stomach churned as she bounced up and down on the back of the horse—though it wasn't just the motions causing her to be ill. Ace was most likely dead with the amount of blood he lost and the fall he took into the ditch—and knowing the kind of men that lived out in these parts, she and Sam wouldn't be far behind. All it would take was someone misunderstanding the situation of her traveling with a Black man.

She tried removing the blindfold from her eyes but couldn't risk falling off, so she held the rider tight. The act of having to hold on to the man that shot at them disgusted her. She considered jumping off the horse and making a run for it, but she wasn't sure she could survive the fall, and she had nowhere to go. Plus, she had no idea where Sam was. These men were likely taking them to the same place.

Annabelle recited her verse, desperately warding off another bout of fits. Without Sam to calm her down, she wasn't sure she could make it through.

"Sam!" she called out. The absence of an answer brought on the overwhelming tears, and she was consumed by them within moments. "Ah!" The rider elbowed her in the stomach, demanding she stop crying. Annabelle did her best to choke down the tears.

It wasn't long before the horse slowed its pace, and the man pulled her off. She fell to the ground, but before she could get up, the man grabbed her by the hair and dragged her.

"Ow, stop! Stop!" She kicked her feet best she could but

couldn't gain her balance. The man continued to drag her from dirt to what felt like concrete. The clanking of metal and the squeal of an opening door tore through the air.

The man released Annabelle, sending her flying across the floor and slamming against a wall. She pressed at her temples, attempting to dull the headache. She breathed deep, inhaling a putrid scent of mold and urine. The jangling of keys clicking in a lock followed the slam of a metal door, and the man who threw her in walked away.

When she thought she was alone, Annabelle removed the bag from over her head. She sat in a cell like a criminal, though she supposed, technically, she was one. Once the pounding in her head dulled, Annabelle ran to the bars to see if she could spot Sam. He was nowhere to be seen, and she hoped he was all right.

There was a rusted bench, a dirty cot with no blanket or pillow, and a corner of the room she would never go to with its yellow-brown stains and revolting smell. She pushed her head against the bars, whispering Sam's name.

A baton slammed against the metal near her face, and she recoiled into the cell. A gruff man laughed as he showed himself. "Well, hey there, darlin'. What's your name?" He had a scar down the side of his cheek.

"A-Annabelle." She crossed her arms and grasped her shoulders, burying her chin into her forearm. She wished to be smaller, to find Sam and leave this place.

"Annabelle." He smiled.

She hated the sound of her name coming from his mouth, the way his lips curled and his tongue danced across them, as if he now owned her name just by saying it. She'd never despised her name more than in that moment, and the man repeated it, this time in a low, come-hither way. A purr. "Annabelle . . . I wouldn't have expected someone as pretty as you to be hangin' around that—"

"Stop! Don't even say it!"

"Oh, you like the dark meat, do you? So, he didn't kidnap you, then, eh? Did he put his hands on you?" The man licked his lips and put his hands through the bars, reaching to touch Annabelle. "I bet he put his filthy hands all over you."

Annabelle swatted the man's hands away, her nails scratching against the back of his palm.

"You little bitch!" The man grabbed out his keys to unlock the door. "Why don't I come in there and you can see what a real man feels like!"

Annabelle backed into the nauseating corner of her cell and screamed for help.

"Get away from her!" Sam sounded like he had just awoken in the cell next to hers. "You lay one finger on her and I'll kill you!"

The guard put his keys back on his belt and sauntered over to Sam, laughing under his breath. "Oh, you have that backward."

Annabelle gasped, covering her mouth. "You can't do that. He didn't do anything wrong!"

"Just look at him!" Spit flew out of the man's mouth and sprayed the bars.

Annabelle walked to the concrete wall that Sam was just on the other side of. She wept; these horrible men would put Sam to death for no reason other than the color of his skin.

"Oh, don't worry, sweetheart. You'll be joining him. That is, of course, unless you'd like to apologize to me and do me a . . . favor." He winked at her and puckered his lips while grabbing his crotch.

Annabelle stared at the guard wide-eyed, shaking her head.

"We take theft very seriously in these parts—especially from the likes of him."

Annabelle lowered her head in shame. She knew it was wrong to steal those horses, and now because of her actions, she and Sam would be hung. Tears fell from her cheeks onto the ground. "I'm sorry, Sam," she whispered. "I'm so sorry."

The door leading outside flew open, and the man who had attacked Sam on the road walked into the jailhouse. With a rifle in one hand and rope in the other, he stood much taller than the other man. Annabelle's stomach dropped. The men came over to their cells and unlocked Sam's door. The look of pleasure on the men's faces made Annabelle sick.

"Please, leave him alone!"

The men ignored her and tottered into Sam's cell. She could hear the bustle of the men charging after Sam. He could usually hold his own, but in his condition, he was on the ground almost instantly. Annabelle heard the men beating on him and Sam trying to contain his screams.

"No! Stop!" Annabelle shook as the tears fell down her face. She pounded her fists into the concrete wall, desperately trying to make her way to Sam, to make the pain stop. Vile names came from the men's tongues, reprimanding him for daring to be with her.

"No! He never touched me! Never! Stop it!" she screamed as she ran to the bars, searching for a way out of her cell, but all she could focus on was the noise coming from Sam's.

Then there was nothing. She couldn't hear Sam anymore. *God no.* "Sam!"

The man with the scar made his way back to her cell, blood splattered all over him.

Annabelle sobbed. "What did you do?" Her heartbeat pounded in her ears.

He scoffed. "Only what he deserved. Let's go." The scarred man opened Annabelle's cell and pushed her into the wall, pressing himself against her, taking in her scent. Annabelle trembled as the man tied her hands together with rope. He led her out the door, where she almost threw up.

Sam was there, barely breathing as he leaned against the outside wall, beaten so badly she struggled to recognize him. She tried to run to him, but the man held her tight. That's when she noticed the tree behind him. The tree with the hanging rope.

She looked into Sam's gentle eyes, and they told her not to worry. They would be together forever after this.

Annabelle swallowed the lump in her throat and followed Sam to the last field they would ever see. She took in the smell of fresh air and flowers and looked to the clear sky as the warmth of the sun kissed her face for the last time. Annabelle imagined a paradise where she and Sam were together in Heaven, away from all the hate of the world. She wished to touch the earth just once more, to have Sam hold her, to kiss his lips.

Visions of their lake flew in front of her eyes. *We never should have left.*

They slipped the noose around Sam's neck. He would go

first, and she would have to live in this world without him. Even if for only a moment, the thought of it made her sick.

The men stood back as Sam climbed onto the stool that would be kicked out from under him. Annabelle looked into Sam's eyes as he mouthed the words, "I love you." The man kicked the stool from under Sam, and he had nothing but two feet of air between his shoes and the ground.

Annabelle let out a scream from the depths of her soul and dropped to her knees. She buried her face in the grass and howled so loud the birds scattered from the tree above. Her heart stopped pounding, and her stomach turned to rocks. Annabelle vomited.

She couldn't move except to fall onto her side. At any moment, Sam's body would be thrown aside, and she would take his place. As she looked up to see Sam for the last time, she noticed the unconscious men on the ground. And Sam stood on an invisible floor. Alive.

CHAPTER FIVE

Annabelle ran to Sam in disbelief. Her hands were still tied together, but after years of unknotting thread, her fingers were nimble enough to easily get the ropes off of Sam. Sam jumped down to help Annabelle free herself. The moment her hands were undone, she threw them around Sam and refused to let go, sobbing as every emotion from the last several days hit her at once. Sam tilted Annabelle's chin to look in her face, tears cascading down his own.

"What happened?" Annabelle couldn't believe her eyes. The man she had just seen, nearly dead from beatings with swollen eyes and blood smeared all over and who couldn't even stand upright, was replaced by the man she'd always known—this strong, healthy man, without a scratch on him.

They looked around for an explanation and noticed two figures on top of the jailhouse waving them over. As Sam and Annabelle walked closer, they saw Elroy and Ace jumping down to meet them. Annabelle sprinted to Ace, throwing her arms around his shoulders, and he hugged her back.

"I thought you were dead! How are you walking right now? What happened? How—"

"Whoa, Annabelle, slow down there." Ace slowly pulled away from her. "I'm glad to see you too." Ace gave her a big smile, and Annabelle returned the gesture. He exchanged a look with his brother, then turned back to Sam and Annabelle. "We need to talk, but not here."

Annabelle and Sam shared confused looks but followed Ace and Elroy back to the road. The stolen horses were in front of the jail. When they spotted Sam and Annabelle, they tried to join the group, but their reins held them back. Annabelle forced herself to look away, her heart breaking as the horses cried out to them, surely upset they were being left behind. She knew better than to take the horses again, so Annabelle said a quiet goodbye and continued on the journey.

The group hurried along in silence for an hour before Elroy spoke up. "Let's sit here," he said, pointing to a tree in an open field with nothing else around for miles. They all walked through the knee-high grass and sat under a tree for some shade—the heat had only intensified with the passing of morning.

Sam and Annabelle sat holding hands, both clammy, Annabelle's slightly shaking. Her heart still raced from all that had happened that morning, and she didn't know if she would ever be able to get over seeing Sam like that. Every time she closed her eyes, she had visions of Sam with the noose around his neck, nausea taking over again.

Elroy stared up at the tree while Ace wove a piece of grass

between his fingers, staring at the ground. Sam cleared his throat, and the men casually looked to Sam and Annabelle.

Ace began, "We weren't completely honest when we told you about where we come from and how we ended up here. Everything we told you is true; we just left out the more . . . eccentric details." Ace hesitated, staring at the ground. "We come from a place called Taegaia. It is not on Earth. Thousands of years ago, there was an event our people call The Ripple, tearing our world from yours. Legend says that the goddesses who created our world gifted the land with magic."

Sam let out a disbelieving sigh and started to stand.

"Sam, wait, you need to know this. I promise this is the truth."

"There is no such thing as magic. What is it with you people telling us about realms and fairy tales?"

"What do you mean, *you people*?" Elroy asked.

Sam stared at the men blankly, as if deciding what to say.

"Please," said Ace. "We haven't wanted to scare you, so we didn't say anything about the oracle. But we have been so curious about how you know about him at all. Please tell us what you know. We can help."

Sam stood with his arms crossed.

"Sam, please just tell them. And besides, what would you call what happened today if not magic? You were floating in the air!" Annabelle wanted answers, no matter how unusual they came.

"I don't know, Belli." Sam slowly sat down. He told Ace and Elroy about what had happened in his house the night with Keres, the warning he'd been given about the Dark Queen, and how Keres had told them where to find the oracle.

Elroy and Ace were baffled.

Ace spoke, "How would Keres even know you? And why would he warn you? He's the queen's trusted advisor."

The group sat there, trying to come up with any explanation for the mysterious events.

"So, Keres said you've been to Taegaia, but that's impossible. Without going through the Rip, that would take powerful magic . . . Chaos from the Dark Queen. But why would the Dark Queen want you there?" Elroy scratched at his beard, talking more to himself than the others.

"Wait," Annabelle said. "How could he have been there? I've seen him nearly every day, and wouldn't he remember?"

"Time in our world does not follow any rules like it does here. Sometimes, a moment in your time can be like a lifetime where we are from, or it can be reversed. That's the worst part. Since we've been here for weeks, our families could be just as we left them, or . . ." Elroy teared up. Annabelle put her hand over her heart and looked at the men in understanding.

"As for not remembering, I'm really not sure. Maybe he wasn't there, then. All I know for sure is that we need to find the oracle."

"So, the oracle can really help us?" Annabelle tried not to sound too excited.

"Yes. That's why we asked to join you—because we need him to get home. He guards the Rip to keep out danger from Taegaia and helps those from our world passing through yours."

"Hold on," Sam said. "I thought you said there isn't any magic on Earth. So, what do you call healing Ace from a gunshot wound and saving us from death?"

Elroy answered, "Magic in our realm is not how you might

imagine. We can bottle it up and bring it to Earth. We luckily had two vials of magic when we were forced through the Rip and thrown into your world. We saved one in case of an emergency, and the other to open the Rip to go back home. We had no choice but to use the first vial to save Ace after getting shot; he would have died otherwise. When we came to find the two of you, Sam already had the rope around his neck, and we had no other weapons to stop any of it from happening. So there went our last vial."

"I'm sorry we lied," Ace said.

Annabelle stared at Elroy with her jaw open, and Sam was expressionless. None of this was possible, but it all somehow made sense—how Ace was alive, what Keres had said, and why Sam wasn't hung.

"I don't know that we believe all this, but Annabelle and I have faith you can get us the help we need. And we will do what we can to help you get home." Sam stood, and the four began their journey again.

WITHOUT HORSES, the pace of the group slowed dramatically. It hurt Annabelle to be the cause of the delay. The men were all in great physical condition—that was evident from their sculpted bodies and ability to walk without growing tired. Though she was thin, she was not strongly built like the rest of her company.

She had always been self-conscious about her appearance, often feeling more like a skeleton than an attractive young woman. The beautiful women she knew sported powdered faces, full bodies, and elegant updos. Her porcelain skin needed no powder, but the rest fell short. Annabelle wore loose-fitting, flowy dresses cinched at the waist to create curves where none existed. And due to the weight of her hair, loose, proper buns were ruled out. Her faults weighed heavy on her heart every time she had to ask the men to stop on her behalf.

"How are you doing?" Sam kissed her forehead. "I know that this is a far way to go, but we'll get there."

Annabelle forced a smile as she looked up at Sam. "I'm fine, thanks." She tried, and failed, to hide her heavy breathing from him. "My feet are just a little sore, is all."

"Okay, then. It'll get better the more we walk, you know. I'm really impressed with you. I've felt a little better since this morning with being able to hold myself up and walk, but this ain't easy. You are doing so well." Sam's eyes lit up, and he reached behind Annabelle, grabbing something off the ground. He came back up with a pink flower in his hands, reached up, and tucked it behind Annabelle's ear. "Perfect. A beautiful flower for my beautiful and strong Belli."

Her cheeks went hot, and she leaned in to his kiss, stomach racing with butterflies. Annabelle took his compliment to heart. Not because she believed him, but because he was trying his best to make her feel better, which worked. He always knew how to do that for her. "How about you? Yesterday you couldn't even walk, and today you can walk in this heat for miles. Shouldn't you be resting more?"

"I don't know how to explain it. After this morning, I just feel a lot better."

"Maybe you aren't sick anymore," Annabelle said with too much hope.

Elroy chimed into their conversation, "Actually, I think the bit of magic we used might have something to do with that. I'm not sure if he's completely cured, but for the next day or so, he should be feeling more like himself."

Annabelle was conflicted. She was glad Sam was more himself but crushed he was not yet cured of whatever sickness he had. She took one final sip of water and hoisted herself off the ground. "Then let's pick up the pace and find him a cure."

The men all smiled, and the group walked on toward the oracle, almost jogging.

SAM SCRATCHED AT HIS ARM, where the bandage covered his scar. He had tried to ignore it since that night, but after what Ace and Elroy had said the day before, he wasn't too sure he could. He'd read hundreds of books and even wrote his own stories, but he never believed anything like this could be real. And if it were, why would it be happening to them? They weren't anyone special. They were just . . . Sam and Annabelle.

Sam kept rubbing at his arm, deep in thought, when Annabelle's soft voice broke through. "Does it hurt?" Her beautiful eyes looked up at him with concern. He hadn't noticed he'd been picking at the bandage so hard until she'd said something.

"No, I think it's fine."

Annabelle gave Sam her sweet smile. "The bandage hasn't been changed in a few days. I don't want it to get infected."

Annabelle always did a great job of making sure he was

taken care of. He knew she would make a great mother one day because of her caring instincts. Her students all loved her for it.

Sam nodded. "You're right." He grabbed an extra bit of fabric from his bag and handed it to Annabelle.

As Sam tugged on his sleeve to roll it back, Ace walked back into camp and glanced over at Sam, narrowing in on his arm. Ace ran to Sam and grabbed his arm firmly. "Where did you get this?" Ace asked Sam wide-eyed.

"I got it the night Keres showed up. I don't know what it is. One moment I didn't have a mark on my arm, the next it was burning. Why, do you recognize it?"

Ace called Elroy over to see Sam's arm. "Yeah, I recognize it." He hesitated. "The three roses . . . it's the sigil of the Dark Queen's kingdom."

Annabelle's jaw dropped. "What! The madwoman who Keres was talking about?"

Ace unbuttoned the top of his shirt and pulled it open to reveal his chest. Over his heart was a tattoo of three seashells, organized in the same manner as the roses. "Each kingdom in our world has a different symbol. Ours is the sea. Hers are the roses."

Sam was baffled, at a loss for words.

Elroy said, "So, this means you really did travel back to our world. Sam, what do you remember? Is my family still there?" Elroy kept his stare on Sam, desperately trying not to show his rapidly increased breathing.

"I—I don't remember anything. If I did, you wouldn't have to work so hard to convince us of your story, and I would know what's killing me."

Elroy nodded, failing to hide his disappointment with Sam's

answer. "Well, the good news is that Sam hasn't aged at all during his time in Taegaia, right? That means that time might be on our side. There's still a chance we can make it before . . . We just have to."

Ace patted Elroy on his shoulder and buttoned his shirt back up. "We will get back to them. Just have faith in Her."

"HOW MUCH LONGER UNTIL we get to the lake?" Annabelle's entire body ached, and all she wanted was to sleep in a bed with a soft pillow instead of the grass and cloak she had been using along the road. Blisters stung her feet, her cheeks were hot to the touch, and she could have sworn she smelled her hair burning. Annabelle could see Sam becoming weaker and couldn't bear the thought of coming so far, only to have it all be for nothing.

Sam turned to Annabelle. "We can't be too far now. It's just past the next town. How about we stop there and get you a room for the night? We can all head to the lake first thing in the morning."

"What about you?"

Sam shrugged. "You know they won't let me stay with y'all down there. I'll find somewhere to spend the night." Sam looked around. "That field looks nice."

Annabelle thought it over. She wanted to get to the oracle as quickly as possible, but she knew they all needed a good night's rest. She noticed more people on the road and figured they must be getting close to Savannah. Annabelle couldn't stop thinking about sitting on anything that wasn't a rock or the ground and being able to clean herself without the fear of another attack. "Why don't you wait here, and I'll sneak you in after dark?"

Sam shook his head, but Annabelle insisted. "I'm worried about you, Sam. What if your heart gives out again?"

Ace and Elroy nodded in agreement.

"See, they know I'm right."

Sam sighed. "Fine, I'll wait just over yonder, by that tree. But you two better watch out for her." Sam narrowed his eyes on the brothers.

"As if she were our own blood." Ace crossed his heart with his finger.

Sam sat down and watched the three head into town to find a place to stay and waited for dark.

ANNABELLE and the brothers made their way through town without any trouble. Elroy asked a local man where they could stay for the evening, and he directed them to a small inn in the middle of town. Annabelle breathed in the city air, the clatter of busy city folk seeming impossibly loud, as she had grown used to the quiet of the road. She smiled at the children playing ball in the streets.

The three passed shop after shop, and one in particular caught her eye—the music store. She admired the beautiful upright piano inside, wishing one day to have one just like it, to fill her home with joyous song and teach her children to love it as she had.

Before heading down the last road to the inn, Annabelle

caught a whiff of a bakery. She stopped in her tracks, breathing in the wonderful smells, wishing she could afford some, but all her money was going toward a room for the night.

Ace approached her. "That smells delectable. Shall we?" He leaned toward the bakery, ushering her to it with his eyes.

"Oh, no, I couldn't possibly." She stared at her feet and began to walk toward the inn but was pulled into the bakery by Ace.

"Come on, Annabelle. You can't resist that smell." He gave her his big boyish grin. "I'm getting"—he scanned the selection —"that one. Care to split it with us?"

"I don't want to take your food."

"Nonsense. It's done." Ace handed over a five-cent coin to the baker, who exchanged it for the large loaf of bread. Ace turned to Annabelle. "Do you like jam?"

Annabelle's cheeks flushed. "The bread is plenty. . . ."

Ace beamed at the baker. "Where is the nearest shop for jam, good sir?"

The baker pointed across the street, and Ace grabbed Annabelle's wrist and pulled her along.

The thought of bread and jam made Annabelle's mouth water, but she didn't want to take away from the brothers. Though if Ace insisted . . .

The two walked into the shop as Elroy waited on the street. The shop was empty, just as the bakery had been.

"So, what will it be?" Ace asked.

"Are you sure? These are so extravagant." Annabelle blushed. She'd been scrimping by her entire life and saved expenses like this for special occasions. She couldn't just expect Ace to buy these luxuries for her.

"Absolutely. I saw a few fat cats out there who I'm sure would be interested in a round of cards." Ace winked.

Annabelle laughed at the thought of the last time she'd seen Ace play cards. He was good, and she was sure he could make up the money he spent in no time if he found others willing to partake.

Annabelle stared at the wall of jam jars arranged in different colors and sizes. She couldn't possibly choose only one. She scanned the wall, reading the labels until her eyes settled on a small jar of apple butter. Her tongue parted through her lips at the sight of it.

"Good afternoon, ma'am," Ace said to the woman behind the counter. "I think the woman has chosen." He giggled. "One large jar of your finest apple butter, please."

Annabelle gasped. "Oh, Ace, that's too much."

"You aren't the only one who loves a sweet treat." Ace winked at her. He handed over several coins and took the jar from the counter. Annabelle followed him back to Elroy. "We got your favorite—apple butter!"

"Apple what?" Elroy lifted an eyebrow and shook his head. "Well, let's have it, then."

Elroy ripped apart the bread while Ace opened the jar, handing Annabelle half of the loaf.

"That's far too much." Annabelle held up her hand, waving it away.

Elroy shrugged. "I'm sure Sam is hungry too."

Her cheeks flushed again. "Are you sure?"

Elroy put the food in her hand as his answer.

"Thank you." She prayed Sam was all right on the hillside and looked up to the sky, wondering how long until nightfall.

Ace poured apple butter from the jar onto his bread, then did the same for Annabelle. She lifted the loaf to her nose, calmed by the scent. Taking a bite, her tongue thanked her for the delicious experience. Annabelle kept eating, almost biting into Sam's portion of the bread, pocketing it before it could tempt her further. Once their stomachs were satisfied, they continued to the inn.

ANNABELLE DID her best to keep a straight face as the woman at the front of the inn stared her down. She placed her dollar on the counter. "Please, ma'am. Our sister will be arriving at nightfall, and I don't want her to go without a room. If I could just have a room with two beds, she would be oh so grateful to you." She kept darting her eyes between Annabelle and the two men. What stories she must be spinning on why Annabelle was there with them.

Ace stepped up to the counter, leaning far over to whisper into the woman's ear. Almost instantly, the woman's face broke from cold to laughter. Whatever Ace said was working. The woman seemed to forget about Annabelle as she giggled at Ace's words. She handed a key to Ace, who gently slid it behind his back to hand to Annabelle. Annabelle grabbed it and headed down the hallway, turning back to mouth "thank you" to Ace, which he returned with a wink.

After opening the door, Annabelle flopped onto the bed, counting the hours until she could go find Sam.

Time seemed to move much faster with a full stomach and a place to rest her feet. As soon as night took over the sky,

Annabelle slipped out of her room and out the back door, propping it open with a nearby rock.

Out on the streets in the dark again, as she was used to whenever she and Sam planned to meet, she hoped she would remember the way back. The scent of the bakery guided her back to the edge of town. A rush of relief ran over her when she saw Sam resting on a hill, right where she'd left him.

Sam made his way to Annabelle as soon as she was in his line of sight. Annabelle grabbed out the bread and jam she had stuffed in her pockets and handed them to Sam. His eyes lit up. "We can't afford this."

"I know. It was a gift from the brothers."

Sam raised his eyebrow at Annabelle.

"They insisted. They wouldn't take no for an answer."

Sam stared at the bread and smiled before chowing it down. "Mmm." He licked his fingers. "Okay, let's go."

Though they were in a town they had never been in before, the inconspicuous walk back was the same as in Charleston. They knew what kinds of streets to avoid, how to listen for the way with fewer people, and when to keep their distance, like their being on the same street was a strange coincidence. This way took longer, but it was just the two of them, and they weren't out of the South yet.

Annabelle looked ahead and recognized a storefront from earlier that day. There was the beautiful upright piano. They were on the right path, with only a few more streets to go.

"Hey, you . . . stop . . . stop the . . . there!" A voice came from the shadows, and Annabelle's heart dropped to her stomach. A man holding a brown bag stumbled out in front of them, blocking the only path she knew to get back to the inn. "Wha—

what . . ." the man hiccupped and staggered to the side, catching himself before crashing into a brick wall, and continued toward them. "What are you . . . doing here?" He was almost yelling, and Annabelle was sure he would draw someone's attention if he kept it up.

"Keep moving, Belli," Sam whispered.

She wasn't about to leave Sam.

Sam spoke to the man. "Sir, go home. You shouldn't be out like this."

The man kept bumbling toward them. "No, *you* shouldn't be . . . shouldn't be . . . be out like this." The drunk man threw his bottle against the wall and shattered the glass. He picked up the biggest piece he could find and pointed it at Sam.

"Annabelle, run!" Sam's voice turned stern, and this time she listened. She ran up the street and hid behind a barrel near the road. She poked her head up to watch Sam.

"I'm not gonna tell you again; you need to leave us alone."

Annabelle had never heard Sam speak so rough before.

"I ain't never . . . seen you around here before . . . b . . . b . . . boy." The man was dangerously close to Sam.

"I'm just passing through. There's no need to cause a scene." Sam slowly backed away, his arms out in front of him, prepared for whatever might happen.

"You think . . . you think you can tell me what to do? You think I will listen to some negro boy?" The drunk man was angrier each time he spoke. Louder. Then he lunged at Sam, and Annabelle gasped. She instinctively covered her eyes, opening her fingers a crack to peek through.

Sam disarmed the man and held his hands behind his back. Legs flailing about, the man struggled to free himself. Sam pushed him away from his body, trying to get the man to leave him alone. But the man spun around and swung at Sam.

Sam easily dodged the blow, then shoved the man again. The drunk was not taking the hint and swung a second time. Sam moved out of the way.

"I don't want to hurt you. Stop this, and we'll be on our way."

The man ignored him and came around for a third swing. This time, Sam pushed the man's hand away and struck him in the jaw. The man shook it off and spat blood onto the dirt. The punch seemed to sober him up a bit, and he lifted his fists to strike again. For the fourth time, the man missed Sam as he swung slowly and staggered around with each bout. He grabbed for the glass on the ground and thrust it toward Sam. Before he came close to hitting Sam, Sam threw a punch directly into the man's face, and he fell backward, hitting the ground like a board.

Annabelle ran to Sam. She looked down at the drunk—he was unconscious. "Oh, Sam. What happens when he wakes up?"

"Don't worry. He's so drunk I doubt he'll remember anything that happened tonight. But we should go before someone else finds us out here."

Annabelle nodded, then grabbed Sam's hand and pulled him up the last street. Her heart raced as she ushered him to the side door she had prayed would still be propped open with the rock she had placed there earlier. She smiled when she saw it was. The two slowed their pace and walked in, acting like they belonged, like they hadn't left an unconscious man in the middle of the street.

Annabelle whispered to Sam, "Just a couple turns, and we're there." She smiled.

As Sam and Annabelle approached their first corner, they heard a door open and instantly froze. Annabelle's entire body went flush, a bead of sweat forming on her brow. A man and woman whispered and laughed. The laughing turned to kissing and moaning, then back to giggles. Surely, they'd just made love, and Annabelle couldn't help but wonder if this was one of *those* kinds of establishments.

But the longer they stood there, Annabelle was sure she'd heard that laugh before. *It couldn't be . . .* The door closed, and footsteps walked toward them. Annabelle was shocked when Ace came around the corner, and her cheeks instantly turned hot.

"Oh! Hey, you two. She was fun." Ace smiled and gave Sam a pat on the shoulder as he walked past them, back to his room.

The couple stood in stunned silence at what they had witnessed, Annabelle unsure of what to do in the awkwardness of it all.

"We should keep going," Sam whispered.

Annabelle agreed, so they shook it off and continued to Annabelle's room.

ANNABELLE HAD NEVER FELT SO clean as she slid out of the tub and gazed at the thick brown water that had been so clear before she'd gotten in. She had scrubbed for what seemed like hours in every crevice of her body, some she didn't know dirt could even get to. She had used oils in her hair, but it was still stiff and dry as she attempted to brush through it. Annabelle grabbed her dress from where it hung and walked back to the room so Sam could take his bath.

When Annabelle opened the door, Sam mustn't have heard her as he took off his clothes. Annabelle saw Sam's backside and instinctively turned away. She had seen Sam without a shirt before while he was working, but never fully undressed. Annabelle gasped with surprise, and Sam hurriedly grabbed for a cloth to cover himself.

"Belli, I'm so sorry. I didn't think—"

"No, no. It was my . . ." Annabelle struggled to find the words, to find somewhere to set her eyes.

Annabelle moved aside as Sam slipped out the door in a towel that barely covered him, and Annabelle tried to hide her red cheeks and racing heart. She couldn't stop her eyes from following his towel out of the room.

Once Sam had closed the washroom door, Annabelle sat on one of the two beds in the small room. She drank the water on the nightstand, trying to cool down.

Annabelle's longing for Sam grew. A flood of feelings coursed through her body at the sight of him. It was becoming more intense, harder to control than in the past. She had no idea what to do about her feelings for Sam. Of course, she knew what they meant, but she had only ever kissed Sam. Sometimes they would lie in a hidden field together and kiss for a good while, but she never let it go further than that. Sam had once asked her if she wanted to, but her face burned bright red at the thought of it. Sam must have known what Annabelle was thinking because he never brought it up again. She would have to come to him when she was ready. Annabelle had always imagined saving herself for marriage, like a good woman, but she could not marry Sam. It was illegal.

Everything about their relationship was wrong in the eyes of the world, yet she still held on to this shred of innocence. Maybe once they had reached somewhere safe, Annabelle would be able to give herself to him fully.

If they ever reached somewhere safe.

CHAPTER SIX

Sam tossed and turned for hours before giving up on sleep. When he rolled over and watched Annabelle slumber, the slow, steady rhythm of her breath calmed him. He had told Annabelle he wanted to stay in town that night so they could all have a fresh start in the morning, but that wasn't the entire truth. While he did want Annabelle to have some form of comfort after traveling for so long, he was scared more than anything. Scared that everything they'd learned was just some elaborate joke. Scared they would find this so-called oracle and be told there was no hope. Scared to die. Sam kept up a strong front for Annabelle, but inside he was crumbling.

Though he was feeling better, he knew Ace and Elroy were right—this magic wouldn't last forever. Sam rolled out of bed and walked to the window, gazing up at the moon. He didn't want to die; he had too much to live for. He wanted to build a home for Annabelle with his own two hands, to have babies with her, and he wanted to grow old with her. Having to face if that dream would ever come true . . . he tried to postpone it as long as he could, but he knew that in the morning, all truths would be revealed.

Sam instinctively grabbed for the notebook from his breast pocket, forgetting the beast had shredded it along with his jacket.

He thought back to his old writings. It all seemed like a lifetime ago. The last page still puzzled him, with the tally marks that had appeared out of nowhere. Far too many mysteries were to be solved, but Sam prayed for answers from the oracle.

Sam took one last look at the moon and crawled back into bed. His last thought before sleep was his greatest fear of all—finding out in one moment if it would be his dreams coming true, or his nightmares.

A KNOCKING sound pulled Annabelle from her slumber. She glanced around the room, trying to remember where they were, eyes falling to Sam, who was deep in sleep. She smiled at the sight. Annabelle had heard Sam tossing about throughout the night as he faced his inner demons, and today, he would be ready for whatever lay ahead.

The door rattled, and Ace called out to them, "Get up, you bums!" Ace wheezed at his own ridiculous joke.

Annabelle giggled before remembering what she and Sam had seen the night before. She dreaded the awkwardness of having to face him but got up anyway. Annabelle unlocked the door and opened it a crack.

"Good morning, Annabelle. Elroy is grabbing breakfast from that bakery down the way, and then we're heading out."

The thought of more delicious bread brought a smile to Annabelle's lips. "Okay, thank you." She closed the door and turned back to the room, trying her best to get ready for the day without disturbing Sam. As she pulled the blanket up to make her bed, Sam stirred awake.

"Good morning, Sam." She walked to his bed and sat on the edge of it. "How are you feeling today?"

Sam sat up and stroked Annabelle's hair. "I'm ready." He put his thumb to her chin and pulled her closer, softly brushing his lips on her forehead, then her cheeks, and finally pulled her in for a kiss on her lips that made her heart soar. Annabelle leaned into him and fell into bed beside him. Sam wrapped his arms around her and held her close. She hadn't anticipated it, but she liked the distraction.

Sam moved his mouth over to nibble at her ear, then continued kissing down to her neck. Goose bumps shot over her entire body, and she arched her back into Sam. Each kiss was like a feather tickling her spine, and the only thing she could do was give in to it. She couldn't think, sure her brain was becoming mush. She could only feel pure desire as Sam moved his hands down her back onto her thighs and squeezed, pulling her on top of him.

Annabelle had never been on top of Sam like this, with her legs on either side of his hips as he caressed her thighs. She felt him under her, firm. Sensations she had never experienced before coursed through her body. Annabelle pulled away from Sam's mouth to gaze into his eyes, uncontrollably panting. Sam tried just as hard to control himself. She wouldn't let it go too far, but this rush was so intoxicating.

"Is this okay?" Sam asked, removing his hands from her body.

Annabelle nodded, putting Sam's hands back on her thighs, and leaned in to kiss him again. She gasped in anticipation as his hands traveled up her dress toward her breasts, her body quivering each time he freed a button. Her heart nearly exploded as Sam slipped his hand into her top. Breathing heavy, she wasn't sure how she was still kissing Sam at that moment. He'd never touched her there before. But it felt so right. It felt—

Ace barged into the room with his arms full of food.

Annabelle jumped off of Sam and turned away to do up her buttons, her face burning hotter than the sun. Sam covered himself with the blanket.

"Well, good morning, lovebirds." Ace grinned from ear to ear. "Sorry to interrupt, but Elroy came back with the food. It's time to head out." Ace just stood there, smiling at the couple.

Sam replied, "All right, give us a minute to finish packing."

Ace placed the food onto Annabelle's bed and backed toward the door as he chuckled. "Of course. I'll give you two a minute to finish . . . *packing*." As he backed out of the room, Ace winked at Sam before closing the door behind him.

"I'm so sorry. Are you okay?" Sam reached for Annabelle's hand, but she pulled it away. Her skin was hot, and he knew exactly what she was feeling. Humiliated. Guilt washed over him, and he wished he could fix it. Annabelle adjusted her dress and quietly finished packing up their belongings.

On her way out of the room, she grabbed an apple and piece of bread off the mattress. When she reached the door, she turned back to look at Sam with flaming red cheeks. "Let's just please forget this, okay?"

Sam nodded, and she closed the door behind her.

He sat on the bed, upset with himself. All he ever wanted was to give Annabelle the world and make her feel safe, and he knew he failed just then. He'd have to have a talk with Ace once he got him alone, but for now, he needed to turn his mind back to more pressing matters.

So, he got out of bed, laced up his shoes, and left the room—slipping out the back door to avoid suspicious eyes—clinging to the feelings he had for Annabelle as he walked toward his fate.

ANNABELLE JOINED Elroy and Ace with her bag, unable to look either of them in the eye as her cheeks flushed red. She appreciated the cool breeze that flew by before the sun set its heat for the day. As much as she wanted Sam, she was still filled with guilt by what Ace had seen. She wasn't sure she would ever be able to look them in the eye again. When Ace opened his mouth to speak, her stomach dropped in anticipation.

"Good morning, Annabelle. I see you two could finally pull away from each other." Ace chuckled as he winked at Annabelle. Her gut dropped, and her cheeks flushed bright red.

"Excuse me, I need to go find Sam," Annabelle said as she ran off. The plan was to meet Sam up the road to avoid suspicions of him staying at the inn, but she couldn't face Ace just yet.

When she spotted Sam leaning against a tree, she stopped in her tracks and waited for the brothers to catch up. The shuffle of dirt followed her quickly, and the four were once again reunited.

Sam addressed the men. "Let's get this over with."

Before they began walking toward the lake, Annabelle noticed Sam make eye contact with Ace and shake his head. Ace seemed to understand and nodded in return.

Loving Sam meant having someone to protect her, even if she didn't ask. He had a gift for reading her, and she appreciated the way he looked out for her when she needed him. Though he couldn't always be so public about it as with Ace, he always made her feel safe, like she had her own guardian angel.

Shifting her eyes forward, so Ace wouldn't notice her stare, Annabelle walked on.

The group became silent, each alone with their thoughts. The only sounds were the chirps of the morning birds greeting the day. Annabelle trailed the group, watching each man contemplate what lay ahead, and knew just what Sam was thinking.

When she looked toward the brothers, she thought of how big this day was for them as well. If there was no oracle, or he couldn't help them, the cost would be their entire families. When she weighed out what everyone had to face that day, she let go of her shame. She did not need to hold on to something that would only slow her down and distract her from what was truly important—Sam's life.

As she climbed the last hill before the lake Keres had pointed them to, the lake she never expected to seek out, Annabelle's knees shook. Sweat dripped from her palms, and her stomach hurt so much she could puke. The lump in her throat grew as she looked at Sam's flushed face. Annabelle used all of her strength to climb the last few feet of the hill, pacing back and forth in her own mind as she struggled with her feelings on whatever may lie ahead. One last step, and she made it. They had made it.

Annabelle fell to her knees as she beheld the beautiful still water surrounded by trees. Nothing could be grander than this lake, their lake of hope. Still waters mirrored the trees, filling her vision with greens and blues purer than she'd ever seen. She closed her eyes and let the soft breeze consume her, breathing the fresh air. It took several moments before Annabelle realized their work was not yet done, and they needed to find the oracle before she could cry with joy.

Sam approached Annabelle and offered a hand. Once she'd helped herself to her feet, both turned to the brothers to see what came next. But as they turned to Elroy, he was already on a path that led straight into the tree line, his face stone. Sam and Annabelle jogged ahead to rejoin him and Ace.

Dense woods provided comfort with its shade. The curve of the trees fashioned a tunnel on the path. The golden-brown hue of the dirt, four companions traveling to a magical source, and an evil witch looming in the distance—*I wonder when I'll get my silver slippers.* The thought made her chuckle.

Sam looked at her with raised brows. "What's so funny?"

"Oh, nothing, my tin man." She giggled.

Sam looked up and viewed their surroundings before

looking back at her with a childlike smile. He leaned in and kissed her nose. "Whatever you say, Dorothy."

The two joined hands as they wound through the woods, enjoying the stroll until Elroy stopped.

"Are we here?" Sam asked.

A curt nod from Elroy was all he got.

Annabelle and Sam looked around for the oracle. They searched the trees, looked for hidden doors in the grass, even gave the birds a second glance, but found no one. Not one piece of evidence showed anyone had ever lived there. As a tear rolled down Annabelle's face, Elroy lifted his hands.

"Oracle, please reveal yourself to us. It is I, Elroy Nephus, and my brother, Ace. We have brought friends in need of your help." Elroy lowered his hands and searched around him. There were no sounds except for the rustle of leaves and the chirp of a bird.

Annabelle became numb—this had all been for nothing. Sam was going to die. A surge of emotions fought their way to the top, ready to consume her whole, when a whisper arose.

A shuffle of grass sounded behind a tree as a young woman emerged. Sunlight illuminated her golden hair, her tall figure gliding toward them. She greeted Elroy, taking his hand, staring at him with her innocent face. "Elroy, thank you for guiding your friends here safely." She spoke with a low, soothing voice. "The journey was tough, but knowing you, you protected them as if they were your family."

A tingling formed in Annabelle's belly as the woman faced her and Sam, nodding to Ace in a familiar manner as she did so. "Hello, Samuel and Annabelle."

Their jaws dropped. Annabelle approached the oracle and fell to her knees.

"Please, ma'am, Sam is dying and you're the only one that can help him. We've come a long way to see you, and Ace told us you could help and—"

The oracle took Annabelle's arms and lifted her to her feet. "I know why you are here, sweet one, but I must apologize; I cannot heal Sam."

Annabelle shook her head. "No, we were told you are the only one who can help."

"Yes, dear, I can help, but I cannot heal him."

A tear trickled down her cheek. "What do you mean? Don't you have magic?" Annabelle motioned to the brothers. "Elroy used magic to heal Ace."

The oracle spoke in a somber tone, "Yes, but this is a different kind of magic. I sense Chaos here. A curse."

"Curse?" Annabelle was taken aback and grabbed Sam's hand, squeezing it tight. "What does that mean?" Annabelle looked to the oracle for answers.

"I can't be sure yet," the oracle said. "I can sense the presence of the curse, but I do not know its consequence. Any information Sam can gather for us is crucial."

Annabelle had never been so confused. "Information for what? Sam doesn't know anything."

The oracle smiled. "For what happened to him these last few weeks. For how to break the curse."

"Weeks? No, we have been together every day for as long as I can—" Then she remembered. She remembered the flash—the feeling of pure terror when she realized Sam was gone.

She stared at Sam. *Weeks? He'd been gone weeks?* Elroy was

right: Sam had been to their world. How had she not put the pieces together sooner? Annabelle looked to the oracle again. "How?"

The oracle walked to Sam and grabbed his hand. "You feel it, don't you?"

Sam slowly nodded. The blank look on his face only made Annabelle more confused.

"What? Did you feel this before?"

Sam shook his head. "Not until she touched my hand."

The oracle spoke to them all. "I have enough magic to help Sam unlock his memories, but I cannot return you to your land. The Dark Queen has sealed the Rip, and even I cannot open it without a piece of the magic that keeps it sealed. Chaos is too powerful."

Elroy clenched his fists, and Ace turned away from the group, both realizing they could never see their families again.

"Do not lose hope. We may still be able to help Sam through his memories and break the curse. He may hold the answers in his mind for a way to open the Rip that we do not yet know." Ace and Elroy looked to the oracle, Elroy on the verge of tears.

Annabelle nodded. None of this made logical sense, but Annabelle had seen enough in this world to know she didn't know everything. Her faith in God went beyond reason or tangible proof, but she knew Him to be true. Annabelle knew what she had seen with the brothers, knew what she felt, and opened her mind to the possibilities of what the oracle was saying. She turned to Sam. "I believe her."

Sam looked into Annabelle's eyes, then spoke. "That's good enough for me." He faced the oracle, bringing Annabelle close in his arms. "What do you need from me?"

The oracle grabbed Sam's hand and led him to a clear area of the woods. "Lie here. You will be protected as you enter your own mind and unlock the memories of when you were in Taegaia. You will not remember your journey to me, but your time there will play out exactly as it happened to you. When you awaken, you should know what your curse is, perhaps even how we can break it." She looked at the brothers. "If we're lucky, you may hold a clue to help get Elroy and Ace back home." Ace gasped and went wide-eyed, looking like a young child full of hope.

"This won't hurt him, right?" Annabelle asked.

"No, Annabelle. He is looking through his own memories. I'm simply here to guide him back to them."

Annabelle sighed and nodded.

The oracle continued. "Now, is everyone ready?"

Sam lay on the ground and looked toward Annabelle. She smiled at Sam, and the two held each other as they said a quiet prayer together. When they finished, Sam turned back to the oracle. "We're ready."

"Good, then let us begin."

The oracle removed a vial from her cloak and sprinkled the dust inside over Sam's body. For a moment, nothing seemed to happen. Then Sam's body locked up and released, but his eyes did not reopen.

CHAPTER SEVEN

A bright flash blinded Sam before everything went dark. Extreme pain surged throughout his body, as if he were being stabbed and simultaneously ripped apart. He screamed but was sure no one would hear him over the loud ringing sound that seemed to be coming from everywhere at once. Just as fast as the pain began, Sam felt nothing. The ringing gradually returned and intensified, Sam's head pounding with the wave of sound. A blue light shone out, and Sam reached for it, desperate to escape the void of pain. Spots flickered in his vision, brought on by the never-ending ring. Sam could hardly remember anything at all, his own name slipping between his fingers. A shimmering wall appeared before him. When Sam touched it, some sort of force pulled him through. The moment he went beyond the shimmer, he was unconscious.

When Sam awoke, he was on his back in what felt like a pile of sand. He gazed up at a massive violet moon lighting up the sky. Exhaustion took Sam once more, claiming him until the sun rose in the sky.

Sam scanned the area around him but saw only a sea of black sand. He tried calling out Annabelle's name, but his throat was so dry nothing came out. *Where am I?* He remembered holding Annabelle by the lake, then pain, and then nothing. Sam started to become less concerned with where he was, but rather how long he'd been there. There was no sign of water anywhere around him. How had he gotten there? He needed to take cover to figure all of it out. Sam squinted through the glare of the sun, continually getting knocked over by the wind. Not knowing where to go, Sam picked a direction and began his journey, a journey he had no clue how long it would take him.

Keeping a straight course proved much more difficult than predicted. Sam kept getting pushed over by the wind, and the sand covered his tracks, so he had no idea which direction he had come from. The sun did not remain constant—or perhaps he was hallucinating. His lips cracked from the heat, and his throat felt like it was being scratched from the inside. He needed water. Now. Legs weakening, Sam fell onto his knees in the middle of the unknown land. With eyes toward the heavens, Sam brought his hands together in prayer.

"WAKE UP," a distant voice called to Sam as his eyes flickered open.

Sam saw nothing but a gloss over his half-open eyes. He tried to remember what had happened. Only two things came to mind—pain and a desert. But now a voice called to him. He was saved. "Annabelle?"

"Sam, wake up!"

A dream, it had all been a bad dream.

Sam wiped his eyes and slowly attempted to blink his surroundings into clarity. A dull pain veiled his head, and he could hear a soft buzzing in his ears. At last, Sam cleared his eyes and looked up to see nothing but boulders surrounding him, and he started itching from all of the sand in his clothing.

He glanced to his left from the makeshift bed he lay on. A black ring glistened on a hand that offered him a glass of water. He took it without hesitation. Sam nearly inhaled the water, thinking only of how it was the best drink he'd ever had touch his lips. Still too weak to stand, Sam faced the one who had given him the water.

"Where am I? Who are you? Where's Annabelle?"

"Just a moment, Sam. There will be plenty of time for questions. For now, just breathe."

Sam found himself standing as confusion and frustration prickled to the surface. The stranger stood a head and a half shorter than Sam, with deep olive skin and well-groomed brown hair. His dark red suit matched the red flower pinned to his coat pocket. An interesting choice of apparel for the middle of the desert. He exuded social sophistication, standing tall with shoulders pulled back, and his shoes were immaculate, despite all the sand that crept into every crevice of Sam's body. If this man was threatened by Sam's size, he didn't show it. He simply looked up at Sam with his piercing green eyes and spoke.

"I understand your frustrations. I really do. But if you would just follow me, we can get this all sorted out."

Sam breathed deep, contemplating whether to hit the man and make a run for it or to do as the man said. Sam peered outside the nest of rocks and recalled the first time he tried wandering out there by himself. As much as he didn't like to, he needed to follow the man. But he would get some answers first. "I'm not going anywhere until I know who you are and where we are going. And where I am. And if Annabelle is safe."

The man considered the terms, then stuck out his hand. "All right, Sam. I'm Keres."

Sam shook Keres's hand and instinctively began to introduce himself. "It's nice to meet you, Keres. I'm Sa . . ." Sam paused and glared at the man, gripping his hand tightly. "How do you know my name?" Sam's eyes narrowed, and his chest rose and fell much faster and deeper as his blood heated.

Keres stared blankly at Sam, then smiled charmingly. "Like I said, Sam, this will all be made clear once I show you. We must go quickly now. The Dark Queen is waiting for us."

Sam shook his head in defiance. "No. I'm not going anywhere with you until I get some answers. And why would I go with you to someone called the 'Dark Queen'?"

Keres sighed and released Sam's hand. "Fine. No need to be so pervicacious. The Dark Queen has given me orders to bring you to her by any means necessary. I was hoping to do this with as little pain as possible. Annabelle is well, I promise."

Sam looked expectant at the mention of Annabelle's name.

"She is back home, safe, but has no idea you are here. The Dark Queen brought you here with her magic, and I found you wandering the desert several days ago and gave you nourishment to bring you back to health." Keres shook his head. "That's all I can tell you for now. We really must be going.

We don't want to upset the Dark Queen by being late." Keres looked down at Sam's bare feet and scoffed. "Really?"

Sam's cheeks flushed, and he shrugged. Anger reemerged, taking over the slight embarrassment, and he crossed his arms. "I'm not going with you. This is crazy." Though as Sam looked around, it became evident he didn't have much of a choice, but this was all he could think of to get the answers he so desperately needed.

Keres stood his ground, unmoved by Sam's defiance.

"I want to know where I am. What's going on?" Sam narrowed his eyes. If Keres wouldn't break, neither would he.

Keres sighed, whispering to himself, "What could she possibly want with this obstreperous fool . . ."

Obstreperous? I'm standing here perfectly quiet.

Keres gathered up the supplies in the cave. "Have it your way, then. Though you'll find the sand and heat to be quite ubiquitous."

Sam scanned the surrounding area of wide-open desert. *Obviously.* This man wasn't making any sense.

"Best of luck surviving another day." Keres performed an exaggerated bow, then stepped out of the cave and walked on, leaving Sam behind without even a drop of water.

Stunned, Sam considered his next move. He had no water, no food, no idea of how to get home, and no direction of civilization . . . except for the direction Keres headed. Sam hated himself for it, but he sighed and walked out of the cave, huffing to himself as he followed Keres into the wide-open desert.

SAM HAD no idea how Keres knew which way to go. Even though Keres lived here, nothing stood out as a reference point —not even the stars or sun as far as he could tell. Everything seemed the same to him—sand, rocks, and more sand. Sam's bare feet burned against it. *Why did I have to take my shoes off at the lake?* Pushing through the pain, Sam focused on the sky and forged ahead.

"Why do the stars and sun move like that?" Sam asked.

Keres ignored him, as he had for the entirety of their walk. Sam rolled his eyes, fed up with his travel companion.

The faintest tree line appeared ahead of them. Hazy, Sam almost thought he imagined it, but the closer he got, the more defined the forest became. *An oasis?* Sam opened his mouth to ask about it when Keres came to a halt.

Keres glared at Sam. "Before we enter the forest, there are a few rules you must follow. Number one: stay beside me the entire time. This forest can play tricks on you. I can't have you getting lost. Understood?"

Sam nodded in confusion. How could a forest play tricks?

"Good. Number two: speak to no one. And number three: don't stare. They don't like it when you do that."

"Wait. What? Who's 'they'?"

Keres ignored the question. "Are we ready?"

Sam gazed blankly at Keres and cleared his throat. "Uh, I think so. Yes." Sam scratched his head and looked back at the desert. There was nothing for him there, so he turned his attention back to the forest.

"Fantastic. We will be to the village by nightfall." Keres pointed his perfectly polished shoes toward the forest and walked between the curtain of the first trees.

Sam tried his best to keep up with Keres, but he had never seen anything like this before. The trees were so tall he must have only been able to see halfway up at most. A fog wove through the floor of the forest and stopped at his ankles. The woods were so quiet, so still, until the beat and hum of music sounded far in the distance.

A hollow sensation took over his stomach. The feeling told him to stay alert. More than once, he thought the trees somehow stared at him, but when he looked again, nothing was out of sorts. When a bird flew past, Sam was sure it had said "hello" and given him a wink. He must be losing his mind.

"Where are we?" Sam whispered as he swiveled his head.

"Shh." Keres hushed Sam and continued walking.

Sam huffed and crossed his arms. He probably looked like a child, but that was exactly how Keres had treated him. Gritting his teeth, Sam rolled his neck and shook out his arms before continuing through the forest.

Limbs heavy and sluggish, the exhaustion did its best to convince him that he couldn't believe his own eyes anymore. He needed to wake up so he would be able to follow Keres however much farther they were to go. As he looked to Keres, Sam noticed he wasn't even breaking a sweat in his suit. How peculiar . . .

Crack! A twig snapped beside him, and Sam whirled around to see what had made the noise. His eyes met with something they had never seen before. At least, nothing they'd seen outside of a book. A magnificent creature stood before him—a black mare. But this one was different than the ones back home. Feathers cascaded from the body of the creature down into wings. Sam reached out his hand to stroke the mare, but Keres yanked on Sam's elbow. "I told you, no staring. We need to keep moving." Several more of the creatures approached behind the first as Keres pulled Sam back onto their path.

"Wha— Was that real?"

Keres kept his gaze forward as he spoke. "Surely, you've figured out by now that you are somewhere quite different than the places you are used to."

"I don't know what I know. I'm still not sure you're even real yet." Sam sighed heavily, his legs threatening to give way if he didn't rest soon. Despite resting in the cave, he still wasn't at his full strength. "How much farther? I need a break." Sam tried to ignore the pain of his feet snapping on fallen twigs.

Keres stopped abruptly and stared ahead. After a moment, he turned to Sam with a big smile on his face. "Why, of course, Sam. There's a nice tree right there; feel free to lean on it for a minute."

Sam looked at Keres, puzzled, but made his way to the tree and lifted himself onto a branch so he could sit. Keres stood where he was, picking off a single speck of dirt from his jacket.

"Aren't you exhausted?" Sam asked.

Keres looked to Sam. "No, but I suppose I'm more acclimated to these parts than you."

Sam reached his hands up to stretch, popping his upper back, and let out a satisfied sigh. "Why do you talk like that?" Sam thought he ought to get to know the man who kept him company.

"Like what?" Keres stared blankly at Sam.

"Well, I mean, it's like you're trying too hard."

Keres let out a low laugh. "Ah, yes. I believe that the way a man presents himself in demeanor reflects the kind of man he is and wishes to be. Don't you?"

Sam thought for a moment. "I guess I see what you're saying. A wishful poet knows the importance of words. But I think actions are more what defines who a man truly is."

Keres narrowed his eyes to Sam, then smiled again. "Absolutely right, Sam. You are absolutely right. I suppose it could be viewed as an unwelcome idiosyncrasy. Would you be more comfortable if I spoke with a more casual lexicon?"

"You don't have to speak differently for me. I was just curious—it's not very relatable to most people. Besides, you're using a lot of the words wrong."

A thin vein popped out of Keres's neck, and his cheeks turned a flaming red. "Very well, then. I wouldn't be opposed to any attempt to speak more informally." Keres spoke through gritted teeth.

Sam shrugged and turned his head down. He'd embarrassed Keres. Perhaps he should just give the man the benefit of the doubt. Maybe Keres wasn't as pompous as he'd assumed.

"Now, are we ready to be on our way again?" Keres seemed back to his normal, proper self.

As Sam jumped to his feet, he screamed as a branch stabbed his foot.

Keres tried to conceal his laugh. "We can get you shoes tonight."

Sam hobbled toward Keres. "Fine, but I'm only continuing on one condition: you have to tell me where I am." If Sam knew where he was, maybe he could get back to Annabelle all on his own. He couldn't be that far from Charleston.

Keres nodded in agreement, then lifted his hands to motion all around him. "We are in the forest."

Sam shook his head. "You know what I mean."

Keres thought another moment. "All right, I'll tell you where you are. But first, we should climb to the top of that hill there, so you can see everything I am going to tell you about."

Sam reluctantly agreed, and the two climbed to the top of what was assuredly a mountain, not a hill.

As Sam approached the peak, he stepped out into the openness, to the clouds lining the treetops and the sky. Keres handed Sam a small telescope and motioned him over toward the edge of the cliff. When Sam looked down, he stood in awe.

Far below, he could make out a village full of unusual homes and bustling people. He admired the houses—square with a central courtyard, but they had a quality that made them feel . . . enchanting. Perhaps it was just the odd structures that struck him as fascinating, as he'd never seen anything like it. Beyond the village, a road snaked through a massive valley, weaving in and out of towns leading away from the mountain.

Each village appeared less cheery than the last, becoming darker the farther he looked. His eyes followed the trail to a beach, where the water went past the horizon. Then Sam spotted what excited Keres most based on his grin—the silhouette of a dark stone palace encased in a cloud of swirling black smoke.

Everything around the castle matched its melancholy nature. It was as if a wave of death had seeped from the walls and suffocated everything in its path, turning grass to black char, trees to rotted corpses, and the sky to a darkness that could only be described as evil. It made Sam cold, even from this distance. Sam thought the palace in smoke would be the most implausible thing he would ever see, until he looked just beyond it.

He had to rub his eyes and look twice to be sure, but his eyes were not playing tricks. Beyond the villages and the river and the smoke was an open galaxy.

Sam searched for the right words. "How . . . what . . ."

Keres stepped in. "That there is exactly what it looks like—the edge of our world. It surrounds us on all sides, but that is the only side you can actually see. This world is held together by magic, far from any other realm."

"So, we really aren't in South Carolina . . ." *Or Earth . . .* Sam began to realize the full extent of his predicament, of how hard it would be to get back to Annabelle. He struggled to come up with some sort of plan.

Keres scoffed. "Not even close."

Sam continued to stare at the overwhelming abyss, marveling at the pinks, purples, and blues all dancing together in a sparkling cloud of electricity that drifted away to meet the rest of the universe. Sam had never seen something so beautiful yet so frightening at the same time. But one memory in his life matched the feeling he had in that instant—the moment he knew he was in love with Annabelle. He would never have thought he could see his absolute love for her in any tangible way, but as he looked to the edge of the world, he knew that this terrifying magnificence would be as close as he could ever come.

That somehow calmed Sam as he glanced out over the entire land, taking in its darkness and horrors along with its charm and grace. For the first time in days, as Sam took the notebook from his pocket and flipped open to the sketch of Annabelle, he could feel her there with him.

"My Belli," Sam whispered as he stroked the picture.

If Sam ever wanted to get back to Annabelle, he had to do the hard thing, the thing that didn't make any sense. This was out of his hands.

Sam turned to Keres. "All right, I've seen enough. Take me to your queen."

Keres grinned, patting Sam on his shoulder, and replied, "Good." Keres looked out from the mountain once more as he spoke. "And welcome to Taegaia."

THE PATH LEADING out of the vast forest led straight to a nearby village. As Sam and Keres approached, the distant music from the forest amplified. It was not like any song he'd heard before, but he enjoyed it. A band entertained a crowd of people at some sort of festival, with instruments he had never seen.

One was as big as a wall, taking three people to blow into it and create the deepest harmony he'd ever heard. The men used their entire bodies to make the sound. Their hands covered holes up and down the instrument, and their feet were beating along the bottom on bags, giving even more wind to the mechanism. One woman played an apparatus that turned like a spinning wheel with one hand, while her other slid down what appeared to be a long, thin piece of metal, creating a backdrop of tinny rain, but that was somehow calming. A third instrument, the most bizarre of all, created the melody, switching between fast and slow tempos in an array of scales unheard of in Sam's world. He heard notes he couldn't even comprehend. They sounded like whispers and laughs and fun. Among all the pandemonium of noise, Sam found his foot joining the music, and a smile crept onto his face as he took in the rest of the gathering.

Sam thought of Annabelle and how she would enjoy the bizarre musical instruments while sitting there quietly singing along, wishing to perform alongside them.

"Wow, it's beautiful," Sam whispered.

Keres laughed, though his face showed no amusement. "More like a cacophony."

Sam shook his head. Keres didn't know what he was talking about—it was incredible.

The lights dancing above the crowd captivated Sam as some people moved to the music and others sat at a table clapping along. It looked like they were all having an evening meal together, enjoying each other's company while celebrating the night under the stars. Then Sam was able to see what he was sure was his imagination back in the forest. There were fantastical creatures, dancing and eating as if they were human. Some were much larger than the humans, with fur and horns and hooves. Others were as small as a bird, glowing different colors and flying about. Some appeared humanlike but existed in every color imaginable.

A woman waved to Keres as she got up from her table and approached them. She was short and stout, her skin a deep magenta, with curly hair a deep shade of brown and styled in a shape that matched her figure. Like most other villagers, she wore a simple peplos dress in a muted color with a rope for a belt. Sam stood in unease until the woman opened her arms to embrace Keres, who paused a moment and hugged her back. The woman then turned to Sam and bowed her head slightly.

"Welcome. I am Carma."

Sam nodded back and introduced himself.

Carma gestured toward the festivities. "Well, Sam, come join in. You look starved. We've got anything you could want." Then she pointed to a home just up the road. "That's my inn; you'll stay there tonight, yes?" Carma nodded and gave Sam a big smile, which made Sam feel oddly welcome in this strange town.

Sam looked to Keres, who returned the gesture. "Yes, we need rest for the night before heading back to the castle."

Carma's eyes widened, and she looked toward Sam. "You're taking him to the Dark Queen?" She grabbed Sam's hand and patted it. "Poor dear," she whispered so softly, Sam was sure Keres couldn't hear. Sam barely made the words out himself.

What was it about this Dark Queen? Surely, one woman couldn't be so bad.

Keres replied, "Yes, she sent a summons for him. I am to retrieve him and bring him to her at once. We will leave early tomorrow." Then he turned to Sam. "Please, join in the fun and food. The rest of the journey is more . . . difficult."

With that, Keres made his way to an empty table and sat to eat.

Unsure what to do, Sam approached the magenta woman. "Excuse me, ma'am. Where should I be?"

Grabbing Sam's hand, Carma walked him over to a stand full of beverages. She took a cup and filled it with a deep orange liquid, then handed it to Sam. He pulled the cup close to his lips and inhaled. Citrus and cinnamon filled his nostrils, and it was one of the most delightful scents he'd ever come across. Sam sipped the liquid—tea—downing the cup quickly and then refilling it.

When he finished, Carma led him back to her table and introduced him to some of the townsfolk. There was a woman who resembled a tree, adorned with flowers from head to toe, another with long translucent wings, who had a slight glow about her, and a creature with a wolf's head but the body of a man.

The sight was like something straight out of a book. Sam was sure he would never remember their names, for he was too distracted by the horns and the wings to focus on anything else, though he tried his best to be polite. But then the scent of the feast grabbed his attention.

He hadn't eaten in . . . actually, he couldn't remember the last time he'd eaten. With a nearby fork, Sam shoveled food on his plate from the center of the table. He grabbed pastries and potatoes, strawberries and squash. Filled to the brim with delight from the dinner and the . . . people . . . he listened to the complex music and took in the stunning scenery around him.

He nearly dropped his fork when one of the villagers lifted her arms toward the sky, and the clouds overhead matched her movements. They turned black, as if a heavy rain were about to fall, and lightning flickered—bright flashes twinkling against the dark backdrop, moving in rhythm to the music. A spectacular show.

Sam almost didn't remember walking to the inn and crawling into bed. As his head kissed the pillow, he fell asleep.

SAM ROSE WITH THE SUN. As he lay in his bed, his heart ached for Annabelle. He'd already been gone for several days, and she had no idea where he was or that he was even alive. It hurt him to think of how she must be feeling at that moment, her believing he had abandoned her or was in some terrible trouble. He had to get back to her—he couldn't let her wonder what had happened to him for her entire life. Sam looked out the window and stared at the hazy pink sky, watching the tinted blue sun coming over the horizon.

A thought sprang into his mind. Sam grabbed his notebook from his pocket and thought back to his first day in this odd place, the days he spent in the black-sanded desert. He put five tally marks on the page, one for each day he'd been there, and tucked the notebook back into his pocket.

A knock rattled on the door, and Sam opened it to find Keres waiting on the other side, all polished and proper with his hair slicked back and in his newly pressed suit. He was clearly ready to go. "Shall we?" Keres handed Sam a new pair of shoes, which Sam happily put on.

Sam nodded, following Keres and closing the door behind him. He trailed Keres into the central courtyard, where there were tables filled with food and Carma standing with a welcoming smile. "Good morning, dears! I hope the room was to your liking."

Sam thanked her for her hospitality. As Keres and Sam started out the front door, Carma caught up with Sam and handed him a bag filled with pastries. Sam hugged Carma goodbye and turned back toward Keres.

"We will be at the castle in three days' time if we stay the course. The Dark Queen will be most pleased to see you." Keres was stone-faced as he stepped onto the path toward the palace, twisting the black ring on his finger as he waited for Sam to join him.

Sam swallowed his food and gave Keres a slight tilt of his head to show he was listening. The lively village became nothing but a memory as he headed toward the Dark Queen.

THE MEN HAD BEEN WALKING for several hours before approaching another town. Sam was intrigued to see how folks in this town lived based on his enthralling experience the night before. But as they walked closer, he did not see anyone in the streets or at the market. Doors were closed and curtains were pulled shut. The only sign of life was a rat that scurried across the road in front of them.

Sam was baffled. *What happened here?* The houses were not draped in color as the previous town had been. There were no bright banners or candles or sounds of celebration. The buildings were covered in deep soot, and many of the roads and homes were scorched. Even the air seemed a bit thicker in comparison to the last village.

A child peeked out of one of the windows. *People live here?* As the two walked on, Sam spotted a group of people huddled under a covering. From what Sam could make out, they were bartering an apple for some bread. The people were somber looking, hunched over and slightly shaking. As soon as the people looked toward Sam and Keres, they fled back into their homes, silent.

Sam began to put the pieces together. The quiet streets, the hushed voices, the dark clothing—these people were in mourning. Sam turned his attention back to the path and continued on, trying to respect their privacy and leave them in peace.

As the men ventured farther from the town, Sam finally spoke to Keres, "What happened back there?"

Keres kept his gaze forward as he replied, "The Dark Queen."

"What do you mean?"

"I mean, when they disappointed her, she took it into her own hands to teach them a thing or two about respect, as she put it."

Sam's jaw dropped. "Why would she do that in her own kingdom?" Was it really possible that she alone caused all this death and destruction?

"Her parents were recently killed, and it snapped something in her. She has sought to destroy all she can so the world around her matches what's inside."

Sam was speechless. "If she is so horrible, why doesn't anyone do anything to stop her? Why do you still work for her?"

Keres turned to Sam. "Some things are much more complicated than they look to an outsider. Our queen has found a way to restrict Harmony to the people and cast out anyone who wields it naturally. She uses Chaos to control the kingdom."

"Harmony? Chaos? What are you talking about?"

"Magic. The queen's dark magic is called Chaos. No one can defeat that sort of power. I chose my path—serve and live."

Sam couldn't believe it. Even across worlds, how could

humans give in to such evil? How could anyone enter a village and burn it with no regard for anyone else's life? Sam's stomach churned as he thought of all the innocent lives lost to such a wicked beast. He tried not to think of the family he lost so young, from people with the same hate in their hearts. When he faced the queen, he would show her all the respect she deserved for how she treated her kingdom.

Keres and Sam arrived in another village just before nightfall. As with the last village, there were no festivities, no welcoming party. Sam stood in the road, looking at the woods surrounding them.

"Get inside," Keres said. "You don't want to be out when it's dark."

Sam took Keres at his word and made his way into the abandoned house that Keres walked into. The room smelled of ash, and there was no proper place to rest, so Sam took a corner of the room on the floor. It took him hours to fall asleep.

Well into the night, Sam awoke to a loud growl outside the window. Frozen, his eyes darted to Keres, who held his finger to his lips. The creature stalked past the window, bumping into everything in its path. The shadow filled the room—a hulking body with sharp teeth—and Sam kept still against the wall under the window. He could hear his own heartbeat; his breath stilled.

Just as it had come, the creature leapt from the porch and ran back into the woods. Sam let out a breath and lay back down, his eyes wide open the rest of the night.

THE NEXT TWO nights were the same. Abandoned homes full of ash for rest, with creatures stalking them throughout the night. Sam was torn between wanting these nights to end and wanting to avoid the castle, however much protection it would provide from the wild creatures. When Sam and Keres stepped out for their last leg of the journey, everything seemed different.

Sam could just make out a pillar of the castle in the far-off distance. He had to figure out what the queen wanted and how he would safely return to his Annabelle. Could magic help him? If magic was even real.

They navigated through several more towns in ruin and were on their final path to the dark castle. Everything seemed darker and colder than when he had first arrived in Taegaia. The ground was covered in thick smoke, and the closer they traveled to the castle, the thicker it got, until it turned into a low fire.

Sam stopped, refusing to walk on a ground set ablaze, but Keres walked right over it. The constant low fire whipped around his ankles, avoiding him as it torched the land. Sam slowly followed Keres into the fire, relieved when the flames avoided him as well.

"What kind of fire is this? Why does it not burn us?"

Keres kept his gaze forward. "It is the Dark Queen's fire. She would not use it on her honored guest and dearest advisor."

Sam gulped at the implication of her using it on anyone at all, pushing the thought from his mind, and kept on.

There was no sound, save for a whisper of the wind and crackle of the flames, warning Sam to turn back while he still could. As tempted as he was to run, he had nowhere to go, and he had to get through this to get back to his home. He couldn't hide from his fate here.

The palace was blanketed in sapphire drapes and surrounded by massive white rosebushes. The bushes covered the entire perimeter of the castle apart from the grand door, met by an enormous staircase at the end of a bridge. Below the bridge was the sound of a rushing river, covered by black clouds that appeared from nothing, and a storm brewed inside with bursts of lightning. Goose bumps formed on his body as he continued to gaze upon the palace. Aside from the roses, only death resided around the castle.

Figures stood tall next to the bridge, as if they were standing guard. Sam's stomach dropped as he and Keres approached. Nearly ten feet off the ground, restrained by vines and thorns which pierced the skin, people stood on a narrow plank—most of them dead.

Sam looked down the line of people and almost vomited. On the nearest stand, a woman coughed up blood. She fought to keep her eyes open, and every time she slipped, the vine tightened, digging the thorns in deeper. Shrieks filled the air as she fell, fully entangled in the spikes. The sight sent chills through Sam, and he rushed to her.

The vines tangled along the posts, no clear sign of a release for the prisoners. The only escape would be someone cutting them free. Rocks piled at the tree line caught his eye, a sharp one near the top perfect for hacking at the vines. As the last limb snapped, the woman dropped from the platform. Before she hit the ground, a fire roared beneath her. She fell into the flames, screaming in agony, until she went silent.

Sam vomited as he stared at the woman's crisp corpse.

Keres approached Sam and pulled him up by the collar. "You cannot help them. Now come, the Dark Queen is expecting you."

Sam couldn't peel his eyes from the flames eating away at the woman's flesh. If the Dark Queen was capable of this . . .

Sam turned and ran back the way he'd come. He didn't care if he had nowhere to go; anywhere was better than the madwoman's castle. He didn't make it five strides before a wall of fire shot up in front of him and stretched out as far as he could see on either side. The only choice was to continue inside as the Dark Queen commanded. Trying to block the horrendous view of the others on their posts from his vision, he turned back toward the castle to follow Keres inside. The sight made him ill.

No life surrounded this palace. Massive vines scattered with white roses choked the castle. An ominous sense of terror enveloped him entirely. The thorns and flames protected the flowers and stone from any intruders.

It was the perfect defense for this fortress. Death and thorns and pain oozed from every crevasse of this wretched castle. This place was haunted, and as Sam took his first step onto the bridge, a shiver crawled up his spine, and he knew only evil awaited him.

CHAPTER EIGHT

A set of stone snake statues coiled like guards at the end of the bridge. A flurry of wind charged toward them and tossed up the crisp leaves that had nestled into the nooks of the palace steps. They ascended the seemingly never-ending staircase until they reached the massive pillars stretching high into the air. Sam hesitated but followed Keres through the grand doors leading into the fortress.

The inside of the castle matched its lifeless exterior perfectly. The cold from the stones raised the hairs on his arms as he walked down the long hallway. The only sounds were his and Keres's footsteps bouncing off the walls encircling them.

Many of the walls had square niches between columns where Sam assumed portraits used to hang. Nothing about this entrance was welcoming, though Sam gathered the queen wasn't inviting many guests anyway. He gazed up at the giant chandeliers adorning the ceiling every few steps and marveled at their chilling beauty as they lit the way into the heart of the castle.

Keres took a hard right through an archway. Two men with breastplates and spears stood guard. One of the guards was so large, Sam didn't even think he was real, that he must have been a statue. But then the man glared down at him, and Sam hurried his pace to keep up with Keres.

The archway opened up into a large room where sapphire cloth wrapped each column; white roses were scattered and etched onto almost every inch of the room. *What's with all the roses?* The floors were not stone like the rest of the castle, but marble. Sam took in the beauty of the room, the intricate stonework on the walls, the painted ceilings telling a story of this world. The largest painting was of three women holding hands, looking down at a village from a mountaintop.

Then his eyes fell upon the center of the room. There, sitting on a throne of silver draped in sapphires and roses, was a woman he could only assume to be the Dark Queen.

Sam didn't know what to expect the Dark Queen to look like—perhaps an old, craggy witch with stringy white hair and a boil on her nose—but not this.

Barely older than him, she was breathtaking. Her skin, olive and flawless. Her long, dark brown hair flowed off her shoulders and cascaded down like a waterfall. Her eyes shone a fierce green, with sharp facial features—distinct jawline, high cheekbones, and narrowed brow. As she stood, he took in the perfect curvature of her elongated figure—a walking goddess.

Was this one woman really capable of all the destruction he'd seen? Certainly, one person couldn't do all that alone.

The Dark Queen took one step forward, the slit up her deep

blue dress exposing her right leg. Not flesh, but a silver limb wrapped in black roses and vines. The stunning design, much like the queen, lured Sam forward. Her presence, like a poison he couldn't escape.

With her next step, an orange flame slowly slithered up her figure, illuminating her body in a glow that simmered red. The fire swam through her veins, pulsating into sparks at her fingertips. A blaze erupted behind her and ran through the room, surrounding them.

Sam fell to the floor and began to pray, with no more doubts about the Dark Queen's abilities, sure she could act alone in the devastation caused to the villages. As the Dark Queen raised her arms, the fires raced back into her. Instantly, she was back to how she'd been before the flames, and Sam was again staring at her figure.

Catching his impure thoughts, he shook off her intoxication. He already had the most beautiful woman in the world, and the one standing before him was a monster. He wouldn't need to remind himself of that again.

Keres bowed deep before his queen. She waved her hand lazily to tell him to stand, hardly giving him any notice as she approached Sam, who stood not knowing what to do. He would never bow to this heinous woman, so he kept his gaze forward as the queen circled him, inspecting him. She stopped in front of Sam, giving him a smirk as she stared into his eyes.

At this distance, he was able to take in the smaller details of the queen. The sapphire ring upon her right index finger, the silver crown made to resemble a laurel wreath scattered with gems placed perfectly atop her head, a silver armlet wrapped around her upper arm, and a tattoo of three joined white roses drawn over her heart. She made her way back to her throne.

Keres stood in allegiance to his queen—a true follower. A timid-looking man stepped forward from beside the throne. "S-sir Samuel Jones, may I introduce Her Royal Excellency, the highest of the high, the most supreme, Mistress of Chaos, Her Majesty, Queen Dorthea Emagine Rayzel—the Dark Queen." The man stared at Sam for a moment as Sam stood his ground, refusing to show any emotion or reaction to this witch. The man cleared his throat. "You will b-bow to the Dark Queen now."

Sam shook his head. "No, I won't." He looked to the Dark Queen. "You brought me here against my will, you killed all those people in the villages, there are people hanging outside of your castle gates . . ." Sam restrained himself from calling her a monster. "I want to go home."

Keres stood still, his face giving nothing away, but the timid man looked horrified as he searched for his next words. He cleared his throat again. "You will—"

"That's enough," the Dark Queen cut the man off, and he quietly backed into his place beside her throne, his head hung low, looking as if he were choking on his own tongue.

The Dark Queen stood, making her way back to Sam—a bit too close for his liking—but as he tried to take a step back, he felt stuck in his place. The Dark Queen sighed. "I haven't given you permission to leave my presence."

At the realization of why he couldn't move, Sam's eyes widened, and the Dark Queen prowled even closer. He could smell her and wasn't at all surprised at the sharp scent of roses dripping from her. Stepping even closer, she got in Sam's face and breathed him in, letting out a sensual sigh as she looked him up and down. "No one here speaks to me in that manner, Sammy. I find that . . . arousing."

Sam was horrified as the Dark Queen gawked at him like some sort of prey. He desperately tried to step away from her, and when she finally released him, she laughed as he stepped backward. The Dark Queen turned to walk out of the room, motioning for Sam to follow. "Come, I will give you a tour of my palace."

Sam tried to resist, but the pull of his feet toward the Dark Queen forced him to join her in the corridor. She glanced over her shoulder before leaving the grand room. "Ilia, stay." The timid man bowed his head and remained at her throne, then the Dark Queen led Sam down the hallway. "It's quite remarkable, don't you think?"

Sam had to agree with her on that point. As horrible as this place was, *remarkable* described it well. The enormous columns lined every hall, making a path where anything could be lurking in the shadows. Sam shivered as he thought he saw movement in the dark corners, but it disappeared before he could identify it.

The Dark Queen led Sam out through another corridor, and Keres followed closely behind. "You have already met my faithful advisor, Keres. He came to me a few years ago after the tragedy of his parents." She said *tragedy* as if she were talking about anything else in the world. Like it didn't matter. "He's been an asset to the castle, running my errands and fetching whatever I may need. Today, it seems that would be you."

Sam listened as he surveyed his surroundings. More stone and echoes.

The Dark Queen continued, "The room you met me in is my grand arena, where the eragats come to beg for whatever they may need."

"Eragats?" Sam asked.

"Yes. Workers . . . the peasants." The Dark Queen waved her hand, as if trying to get the thought of the *peasants* out of the air. "Through here is the dining hall, where you will meet me every night for dinner. I've assembled the best chef and staff in the realm, so you won't have to suffer through the filth they eat in the villages. Through this corridor . . ."

Sam tuned the Dark Queen out as he retraced her words. *Every night.* What did she mean by every night? Surely, she couldn't believe he would stay here with her willingly, or at all. As unbelievable as all of this was, he just wanted to return to his simple—well, soon-to-be simple—life with Annabelle. Sam continued to fantasize as the Dark Queen waved her hands, pointing to different sections of the castle. He wasn't taking in a word she said. The Dark Queen stopped abruptly outside of a door.

Sam admired the intricate details along the door's edge, losing himself in the art as the Dark Queen's voice pierced through again, "I expect you will find your chambers comfortable. They are the finest in the palace, besides my own, of course." The Dark Queen scanned the corridors, her eyes narrowing on a young red-haired woman just coming down the hall. "This servant will be yours now." The Dark Queen snapped her fingers. "Servant girl, come here! This is my sweet Sammy."

"It's Sam," he interrupted. He wished she would stop calling him Sammy—he hadn't been called that since he was a small boy.

The Dark Queen ignored the interruption. "You will give him whatever he may need. I am deeming *you* his charge for the duration of his stay. He will be bathed and dressed in fine silks for dinner this evening. You think you can handle that?"

The young woman trembled as she replied, bowing, "Y-yes, Your Greatness. Anything he needs."

The Dark Queen half smiled at the woman. "Good. I expect I will not be kept waiting this evening, or it will be *you* who suffers the consequences."

The woman nodded and hurriedly opened the door, motioning Sam inside.

Sam followed, hoping to save this poor young woman from whatever consequences the queen may try to bestow upon her.

The Dark Queen's voice seeped into the room as the young woman closed the door. "Persephone will keep an eye on you."

The young woman went stiff before turning to Sam. She backed toward his bathing room in her emerald dress that touched the floor. It cinched high at the waist and was adorned with gold embroidery. The woman wore a swirling gold armlet on her exposed arm. As he got a better look at her, he could see she was not a young woman at all, but a girl. "I—I will start a bath for you, good sir. Do you have a preference of oil?"

Sam shook his head, and the girl went into the next room. Once Sam heard water fill the tub, he darted around the room, looking for some way to escape, or at least find—well, he didn't know, but he was going to search anyway.

He started with the most obvious place—the window. Sam unlatched the oversized glass panes decorated in various shades of blues, and pushed them open. A breeze hit Sam in the face, and as he looked outside, he immediately knew he could not escape this way. There must have been three hundred feet of stone that touched nothingness, only dropping into the river below. He could never survive a jump like that. Even if he managed to scale to the bottom of the castle, the drop into the water would kill him instantly.

Sam scanned the room. There had to be another way out. He ran to the bed, the largest and most lavish bed he had ever laid eyes upon, and crouched down onto the floor to see underneath. Nothing but more stone waited. He then turned his attention toward the paintings on the walls. One by one, he took them down, hoping for some sort of passage behind them. Again, he met no luck.

As he turned to look for a new idea, a knock sounded on the door, and Sam froze in place. The door opened, and Sam had to stifle a scream when a man walked in.

No ordinary man stood before him. With skin the shade of ash and deep-set onyx eyes, the creature glared at Sam. Intricately styled hair in the purest of white fell to his waist and contrasted the hue of his irises. His long, pointed ears extended well past the back of his skull.

An elf, Sam recalled, as the creature straightened to its full height, the top of his head nearly eye level to Sam. Like Keres, he stood poised and proper, and wore a silver-blue satin tunic.

"I'm sorry to disturb you. My name is Gadriel, and I am the palace overseer. The chef is preparing tonight's meal, and I am here to see if you have any special requests."

Sam crossed his arms and narrowed his eyes, taking in Gadriel's presence. Every humanlike being he came across filled him with awe—a true reminder of how far he'd slipped from Annabelle. "No," Sam said firmly. He began to turn away, then had a second thought. "Actually, I don't eat meat. But anything else will do."

Gadriel gave Sam a smile and bowed as he backed out of the room. "Of course, sir. I will tell Chef immediately." He closed and locked the door behind him, leaving Sam back to his task of making his escape plan.

The servant girl reappeared into the room. "It's ready. I hope you like hot baths." She spoke sweetly—her voice reminded him of honey.

Sam cleared his throat as he nodded to the girl. "That will be fine, thank you."

Sam walked into the bathing room and gasped. The bath was as large as his whole house, filled with oils and bubbles. Detailed works of roses on silver scaled up the walls, with accents of blue drapes kissing the ceiling. There was even a painting of the pink sky on the wall where a window would have been. Sam wanted to search this room as well, but his back and feet ached—his body begged for a warm bath. So, Sam undressed and stepped into the tub.

A surge of relief coursed through his body, and he told himself he would search the room after his bath. He walked to the far end of the tub and nestled into a seat under the water that perfectly fit his curvature. While Sam knew he could never let the queen know of his enjoyment, he let a smile creep onto his face as he closed his eyes and slowly drifted off into pure relaxation.

Sam had no guess as to how much time had gone by as the servant girl called him awake. Once he realized where he was, he quickly covered himself with his hands.

The girl looked at Sam unashamed. "Sorry to disturb you,

but the Dark Queen expects you for supper soon. We need to get you dressed."

Sam nodded and sent the girl out so he could change. He wondered why everyone was apologizing to him when it seemed they were only doing their jobs. Was the Dark Queen really that terrible to live with? Was it not just the villagers she bestowed her wrath upon?

Grabbing the towel the girl had put next to him, Sam walked over to the counter, where a fresh razor lay waiting. Once the mirror cleared of steam, Sam stared at his scruffy face. He preferred a clean shave, unused to seeing himself with a beard. He'd be happy to see it go.

Stroke after stroke, the razor glided effortlessly across his face, giving Sam a piece of himself back as he rubbed his palms over his smooth cheeks. He patted himself dry and walked back to the chair he had placed his clothes on. But when he got there, his clothes had been replaced by an extravagant deep blue suit.

The silk suit fit his form perfectly, covered in a design of large white and silver roses. Silver buttons fastened together down the front, with three linked roses carved onto each of them—just like the tattoo he'd seen on the Dark Queen's breasts. Annabelle would marvel at the craftsmanship. He'd never worn anything so luxurious, and he couldn't help but enjoy the feeling of the silk as it tickled his skin. He thought the pants and white tunic were enough but threw the jacket on anyway.

After he was dressed and slipped on his shoes, Sam looked at himself in the full-length mirror. He looked handsome, and only wished it was Annabelle who got to see him this way for an evening together.

Sam stepped back into the room, and the servant girl sprang up from sitting on the bed to examine him. "The Dark Queen will be very happy with you."

He smiled at the girl. "Thank you for your help. The bath was lovely."

The girl tried to hide her smile.

"By the way, we haven't been properly introduced. I'm Sam." Sam stuck out his hand toward the girl.

She hesitated, then grabbed it. "I'm Mara." She let go of his hand and pointed at the clock above Sam's door. "Time for dinner."

Sam followed Mara to the door and down the hall to the dining room. Before entering, Sam paused, taking a deep breath, and entered the room with his head held high.

CHAPTER NINE

Dorthea gazed up at the portrait of her parents. She stared at it every day and could paint it from memory if she had to. Her eyes landed on her mother first, always first. Her long hair in perfect ringlets, the pearl necklace upon her prominent collarbone, her sharp cheeks that made her appear more intimidating than nurturing. Dorthea took after her mother in that way. It didn't bother her, but rather, she embraced it. She held herself with confidence beyond what her mother could dream. She commanded any room she walked into. All eyes were on her, and people listened. Not just because of her impossible beauty and her powerful presence, but because she owned them. She owned everyone and everything, wherever she walked. That's a power neither of her parents ever knew. They didn't have the guts to take what they wanted. But she did.

Dorthea shifted her gaze to her father. She had no respect for that man—if one could even call him that. "Pathetic, worthless excuse of a man," she whispered to the painting. He always talked to her about fairness, kindness, and empathy. Weakness was more like it. He was a weak man and a hypocrite. She looked at his bearded face with the crown atop his head and thought only of how he never deserved it. She would feel sorry for her mother, but that showed vulnerability, another weakness. Her mother should have left him, banished him, killed him. If they were still alive, Dorthea would be up for the task. He'd been an embarrassment to the family. But death suited him, so she'd settle for that. It had been unexpected, and she still couldn't explain how it happened, but she was better off with them dead.

Every time he left on a *mission,* Dorthea knew what that meant. It wasn't to make peace with others or even to bring home new wonders. Just an excuse to bed another woman. Her father couldn't help himself; he would fuck any woman with big tits. He knew his wife would never find out, and if she did, she wouldn't do a damn thing about it.

Her mother put him on a pedestal and could find no fault in him. He had the entire kingdom fooled, just like her mother. But Dorthea knew. "You think I didn't know what else you did every time you came home with a *special find*? Fucking bastard."

Dorthea stopped spitting on his portrait a while back, but maybe she should start up again. After all, his smug face would always be staring at her. Taunting her. Telling her he had gotten away with everything, being immortalized as the kingdom's perfect ruler. But she knew the truth. She took one step closer, hovered a moment, then walked off, trailed by her advisor. Her servant scurried frantically to the portrait, wiping off the dribble running down the Fair King's face.

CHAPTER TEN

Sam walked through the grand entryway, captivated by the wall of glass holding back a reservoir of water. The tank was vast, containing an array of rocks and plant life, but there were no signs of fish anywhere. He stared at the glimmering water, wondering its purpose, when the Dark Queen cleared her throat. Sam turned around and walked toward the single table in the middle of the room, taking the only other seat—opposite the Dark Queen.

"So, you can take an order." The Dark Queen swept her tongue across her teeth as she examined Sam. When she finished, she snapped her fingers, and the servants sprang into motion.

They filled cups with sparkling beverages, served appetizers of cheeses and breads, and several ran to the kitchen for the main course.

Their attire surprised Sam; it wasn't like anyone else's he had seen in the palace. By the way the Dark Queen talked about her subjects, Sam expected them to be dressed in rags, as if they were all lowly and dirty peasants. Folds of fabric danced around the women's figures, with a simple belt wrapped several times around their waist and peplos dresses in shades of creams, grays, and blues.

The men's clothing had a similar quality, though remarkably shorter than the women's floor-length dresses. Open sandals wrapped up to their mid-calves or knees—in various earth tones—adorned the feet of both men and women. Their attire hinted a simple reflection of the Dark Queen's lavish gown. While she was draped in silk and jewels, their wardrobe looked to be made of a thin, almost translucent cotton, with no extravagant accents or jewelry.

The chef emerged from the kitchen with a nervous smile painted on his face. Gold accents embroidered his clothing. He bowed to the Dark Queen before having the others serve the main course onto Sam's and the Dark Queen's plates. Consumed with watching the people shudder as they did their best to evade the Dark Queen's attention, he noticed a moment too late what he'd been served.

He searched for Gadriel in hopes of sorting out the situation, but when Sam spotted him, he was already walking out of the hall. Keres stood alone by a pillar, watching over the room. When had he gotten there? As Sam turned his focus back to his meal, he thought he caught a glimpse of a large fin in the tank, but it was gone as quickly as it had appeared.

Sam sat in silence, picking away at the array of breads and fruits splayed out in front of him, ignoring the hunk of whatever carcass lay on his plate.

The Dark Queen simply watched Sam before speaking, "Is there something wrong with your dinner, Sammy?"

He swallowed the lump in his throat before answering. "It's just that, well, I don't eat meat."

The Dark Queen stared at Sam blankly for several seconds before a smile crept onto her face. "I see. Chef?"

The chef ran to her side, bowing, avoiding her eyes. "Yes, my queen?"

"It seems you have prepared a meal that is unsuitable to the needs of my guest."

The chef's eyes widened. "My queen, I apologize. I will fix this right away."

"No need. You've already proven your incompetence." The Dark Queen lifted her hand toward the chef. The only sound in the room before the man hit the ground was a mind-numbing crack.

"No!"

The chef's lifeless body lay on the floor, his mouth open for one last scream that never left his lips. The other servants in the room stood frozen, afraid to be the one to catch the Dark Queen's attention next. Sam's stomach twisted—he had caused an innocent man's death.

Now he understood the true horrors that came with disappointing the Dark Queen. Sam's blood was hot, and he saw red.

The Dark Queen ignored Sam and turned toward her staff. She scanned back and forth, each member careful to avoid her eyes, until she stopped on one. "You."

A young man met her gaze, inching his feet forward. "Y-yes,

my queen." The man looked like he was about to burst into tears.

"You are his protégé, yes?"

The man nodded.

"Prepare for us something edible."

The new chef bowed low to the Dark Queen. "O-of course, Your Greatness." He spun toward the kitchen doors and ran through, with several more servants trailing his heels. Once the staff had left, the Dark Queen turned her attention back to Sam, studying him as she placed her hand gently under her chin.

He glared back at her with narrowed eyes. The two stared at each other for several minutes, a tension building between them that Sam could feel in his bones. The Dark Queen broke the silence.

"So, what do you think of my queendom?" She spoke as if she hadn't just ended a man's life and was catching up with an old friend.

Sam clenched his jaw, tightening his fists beneath the table. The Dark Queen cleared her throat, the only reminder Sam needed. Play along or die.

"I enjoyed the festivities on the outskirts of the . . . queendom. I can't say I'm quite a fan of the lifeless air the innermost villages breathe." Sam thought maybe he'd gone too far, but he couldn't help himself. This woman was a murderer. She needed to answer for the unspeakable things she'd done.

The Dark Queen simply smiled back at Sam. "Thank you for noticing how much work I've put into making this a place I can truly call home. Those before me had the Empire of the Mother crawling with filth, constantly having celebrations for who knows what. The only thing they should have been celebrating was me. They know that now."

"The Empire of what?" Sam asked.

"The Empire of the Mother. My queendom. Though, I suppose this whole world is all mine now." A smirk lined her face as horror took him over. She sounded like a petulant child.

Before Sam could reply, the servants opened the door and rushed inside with trays full of food. They scurried around the table, shaking as they placed Sam's entrée before him. Sam smiled and thanked them for the delicious meal. They stepped back to stand against the wall as Sam and the Dark Queen ate, but she lifted her hand and shooed them away. Sam watched them all race back into the kitchen.

Out of the corner of his eye, he caught Keres fidgeting with his hands as he stepped behind a pillar and stayed in the dining hall.

Sam slowly picked at his food. His body was hungry, but just sitting with the madwoman before him made his stomach churn. It took all of his courage to look to the Dark Queen. "Why did you bring me here? I was with the woman I love, about to start our lives together, and you took that from me. Why?" A tear formed in Sam's eye, and he used every ounce of strength within him to keep it from falling onto his cheek.

The Dark Queen grinned. "Exactly. That's the kind of man I need, one capable of grand love. Love is power, and I want it." She said it so matter-of-factly, Sam didn't know how to reply. Was she this delusional to think Sam, or anyone, could ever love her? That anyone would willingly give her any more power?

Sam shook his head. "I will *never* love you. My heart belongs in whole and permanence to Annabelle."

"I don't need you to love me. The power rests in your heart, ready for me to take whenever I want. You will stay here with me, allowing me to use that power how I please. Forever."

Sam stared at the man still lying on the floor, then into the Dark Queen's eyes, and saw truth.

"I will get back to her."

The Dark Queen scoffed. "Oh, Sammy. You can try, but that would only kill her."

Sam shook his head. "What?"

She took a sip of her wine. "Oh, now this is divine." She swiveled the cup and inhaled its scent. "Don't you agree?"

Sam's jaw dropped. "Tell me what you've done with Annabelle, or I suwannee . . .!"

"You'll *what*?" The Dark Queen laughed. "Oh, you Southern boys and your sayings."

Sam narrowed his eyes at her, a vein throbbing in his neck as his heart rate quickened.

The Dark Queen sighed. "I see we aren't going to drop this. Fine. I have placed a curse upon your beloved, and the moment you touch her begins a countdown to her death. The beauty of my curse is that it will appear as if *you* are the one in danger. By the time she starts showing signs of withering away, it will be too late. And the only way to break a curse is to have it removed by the one who conjured it. I can promise you that will never happen." The Dark Queen grabbed her utensils and began to eat, as if what she had just said didn't destroy Sam's life. "Happy now?"

Sam contemplated how she could do such a thing. She was

truly delusional. "But you just told me your plan. I can get back to her and get her help, no matter what you do to me!"

The Dark Queen cackled.

She really leans into this whole wicked-witch thing.

"Oh, sweet Sammy. You don't honestly think I would tell you something and let you go free, do you?"

"I don't need you to let me go! I will escape, and I'll warn her!" Sam screamed.

"Not if you can't remember what I've told you."

"What? How would you even do that?"

The Dark Queen sighed, seeming bored with the discussion. "I have my ways."

"No!" Sam leapt from his seat and lunged at the Dark Queen. His body turned to stone, refusing to move any farther.

The Dark Queen continued to eat. "You should know by now, Sammy, there's nothing you can do to stop me. I command you."

"Why me? Why us?" Sam needed to know.

The Dark Queen shrugged. "Why not? My magic sensed great power in your heart, more powerful than anyone else I could have chosen. Lucky you."

Sam's body fought him as he sat back down and picked up his silverware, cutting into the meal before him. Sam opened his mouth to speak but was stopped by the fork the Dark Queen's magic lifted to his lips.

CHAPTER ELEVEN

Staring out the tower window, Dorthea took in the magnificence of her kingdom as she stroked the creature next to her before it slunk away. She was creating exactly what she wanted—giving her kingdom a chance. The lies had grown tiresome. She would save her kingdom from itself. Few truly appreciated the genius of her plan, to wipe it clean of the ever-looming deceit and betrayals. Soon, this world would be clean of its indiscretions, all she needed was a bit more power . . .

Sam would do perfectly. He was already coming in handy. In all her time purging the realm of its depravities, she'd been too reckless to check on the outer edges of the kingdom. Her power only went as far as the eye could see, so she'd simply forgotten to teach them their lesson as well. Foolish to think they would get the message without her paying them a visit in the flesh. Perhaps it was about time.

Dorthea made her way down the tower into her

bedchambers, laughing to herself as she looked upon her bed, taking in the man under the covers, fast asleep. She had always been an excellent lover, and Enos fell asleep after each bout. He was her favorite bedfellow, so she had stopped taking other lovers a while back.

Past Enos, Dorthea slunk over to her chest, quietly opening it to not wake him. He needed his rest. She'd be ready for another round once he regained his strength. Dorthea pulled out several relics—a chalice, a branding iron, a key—before settling on a silver necklace she placed around her neck.

A venomous sneer slithered onto her face as she closed her eyes, a veil of weightlessness blanketing her, and evaporated into the air.

CHAPTER TWELVE

"Gahhh!" Sam slammed his chamber door. He picked up a nearby vase and threw it across the room, watching the shattered pieces fall to the floor, his heart feeling the same.

"Oh!" Mara's head popped up from behind the bed.

Sam's head whipped in her direction, and his anger quickly stepped aside. "Mara, I'm so sorry. I didn't know you were in here. Are you all right?"

"Yes, I'm fine. I was just cleaning up before you went to bed. I'm sorry, I can leave."

"Don't rush out because of me. I'm sorry, I'm just so . . . so . . ."

Mara sighed. "What'd she do to you?" She patiently waited for him to answer.

"Besides kidnapping me and taking me away from the love of my life?" Sam huffed. "She said she cursed my Annabelle to die if I ever escape."

Mara shook her head and walked over to Sam, grabbing his hand and ushering him to sit on the bed. Standing in front of him, she was at eye level. Her hand on his shoulder calmed him a bit. "She hurts people to get what she wants. She's wicked."

Sam nodded. "Who is she using against you?"

Mara dropped her head, her voice turning soft and low. "No one anymore."

Sam gasped, bringing a hand to his chest.

"She took them all from me. That's why I'm here now. I have nowhere to go and no one to go to." A tear slid down her face as she looked back up to Sam. "She destroyed my entire village, burning it to nothing. When I sleep, I still hear the screams of my family as I run toward the woods." Mara paused to wipe a tear from her cheek. "I thought I had escaped, but she captured me. I thought for sure she was going to incinerate me along with the rest of my village, but she let me live. She brought me to work here and knew I would be loyal because everything else was gone forever. This palace is all I have. She takes everything precious to a person and uses it to get what she wants."

Words refused to form in his mind. All he could think to do was take her hand as she began to sob. Mara leaned into Sam, and he stood to hug her. He tried not to think about the same pain he would feel if he lost Annabelle, if the Dark Queen kept her word. Suddenly, Sam was crying as well, and Mara looped her arms around his waist. In that moment, it didn't matter that they were strangers—they were in this together. Sam there for Mara's grief, and Mara there for his hopelessness. He lost track of how long he stood there, embracing a stranger.

When they separated, a stranger no longer stood before him, but a friend.

Mara cleared her throat. "That's the first time I've let myself feel it."

"What? Why?"

"You don't exactly get much time to grieve in a place like this. It's never ending."

Death seemed to be around every corner of the castle, and he didn't imagine the Dark Queen would take too well to her staff constantly breaking down. "So, what do you do?"

Mara wiped the tears from her cheeks. "I have hope this soon will end, that maybe one day we'll be brave enough to fight back." Mara's demeanor changed. She no longer looked like the scared girl she'd let him see.

"How can anyone fight back? She kills anyone who defies her."

Mara smiled. "Don't lose hope, Sam."

"I won't."

THE NEXT MORNING, Sam awoke to the sound of a tap on the door. He rolled over to the blur of Keres walking toward him. "What do you want?"

Keres gave Sam an apologetic smile. "Sam, please don't be angry with me. You yourself have seen the power of the Dark Queen. I only do what I am told. But today, I thought I would try to do more. I was hoping to show you around the palace and its grounds so you could see all it has to offer."

"Why would I want to do that?" Sam huffed.

"Well, sir, because I thought you would want to get to know your new home."

Sam's heart ached at Keres's words. *New home.* Would Sam really never see Annabelle again? Would he truly be stuck here forever? Sam sighed and grabbed his shoes from beside the bed. If nothing else, maybe he could find a way to escape this place and get back home to Annabelle.

"Fine . . . where are we going?"

Keres smiled. "You'll see, just have patience."

Sam grumbled and asked Keres for a few minutes of privacy to get ready for the day. He grabbed his notebook from his pocket. *Tick.* Sam had just arrived at the palace, yet he'd already been gone nine days from his sweet Annabelle. Sam said a prayer to ease her fears and worry as she waited for Sam's return. He hoped it wouldn't be much longer.

Sam dressed and finished getting ready, then followed Keres out of his chambers and down the hall. But instead of going back in the direction Sam was familiar with, Keres turned to the right, toward the back of the castle. They wound through several hallways until coming to a small door that Keres pushed through, letting a ray of light into the dim castle hall.

A burst of fresh air hit Sam. The door opened into a beautiful garden fenced with large hedges, with no other entrance or exit than the door they'd gone through. The garden, completely different from the rest of the grounds, full of rosebushes pressing into every corner, breathed life into the castle of death. Sam looked questioningly toward Keres.

"The Dark Queen kept only one place alive through her destruction—her precious rose garden. She comes here every evening, so we are free to use it in the morning and midday."

The two men walked the garden's perimeter. Sam admired the white roses adorning bushes and benches, and the array of statues posted at different parts of the garden. "How long is she planning on keeping me here? Doesn't she just need to take whatever power she wants and then let me go?"

Keres bowed his head. "Well, Sam, I'm afraid what I have to tell you will only upset you further."

Sam swallowed. "Go on."

"Time here is not what you are used to or would expect back home. While our days seem normal to us, our worlds do not connect in time."

"I'm not following. How can your days be normal but also not normal?"

"Time in our world works properly when you are here, but it dances around your time. Sometimes slowly, and other times very quickly. While one day here could seem like just a day, it could be one day in your world, or one moment, or one lifetime."

Sam's stomach churned. "So, what you're saying is that even if I got back home, I could be going back to a life I know nothing of?" He could hear his own heartbeat pounding in his head.

"Precisely. We have no real way of knowing how the time in your world is moving presently."

Sam dropped onto the bench beside him, shaking his head slowly. "No, I have to try. I won't give up. I can't let Annabelle live a whole life without knowing what happened to me."

Keres nodded and motioned toward the door leading back into the castle. "Let's continue."

"I don't want a tour right now! I need to figure out how to get out of here!"

Keres simply opened the castle door and ushered Sam back

inside. "Come, I will show you more of where you will be staying."

Sam didn't have much of a choice if he wanted to learn more about the castle and a possible way to escape, so he followed Keres inside.

Keres showed Sam so much of the palace that he was getting exhausted. Up a spiraling tower that looked over the castle grounds, he could see the kingdom like he had from the mountaintop, only this time he could see only blackness and pain, happiness being too far off in this distance.

Perhaps that is how they had escaped such horrid conditions. They were far enough away from her sight that she simply forgot to torture them as well.

From here, he was able to get a much better look at what lay behind the palace, and it still shook him. A vast mountain expanded in both directions. To one side lay a beach with dark and destructive waves crashing ashore. In a far corner of the palace grounds, he could make out a white, circular structure decorated with columns. On the other side of the palace, an expanse of purples and blues mixed together, trailing off into nothing.

"What did you mean when you said that was the edge of the world?"

Keres stood in silence for a moment, then cleared his throat. "Our world was not shaped like yours. Ours is simply a fragment of another world, ripped away and suspended here in a piece of space far from it."

"From Earth?"

"Yes, Sam. The goddesses gave us this land and our magic as a gift, but they created our world from yours."

Sam slowly nodded at Keres's words. He didn't know whether or not to believe him, because how would that even be possible? Then again, how was any of this possible? Sam decided not to question Keres any further, making note to avoid that part of the grounds at all cost. Whatever it was, he didn't want to be at its mercy.

Sam followed Keres from end to end of the castle, passing artwork that had been shredded and rooms that had been emptied. It was as if he was getting a tour of the queen's dark heart rather than a palace. He couldn't believe someone would choose to live like this, and make others live in her wretched feelings as well. She wanted everyone to suffer right alongside her.

Out of the corner of his eye, Sam spotted someone rounding the corner. It looked just like . . .

Sam took off after the figure, and when he turned the corner, Gadriel stood there, waiting for Sam.

"You!" Sam swung at Gadriel, perplexed when he drove his fist into the air; the elf was gone. Sam stood in bewilderment until he heard a throat clear behind him, then turned to see Gadriel standing there. Before Sam could take another swing, the elf stood behind him again, holding Sam's hands back. Sam struggled to free himself, but Gadriel was too strong—inhumanly strong.

Keres walked around the corner then, but stood watch from a distance as the two fought.

"I'll let you go if you stop attacking me," Gadriel said.

Reluctantly, Sam agreed.

Gadriel let go of Sam's arms and spoke. "Now, that's better. What seems to be the problem, Sam?"

"You know what the problem is! I told you what not to serve, and a man ended up dead!" Sam panted, using every ounce of restraint he had to hold himself back.

Gadriel kept a calm stature. "I was just as upset as you were about that. Why do you think I left the room when I saw the mistake? I can't help the ineptitude of others." Gadriel softened his voice. "It seems your anger is more appropriately directed at the Dark Queen."

Sam studied the elf, trying to decide if he should believe him. "Fine. But you're supposed to be in charge of the staff. Their mistakes are your mistakes."

Gadriel smiled. "I see. I best be going. I have a lot of people to take care of."

Sam glared at Gadriel's shifty smile and turned back to Keres, still unsure how much he could trust those in the palace of thorns.

Depressed and defeated by what he had seen and the world in which he was now expected to live, Sam told Keres to show him back to his room so he could sleep.

"Just one more stop. I promise you won't be disappointed."

"Fine," Sam said, "but make it quick, please."

A set of double doors invited them in.

Sam's jaw dropped as Keres opened the doors to the largest collection of books he had ever seen. Stacks and shelves stretched from floor to ceiling, end to end. Masterful staircases wound their way up for access to each book, with tables and chairs in every corner to cozy up and read for pleasure or research. Sam imagined every book ever written ought to be in this room. No corner went without beauty.

Even the ceiling had intricate sketches in colors that made

the ideas come to life. Sam could have sworn the paintings actually danced and swayed but brushed it off as a tick of grandiose by a brilliant artist. He scaled a staircase to observe the library from a better vantage point. He was not disappointed. Sam found himself in a sea of knowledge and tales that expanded far beyond the walls of just one room. It held the most beautiful and mesmerizing things he's ever seen, and it took a moment before he realized he shouldn't be enjoying it.

This was just a trick to make him forget about going home, to distract him from what truly mattered.

"This is cruel. I don't want to see this. I want to leave. Why won't you help me leave?"

Keres contemplated his question. "I serve my queen loyally. I'm sorry for what she has done to you, but I simply cannot defy her and let you leave. I would be the one left with her in the wake of your disappearance."

It wasn't fair of him to ask Keres to put his life in danger just to save himself. "I understand. I just wish there was something I could do to get out of here."

Keres looked Sam in the eyes. "Let me give you a tour of our library."

"Keres, I said no."

Keres continued anyway. "Here, we have stories of adventurous tales; over here, are some of the finest recipe books in the land, and over there you will find resources containing everything there is to know about our world and the magic that comes along with it."

Sam didn't care about what Keres was saying. Unless . . . "Wait! Repeat what you just said."

Keres gave Sam a smile. "You heard me." Then he turned to the doors and left Sam in the brimming library to do what he could.

Sam whispered after him, "Thank you."

THAT NIGHT AT DINNER, Sam sat in silence as the emotions of the day poured over him. His heart could barely handle the weight, so he tried to keep his focus on the words Mara told him to hold on to—hope. And not be consumed by his anger toward those in the palace. He almost didn't hear the Dark Queen when she spoke.

"Are you already bored of my palace?"

Sam looked at the Dark Queen, who met his gaze with raised brows. "I'm fine."

The Dark Queen scoffed. "Nonsense. I will bring out the entertainment. I find myself rather jaded tonight."

Sam grimaced at the thought of the poor soul who had the job of entertaining this beast. Confusion struck when she didn't call for anyone, but her hand rose. She was using magic. But on who?

Sam sat quietly until he heard the cracks of glass coming from beside him. He watched in horror as the water behind the glass wall swirled, a figure caught up in the whirl.

Oh, God. She's going to drown someone for her own amusement!

Sam stood and rushed to the glass wall, looking for a way to get the prisoner out without killing himself in the process. The Dark Queen laughed as the waters settled and the figure became clear.

It was a man with long brown hair, a muscular build, and soft facial features. But this man had no trouble in the water—a half fish, donning a long silver-blue tail in place of his legs. Sam could only stare as the man . . . fish, looked back at him. *Merfolk.*

Sam recalled the myth of the merfolk that sailors had told tales of when making port, and this was definitely one of them. Part man, part fish, living underwater.

Annabelle wouldn't believe what he was seeing. She loved the water, and always said she wished she had fins of her own.

Sam stepped forward and put his hand to the glass. He stood in amazement as the merman made his way closer to Sam, staring at him with deep brown eyes. The merman put his hand up to Sam's, but the moment he touched the glass, the merman began writhing in pain. Sam looked to the Dark Queen, who enjoyed torturing the man in his cage.

"Stop! You're hurting him!"

The Dark Queen did not stop. "Precisely."

After several moments, she released him from her hold, and the merman stayed where he was, looking at Sam.

Why wasn't he swimming away? Then Sam realized; he had nowhere to go. He was the Dark Queen's jester, under the control of her will just like Sam was.

Sam slowly walked back to his chair, praying and hoping there was some way to help this poor creature. As Sam sat in his seat, he heard a voice in his head.

"You can't help me."

CHAPTER THIRTEEN

Sam couldn't get to the library fast enough after dinner. He had much to research about this land and how to escape it. *Annabelle.* He needed to figure out how to break her curse before he could return to her. Otherwise, it would all be for nothing.

Sam dashed through the halls and had the library doors in his sight but stopped in his tracks. *No.* Sam fought to continue on his mission as his feet stuck to the floor. The pricks of heels on the cobbled floor told him he wouldn't be going anywhere.

Sam stopped struggling and slowly turned around. The Dark Queen released him as he met her gaze, knocking him off-balance. By the time Sam stabilized himself, the Dark Queen had already caught up to him, two men following closely behind. One he recognized from the moment he first met the Dark Queen—the nervous man who had introduced her.

What is his name again? Sam thought back to the moment

when the name escaped her lips. *"Ilia, stay."* How could he forget? The Dark Queen spoke to him as if he were nothing more than a trained pet. He didn't fault Ilia for his nerves. Sam watched as the man trembled before him now, looking to the Dark Queen and awaiting her next command.

Sam's gaze fell to the second man, whom he did not recognize. He struck Sam as quite peculiar. The man stood several inches shorter than the Dark Queen, though he imagined they would stand the same height if it weren't for her overwhelming choice in footwear.

White with sun-kissed skin, his scruffy brown mane was the only hair Sam could see on his body, which he could see most of. He stood in the grand hallway in loose-fitting silk trousers with his torso draped in jewels. In his exposed state, Sam could make out every muscle on the man. He was in peak physical condition, from his molded abs to his forceful arms. The calm look on his face, and the proximity in which he stood next to the queen compared to Ilia, showed no signs of fear.

The Dark Queen cleared her throat, and Ilia stepped forward, just a pace behind her. Ilia looked at Sam and spoke. "S-Sam. The Dark Queen would like to remind you of the c-civility expected in her palace. Running is an activity b-best suited for the outdoors, and not in threads of silver among these great halls."

Sam looked upon the Dark Queen, who was baring a smug grin. He took a moment, then gave the slightest jerk of his head to her. "My apologies." As much as the words stung coming across his tongue, he needed to get back to the library as fast as possible.

The Dark Queen gestured back to Sam. "Thank you, dear

Sammy. Where are you off to anyway? Your chambers are nowhere near mine." That's when Sam noticed the door to his right. The Dark Queen's chambers. This would be more difficult than he'd anticipated with her so nearby.

Sam struggled for the words. "I was looking for . . ." *Think!* Should he tell her he's going to the library to read? She couldn't possibly be upset about that . . . could she?

"Sam, I think you found what you were looking for." Her eyes flitted to her chamber doors. "Do you care to join Enos and me inside? I'm sure he wouldn't mind sharing."

The second man spoke for the first time. "Of course not. There's always room for more."

Sam stood in confusion, wracking his mind for something to say. "No, thank you. I was just lost, is all. I best be getting back to my room." Sam lifted his arms and attempted a yawn.

The Dark Queen gave Sam a repulsive grin. "Another time, then."

Sam was still confused but kept his ground.

"Ilia!"

"Y-yes, my queen?"

"Be gone. I am done with your blubbering for tonight."

"Of course, Your Majesty." Ilia bowed to leave, but as he turned to go back the direction he'd come, a rip tore through the air.

Ilia froze, and the Dark Queen's eyes narrowed. Sam looked down to see Ilia's boot on the Dark Queen's gown, and a large tear now ornamented the bottom. Ilia began shaking uncontrollably. "M-my queen, I am s-so s-sorry. P-please forgive m-me, I can fix it im-mmediately, g-good as n-new."

His voice wavered, so Sam could barely comprehend what

he was saying. But how was he still speaking at all? Sam was sure he would be dead before he parted his lips.

The Dark Queen simply looked at Ilia, her face unreadable. "No. I said be gone."

Ilia didn't need to be told twice and shuffled away as fast as his trembling feet could take him.

The Dark Queen turned her attention back toward Sam. "I needn't waste my time on him now. I have other, more important, things to attend to." With that, she grabbed Enos's bicep and maneuvered him toward her. She spoke in a low, smooth tone. "Carry me in tonight, lover."

Enos smiled at the Dark Queen and replied with a grunt. Before Sam knew what was happening, the Dark Queen hiked up her gown, revealing her thighs all the way up. Enos lifted her toward him, and she wrapped her legs around his waist as he buried his face in her chest.

Then it hit Sam, and his body became tight, unmoving. How could they invite him to join—think that he would ever be with her in that way? He could only watch as his body betrayed him, unable to move. The chamber doors opened, and Enos lifted a hand to the queen's bosom, holding her up with only one arm. He slipped his fingers into her gown and pulled her breast free, grabbing her nipple with his teeth. Sam somehow forced his eyes shut and listened to Enos lead her into the room. Sam's stomach churned as the last noise he heard before the doors shut was a loud moan from the Dark Queen.

Sam's feet began walking on their own, taking him away from the Dark Queen's door. His mind was cloudy, trying to block out the image he had just seen. *Why couldn't I just look away?* Sam didn't recall walking back to his room as he stood in the doorway, glancing upon his bed.

He stood there for several minutes until someone tapped his shoulder, and he jumped.

"Oh! I'm sorry, I didn't mean to frighten you."

Sam heard Mara's voice and calmed himself, meeting her gaze.

"What's wrong?"

Sam still couldn't speak, so he made his way into the room instead, Mara slowly following behind. He took a seat on the bed and stared at the ground, trying to shake the thoughts from his mind. Mara approached Sam and grabbed his hand, giving it a slight squeeze.

"Do you want to talk about it?"

Sam lifted his head to meet Mara's eyes and shook his head. "It was horrifying. The Dark Queen. And that man." Sam's body shuddered.

Mara's face turned knowing. "Ah, I see you've met Enos."

Sam looked at Mara with disgust written on his face. "They're always like that?"

Mara nodded. "Yes. But it's not just them. You can find many people in all corners of the palace embraced."

Sam shook his head. "How can they just do that out in the open? Have they no shame?"

Mara half laughed, seeming confused by the entire situation. "It's not really a big deal here, as long as the Dark Queen doesn't catch someone she cares about."

Sam scoffed. "I doubt she cares about anyone."

"You'd be surprised. The Dark Queen has taken many

lovers, and once you've been with the queen, sometimes there's a lasting connection."

Sam's stomach churned, wondering how anyone would want to be with such a monster. "Who would agree to be with her? Does she . . . force them?"

"No, not at all. I've heard rumors that she is an exceptional lover. But I think it has more to do with power. Getting close to the Dark Queen has its benefits." Mara shrugged. "Though once Enos came around, she hasn't taken any other lovers. She must be very fond of him."

Sam nodded, understanding why someone would want to be on her good side. He couldn't hold that against them. Still, he wanted the image removed from his eyes, for it to stop playing over and over again. "I need to think about something else. Anything else."

Mara smiled. "I've got just the thing."

Before he knew what was happening, the pair were out the door. He'd told Mara it was ridiculous to cover his eyes when he didn't yet know his way around the castle, but there he was, eyes closed, holding Mara's shoulder as she wove them through the palace hallways.

He tried to memorize their turns, but this place was so enormous, he'd lost track after the first dozen movements. He listened to see if there was anything distinctive about where they were, but Sam could only hear his own breath. Mara's footsteps were almost imperceptible. If he weren't holding her shoulder, he'd have thought himself alone in the chilly castle hall.

Mara slowed her pace, and Sam felt her shoulder rise as she stepped forward. *Stairs, great.* He did his best to step up and follow her up the winding staircase, only tripping a couple times before they were back to even ground. He hadn't been in this part of the castle yet. The only stairs he'd ever ascended were the tower, and they hadn't climbed nearly as high as then. Mara led him through several more turns before she abruptly stopped.

There was the slightest tap, then the creak of a door as it opened before them. After a brief pause, Mara stepped forward, pulling Sam along with her through a doorway.

As soon as he stepped into the room, Sam sensed a shift in the air. He was no longer chilled but was filled with the warmth of a crackling fire that imbued the space. The smell of cinnamon and citrus intertwined, filling his nose and calming his nerves as he recognized the scent.

Mara told Sam to open his eyes, but the room was completely bare—no fire, no cinnamon and citrus.

"What is this?" Sam turned to Mara.

"Oh, right." Mara giggled. She grabbed Sam's hand and placed it on the wall behind him. "Do what I do."

Sam followed along as she traced random lines on the wall with her finger. When they finished, the room filled with noise. Sam jumped as he turned around to a room full of people and someone holding out a cup of tea in front of him.

"What? How?"

"This room was warded before the Dark Queen took away Harmony from everyone. What I showed you was a way of revealing something that's been hidden by magic," Mara said.

Sam shook his head. "That's . . . amazing. So, y'all just hide in here?"

He looked around the space at all the eyes now on him.

People stood wall to wall, easy to do in a room of that size, with sofas and chairs scattered about. It was hard to make out any more details with all the people, so he turned his attention back to Mara.

"Not always." Mara smiled.

"Eh-hem." The man holding out the tea cleared his throat.

"Oh, sorry." Sam took the drink and thanked the man who'd given it to him; he looked familiar but Sam couldn't quite place him.

Mara had walked off with her own cup, cozying up in a chair closest to the fire. He decided to join her, missing the feel of warm air filling his lungs over the frigidness in the rest of the palace. Mara gave Sam a gentle smile as he stood next to her, nodding in assurance for him to take the seat beside her. As soon as he got comfortable, he gazed out at all the faces, trying to gauge what he had walked into.

It wasn't until he saw the table of food in the corner, decorated with a painting of the man the Dark Queen had murdered before his eyes, that Sam recognized his host. It was the new chef. The other faces became clear to him then. There were several people he knew to be the kitchen staff, a couple other maidens like Mara, and a few he did not recognize.

Turning in his chair, Sam faced the new chef and his staff, all of whom had a hint of sorrow behind their eyes. "I am so sorry for your loss." Sam met soft nods of acknowledgment and decided nothing else needed to be said.

Sam twisted back in his seat and leaned in close to Mara and whispered, "What is this?"

Mara whispered back. "Tonight, it's a remembrance. A life celebration."

A twinge emerged in his stomach as he replayed the man's death over in his head. The snap of his neck was cemented in his memories. "Why did you bring me here?"

Mara gave Sam a gentle smile. "You were a part of his life, in his final moments. You should be here. Plus, we don't want you going crazy in your room all by yourself."

Sam nodded, not sure he fully understood what Mara meant about being a part of the man's life. He didn't know anything about the man, except he had caused his death. Why did Mara think he should be here?

With shaking hands, Sam brought his teacup to his lips and enjoyed the rush of warmth, savoring the taste on his tongue. He let the flavor take him back to the first time he'd had the tea in this realm, the night of the festivities. Though it had only been days, it seemed like an eternity. An eternity since he'd been with Annabelle. Now here he was again, drinking the same transfixing tea, only this time under much different circumstances.

A man cleared his throat, and Sam looked up from his cup. The new chef spoke. "Thank you all for coming to remember our dear and departed friend." The man gestured toward the portrait on the table. "Tonight, we send him off to paradise." The new chef lifted his cup, and the others followed suit. "Goodbye, old friend." Those among them repeated the sentiment, and a sudden shift entered the room.

Sam sat bewildered as folks around him stood and clapped, and the women began to sing what sounded like a joyous song. The men chimed in, and soon the small gathering was dancing around the room with smiles on their faces. Mara grabbed Sam's arm and pulled him, urging him to join. Sam hesitated, but Mara grabbed his cup, set it on the table, and kept insisting. Sam grinned slightly as he watched everyone gracefully make their way around the room, and decided to join, as he was here for them more than himself.

With a heave out of the short chair, Sam lifted his large body and stepped forward. He tried to watch the movements to learn the steps, but he had never been much of a dancer and found it hard to follow along. Mara took hold of Sam's hand and pulled him in her direction; he lost control of his feet beneath him.

As he stumbled to the side, Mara twisted him around and Sam caught himself, realizing she was helping him with the steps. She grabbed his hand again, and he held tight, desperately trying to avoid a fall. The duo wove through chairs and tables in the small room, and without realizing when it happened, Sam felt a smile on his face. He gave in to the music and twisted and spun, finally picking up the moves.

After several songs, Sam plopped back down into his chair, wiping the sweat off his brow. Mara fell on the chair beside his in a fit of giggles, which made Sam laugh. Soon enough, laughter filled every corner of the room. It was enough to make Sam forget about what he'd seen between the Dark Queen and Enos, and the fact that he was at a remembrance.

Once the laughter settled, Sam picked up his cup and took a long sip, surprised to find it still warm after his lengthy absence. The others indulged in their own cups, calming themselves and starting quiet conversations in twos and threes. A few walked toward the table and made a plate of food.

Sam turned to Mara, amazed at her ability to dance for so long. He always thought she looked a bit sickly with her frail body and sunken cheeks, but tonight she seemed full of life. It was the first time he was able to see her true youth, as before her haggard appearance had made her look well beyond her years. But now, he could see the spirited girl behind the pained mask. Judging by her smooth skin and large eyes, this girl was no older than 14, and he became sorry for her all over again. This lost girl reminded him of Annabelle, but where she had Sam, Mara had no one.

But as Sam looked around the room, he thought maybe she had all she needed right here. Mara was right: he did need to be here tonight.

Sam listened to the whispers in the room, not knowing what to do next as Mara chatted with the fellow on her opposite side. He couldn't help but think of all the people willing to defy the Dark Queen as he scanned the room again. In a palace that was stripped of any joy, he'd somehow found some. There was still hope in this place.

Sam stood to get closer to the fire, hoping he would look less awkward by himself there. He stared into the flames as they whipped around and climbed their way out of the chimney by way of ash, taunting him as they escaped from the castle that he could not.

Sam spun around as he sensed the presence of someone near him. Expecting Mara, he instead met the gaze of a beautiful woman he'd noticed earlier in the far corner of the room. Her deep and rich brown skin was darker than his own. Violet eyes shone bright, and he couldn't help but notice the large golden flowers crowned atop her full brown curls. She dressed far more stylishly than the rest of the crowd.

Like the other women, her gown kissed the floor, but hers was made of silks in a blush color that matched the clouds. The woman didn't say anything. She just smiled at Sam as she refilled her cup from the pot over the fire, then walked back to her friends. Sam turned his attention back toward the fire, until he felt a small tap on his shoulder.

Mara looked up at Sam. "Ready?"

Sam nodded. "Lead the way."

Before Sam closed his eyes and placed his hand back on Mara's shoulder, he took in the room once more, savoring the feeling of home, and followed Mara back to his chambers.

NO MATTER how often he turned and flipped, Sam could not get comfortable. Be it the fluffy pillow, the smooth mattress, or the silky sheets—all of the luxuries fell short in the dark palace. He longed for the familiarity of his home—for Annabelle.

Sam got up and dressed in his own clothes, which oddly provided him some comfort. Though they were almost rags, he didn't have much else from his world. He grabbed his notebook, lit the candle by his bedside, and started flipping through the pages, reading his old words—words from another world. Once he finished, Sam tiptoed toward the door and slipped out of his chambers.

He wanted to get to the library early since he'd lost his chance the night before. As he made his way through the palace, he passed the dining hall, where something caught his attention out of the corner of his eye. Sam peered in and saw the merman in his glass cage, sitting on the oceanic floor. Sam contemplated letting the man be and continuing on his way, but something drew Sam closer, like he couldn't leave him alone.

Sam approached the tank and looked into the man's eyes, and the merman stared back at him in fear. "It's okay; it's just me." Sam shook his head. *What a stupid thing to do. He can't possibly hear me behind that glass.* But then Sam jumped as he heard another's voice in his head.

"I can hear you just fine. You need to leave."

So, Sam had heard right before. This man was somehow talking to him in his own mind. Sam spoke back to him. "You can hear my thoughts?"

The merman nodded. *"The ones directed toward me."*

Wow. This was incredible! "How?"

The merman shrugged. *"It's a gift."*

Excitement almost overcame him before the realization of the terrible predicament they found themselves in. When Sam placed his hand on the glass, he flinched at the cold sting of ice. "Aren't you freezing in there?"

"Doesn't bother me. I'm used to it."

"What's your name?"

The merman was taken aback, giving Sam a look of confusion. *"Why?"*

Sam stood still for a moment. "Why not?"

The merman shrugged slightly as he contemplated Sam's answer. *"Zael."*

"I'm Sam. I'm sorry we have to be meeting like this."

Zael gave Sam a blank look that turned to sorrow. *"Yeah."*

"How are you today?" Sam tried to lighten the mood, if that were even possible.

"You shouldn't be here."

"I'm sorry. I just thought you might be lonely and wanted someone to talk to."

Zael pushed off the floor and bobbed in front of Sam, emotionless. *"I'm not someone you want to talk to. You should leave."*

"All right." Sam hesitated. "Maybe I can come back another time."

Zael didn't answer, and instead swam away to the back of his cage, disappearing from Sam's sight.

"Bye," Sam whispered. He turned on his heel and headed into the hallway, looking back at the empty water as he made his way to the library.

The winding halls still confounded him, with the columns of stone and marble and the never-ending paths they seemed to take. It was enough to play tricks on the mind—at one point, Sam thought he'd seen an enormous tail slip down a corridor, but by the time he caught up, the hall lay empty.

Sam walked as quietly as he could manage when he'd reached the Dark Queen's chamber doors. He didn't want to risk waking her and ruining his plans for the day. He couldn't hear any movement coming from her chambers but held his breath until he had cleared the hall. He kept walking and finally reached the entrance to the library, eager to get inside and close the doors behind him. When he spun around to face the open room, Sam was startled by Keres, who sat in front of a tray of drinks and pastries.

Sam made his way to the table and whispered at Keres. "What are you doing here?"

Keres smiled, gesturing toward the tray. "Isn't it obvious?"

Sam was confused. "I mean, why are you here? The Dark Queen is out there. She'll kill you if she sees you helping me."

Keres gave a slight shrug. "I'll worry about the Dark Queen. I just wanted to make sure you were properly nourished for the day. I'll be leaving now." Keres tipped his head at Sam, who returned the gesture.

Once Keres had left the room, Sam looked at the tray on the table. He hadn't been hungry, but once he caught a whiff of the pastries and—he sniffed the cup and smiled—coffee, his stomach began to rumble. He raised the cup to his lips and let the coffee fill him, a burst of energy coursing through him. He'd only had coffee a few times before, but this was by far the best he'd ever tasted. Crumbs fell to his lap as he cut open the bread to spread jam on top. He ate as quickly as he could, but the delicious delights slowed him down as his tongue begged him to enjoy the flavors.

Swallowing the last bite, Sam turned his attention back to the library, scanning the bookshelves for where to start. He shuffled to the bookcase closest to him and grabbed a stack of books, setting them next to the pen and paper on the table, and got to work.

A THUMP at the door forced Sam out of his trance. He looked up and saw Mara poking her head into the room wide-eyed.

"What's wrong?"

The look on Mara's face frightened him.

"What are you wearing? The Dark Queen will be furious if you show up to dinner like that."

Sam brushed it off. "I've got plenty of time until then."

Mara shook her head. "No, dinner starts in fifteen minutes.

I'm supposed to be taking you there now. I've been looking everywhere for you."

Sam's stomach dropped. Had he really been working all day? Sure enough, as he looked out the window, he saw the sun low in the sky. Sam hopped up from his seat. "I can't be late. She'll kill you."

Mara nodded, confirming his fears.

Sam did the only thing he could think to do, and sprinted past Mara, going as fast as he could toward his room. If he could get there fast and change, maybe he had a chance of making it to dinner on time. Sam's heart raced as he surged around each corner, trying not to count the seconds going by in his head. Sweat dripped from his forehead, and not because he was out of shape. He needed to get there in time. He needed to save Mara.

Sam barreled through the door and looked around for something to wear while tearing off his clothes. He grew frantic as he couldn't find any in sight and ran naked into the washroom.

Steam filled the room, but he ignored the bath drawn for him and narrowed in on the clothes laid out on the chair. He pulled them on his body as fast as he could, not bothering to button up as he put on his shoes. Sam glanced in the mirror at the mess that stared back at him, but he couldn't stay to fix himself. Mara's life depended on him.

He hurried back out of the room and ran into Mara in the hallway as she was trying her best to follow him back to his chambers. He grabbed her hand and pulled her along with him toward the dining hall. When he had it in his sights, Mara pulled against him, forcing him to stop.

"We have to go!" Sam tried to pull Mara, but she was adamant.

"Sam, I can't send you in there looking like that." She pulled a rag out of her pocket and wiped at his face. She grabbed a vial out of her other pocket and sprinkled it on the rag. Sam winced as the cold water touched his forehead, but he let Mara continue, forcing himself not to count the time slipping by. Mara put the rag away and began tugging at Sam's shirt, buttoning up near his neck and adjusting it to where it fit. She looked Sam up and down, her face giving him no comfort, then nodded.

"That's all I can do."

Sam prayed it would be enough.

Rounding the corner into the dining room, where the same table sat adorned with breads and fruits and wine, a rush of relief fell over him at the Dark Queen's empty chair. He'd made it. Mara was safe.

Sam tried to calm himself as he made his way to the table, leaving Mara standing in her place by the entryway. Before he could sit, the clicks of the Dark Queen's heels made their way into the hall. He tried not to look her in the eye, but his nerves got the better of him, and he met her gaze as soon as she appeared. Sam couldn't believe what he saw, and tried his best not to look as his heart beat faster.

The Dark Queen wore a gown of fabric strips lazily wrapped around her body. Though Sam wasn't sure he could even call it a gown. The white and gold fabric did little more than cover her breasts and hips. He tried forcing his eyes away, but his body fought him again. The Dark Queen's breasts were hardly covered, Sam thinking he had more fabric on one pant leg than she had in her entire gown. The smirk on the Dark Queen's face assured him she wore it just to toy with him.

"Like what you see? Of course, it's not as much as you saw last night, but we can fix that if you decide to join me tonight."

Sam shook his head, coming to his senses. "Never." He almost forgot about his close call, until the Dark Queen stopped walking and looked him up and down, her eyes studying him.

Please have been enough. Please. Sam tried to will his clothes to look more presentable, for his body to calm so she wouldn't suspect a thing.

The Dark Queen smiled again. "You're looking quite fetching yourself this evening."

Sam was stunned and turned back to Mara. He could see she was trying to keep a blank face but saw the hint of relief behind her eyes. Sam turned back to his chair and sat. It was then that Sam noticed a man trailing behind the Dark Queen, a man he hadn't seen before. He looked to see who else had followed her into the room, but only saw Keres, Gadriel, and a few kitchen staff. *That's odd. Ilia almost never leaves the Dark Queen's side.*

Sam stared at the stranger's face; he had a familiar look about him. He was trembling in the way Ilia always did, fearful of his queen and doing his best to obey her every whim. The Dark Queen snapped her fingers, and the man rushed to the table.

"D-dinner is served," he announced, as staff made their way out of the kitchen and began serving plates.

Sam's eyes went wide. "Where's Ilia?"

The Dark Queen smirked, and Sam's stomach twisted up at the look. "I found the time to deal with him."

The realization hit Sam in the chest like a brick. He couldn't breathe. His mind went to the terrified man that had introduced him to this wretched beast—the Dark Queen's latest victim.

CHAPTER FOURTEEN

Sunlight broke through the curtains, hitting Sam in the face. His eyes popped open, searching for the culprit who woke him, but found the only criminal was the sun. Sam flipped over, pulling the blanket over his head. He was even more tired than when he'd crawled into bed the night before. Every day in this godforsaken castle felt the same.

Wake up. Go to the library. Find nothing useful. Somehow stomach a dinner with the Dark Queen where all she did was torture and inflict fear and pain on those around her. Bed.

It had been days since Ilia's death, but Sam was still on edge. He knew the Dark Queen demanded perfection, and even knowing her vile ways, he had hoped something so trivial as a ripped gown would get a pass. That was foolish. Sam made sure never to have a close call again with the Dark Queen. He couldn't risk anyone else's life.

He'd gotten up early every day and gone to the library,

making sure to keep an eye on the clock. Though his time in the library had yet to yield results, Sam remained hopeful. He only had one plan, and he wasn't about to give up on it. He'd only learned more about the magic Keres had told him about, and a few other helpful terms.

Harmony was the magic that the world ran off of and was the good sort of magic. Chaos was what the Dark Queen had given in to, an evil and powerful magic that came at a steep price. The books weren't clear on what that price was, though the closest it came to a description was the person's humanity. Between the two magics of Chaos and Harmony was Alchemy. Unlike the other two, Alchemy did not come from within—it was more like witchcraft with brewing spells. Then there were the magical creatures, who each had their own set of powers. Like Zael with the mind reading and Gadriel with speed and strength. It was all a bit confusing.

Though Mara was becoming a friend, he wasn't sure how much he could trust her to ask for her help outside of the library. He'd save that for later. He couldn't let it get back to the Dark Queen that he was asking those sorts of questions to Mara or anyone else.

The only person he could have small conversations about escaping with was Keres. Sam wasn't sure what made him different, almost immune to the Dark Queen's terrors, but nothing had come from those conversations either, as he had to keep them short and few.

Sam made his way out of his room early as usual. He wound through the hallways, trying to keep himself positive by humming, almost silently, a song that Annabelle used to sing by the lake. It wasn't much, but he wanted to feel close to her. This time apart, with all its uncertainty, was weighing heavily on his heart.

Sam peeked into the dining hall, curious to see if Zael might be there, or if he was hiding as usual. The only time he'd seen him in the last three days was at dinner, when the Dark Queen forced him to entertain her. Sam felt sorry for the merman, they were in the same situation, but at least Sam could explore his surroundings and have connections with others. This man had no one.

But today, when Sam looked into the tank, he saw Zael. Sam pointed his toes to the room and walked in, approaching the glass wall slowly. "Good morning!"

Zael jolted and spun toward Sam, covering his body with his large silver-blue fin. *"What are you doing here?"* Zael almost sounded upset.

"I—I thought you might be lonely."

Zael grimaced. *"You can't fix that."*

"Why?"

"I'll be alone forever."

Sam thought about storming out of the dining hall. He didn't have time to talk to such a rude individual. But then an idea came to him. "Where's your family?" The merman's face softened, and Sam knew. Just like Mara's family, like the chef and Ilia, they were gone. "I'm sorry."

Zael nodded. *"I guess you can stay."*

Sam smiled. "All right, then." He walked over to the table and grabbed a chair, dragging it over to the glass wall. The pair sat in silence for a good while. This man didn't need to talk about anything, he just needed someone who was there.

The clanking of dishes came from the kitchen, and Sam

realized the rest of the palace was beginning to stir. He needed to leave before anyone else found him here, especially the Dark Queen. Sam looked at Zael, who gave him a nod and swam to the back of his cage, giving Sam permission to leave. He quickly put the chair back at the table and headed off toward the library.

Sam stepped out into the all too familiar hallway, frustrated he was still even there. He thought he'd at least by now have an idea of how to get back, or maybe how to break the curse the Dark Queen had put in place to kill Annabelle. Sam was about to round the last hallway when he bumped into someone walking in the opposite direction.

"Sorry, I didn't see—" Sam saw who it was and stopped his apology.

"Up early again I see." Gadriel sneered at Sam, waiting for a reply.

"I suppose I am." Sam still didn't trust Gadriel and preferred the conversation to end quickly.

"Where are we off to this morning? The only rooms down this way are the Dark Queen's chambers and the little library. I've seen how you interact with the queen . . . what could you possibly need with the library?" Gadriel eyed Sam suspiciously. His deep black eyes made Sam uncomfortable.

"What's it matter to you?" Sam was done talking to the elf. He tried to sidestep him, but Gadriel was too fast and blocked Sam's path. He made the movements look effortless, casual even.

"I've noticed the books rearranged on the shelves. Are you enjoying learning about our world's history? Those books can be quite telling."

Sam's heart beat faster. What was Gadriel getting at?

Gadriel continued, "I would hate for the Dark Queen to think you were doing something to ruin her plans with you."

Sam stumbled over his words. "No, it's just, I, well, I wanted to know more about where I am. What's the harm in that?"

Gadriel looked Sam up and down. "Mhmm." The elf stepped out of the way. "Go on, then, I'm sure the Dark Queen wouldn't mind your company in the library this morning."

Sam's stomach dropped. "The Dark Queen is in there?"

"Of course. She is an avid reader. I'm surprised you haven't come across her before."

Sweat dripped down Sam's forehead, and he wiped it away as inconspicuously as he could. "Actually, I was thinking I might head to the rose garden for some fresh air."

"A fine idea." Gadriel gave Sam a slight nod.

As Sam turned to head back down the way he'd come, Gadriel whispered out to him, "Don't worry, I won't tell the queen your secret." The taunt in Gadriel's voice made the hairs on Sam's neck prickle.

Tracing his steps back, Sam walked several halls before coming to the garden entrance. He pushed on the door, relieved to see the space was empty, and made his way to the far side of the garden.

The breeze on his cheek was a welcome change. Sam sat on a garden bench, soaking in the feel of the morning air. He hadn't realized before now how cooped up he'd been. Finally, he could breathe.

As Sam studied the beautiful roses—the only thing the Dark Queen had not killed—he spotted a tail near the bush, wiggling about. *Just a tiny little snake,* he thought.

Once it slithered away, Sam's attention transferred to the silence. No birds chirped. No wind blew. No threat stood nearby.

Peace existed within the secluded walls of the garden, even if just momentarily. Taking the opportunity to shut his weary eyes, Sam stretched out on the garden bench, soaking in the rays of sunshine. As the warmth tickled his skin, a longing stirred within Sam's heart . . . for home. For Annabelle. For everything he once knew.

The leaves shifted, and a low hum fluttered through the air. Now alert, Sam spun around to find the culprit amidst the thorny bushes. A single touch and the roses bloomed before the transfixing woman, multiplying and adding beauty to the garden. When the woman reached the tree, her fingers ran along the bark as if speaking to the leaves. With the lightest tap on the stem, two oranges appeared from nothing.

Wow, Sam thought as his jaw dropped. *If only growing food were that easy back home.*

After gently plucking the oranges from the tree and slipping the fruit inside the pocket of her gown, the woman with the golden flower crown and big brown curls turned toward Sam, who quickly averted his gaze to something less stunning.

Then a thought surfaced: Sam knew this woman. He'd seen her at the remebrance, and by the looks of it, the recognition was mutual.

Like a young child, the woman skipped toward him, causing Sam to shift rather awkwardly in his seat.

"Hello." The woman's voice was soft and steady.

"Hello." Sam nodded; his lips tight.

"Samuel, right?"

Sam was taken aback. "How'd you know?"

The woman giggled. "Everyone here knows who you are." She curtsied to Sam in her long flowing gown. "I'm Octavia." She waited for Sam to reply, then dropped her voice to a whisper and leaned in. "I don't bite."

Sam laughed. "Sorry, where are my manners?" He stood and gave Octavia a slight bow, then gestured to the bench. Sam did his best to avert his eyes from her chest, as her dress cut down almost to her navel. Octavia smiled and accepted his offer.

Sam turned to Octavia. "So, you have magic too?"

Octavia looked at the tree she had been tending to. "Yes, but it's not like Dorthea's, or anyone else's you may have seen."

"How so? Wait, did you just call the Dark Queen . . ." Sam lowered his voice. ". . . Dorthea?"

Octavia smiled. "Of course. That is her name, after all."

Sam was baffled. "And she doesn't care when people do that?"

"Well, she doesn't care when *I* do. Some of us have special privileges. People like me or Enos, we have a little bit of freedom with Dorthea."

Sam stumbled around his thoughts. "Are you like her closest friend or something?"

"Or something." Octavia smiled to herself.

Then it clicked. "Oh, you're her . . ." Sam wasn't sure why the word *lover* was refusing to pass his lips.

"Not anymore; that was a long time ago."

Sam nodded slowly, taking in the new information about the Dark Queen. His upper lip curled, and his nose scrunched up.

"She wasn't always like this, you know." Sam met Octavia's

doe eyes. This didn't make sense. Enos, sure. He seemed to be just the kind of person the Dark Queen would go for. But Octavia? This calm, kind woman was nothing like the Dark Queen. What did she see in Octavia? What did Octavia see in her?

Octavia continued, "Oh, I wish you'd known her before. You two would have really gotten along."

Sam scoffed.

"No, really!" Octavia stood and grabbed the skirt of her dress, spinning in a circle. "She was absolutely splendid!" Octavia kept twirling, arms over her head, looking lost in a dream. She plopped back onto the bench.

Sam sat stunned. This woman had at least ten years on him, yet she acted so carefree. "Is that why you two . . . stopped? She was no longer splendid?"

Octavia giggled. "Oh, no. We ended long before she gave in to Chaos. Our time together had just come to an end." Octavia said it so matter-of-factly, Sam wasn't sure what to say next.

The conversation was going somewhere he'd never anticipated, and he wasn't sure he wanted to go any further. He searched for any words to change the subject. "Those flowers in your hair are lovely." Sam gestured at the golden crown of flowers on her head. "Are they real? I haven't seen anything but roses growing around here."

Octavia beamed. "Thank you! I grew them myself. They're chrysanthemums." Her eyes twinkled at the word.

"Ah, I've never seen those before." Sam fidgeted with his hands. Why was it so painfully awkward to talk to this woman? Perhaps it was her cheerful disposition. She lived so carefree—

it didn't fit the palace at all. Odd that someone so kind and beautiful could seem so out of place.

Before he could think of the next thing to say, Octavia popped up.

"I should get back to my darlings. They need my love. Thanks for the company." Octavia bowed low, and Sam returned a nod.

"Goodbye."

"Bye!" Octavia danced off, touching the flowers as she went, giving them her love.

IT HAD BEEN A LONG, boring day, and the soup in front of him did little to keep his attention as his eyes fought to stay open. Going to the library and possibly seeing the Dark Queen was a risk he couldn't take, so he stayed in his room after leaving the garden.

I should have taken a nap.

Everyone in the palace had been busy with their daily tasks, so Sam sat on his bed all day, not knowing what to do with himself. Luckily, he'd stumbled across some parchments and pens, but inspiration evaded him in his attempts to write. Outside of this palace, he would have enjoyed a day of doing nothing for once.

He never had a chance to just sit in bed all day with all the work that had to be done on the farm. His only time off was for sleep and church. Even though Mr. Anderson wasn't a church man, he always encouraged Sam to continue going, and would give him the morning off to attend. Sam wondered how Mr. Anderson was faring without his help on the farm. He hated the thought of Mr. Anderson thinking Sam had abandoned him. He hadn't even been able to write his goodbye letter yet.

SAM'S EYES CLOSED, and his head bobbed when the sound of shoes entered the dining hall. It must have been the Dark Queen. She was running late to dinner this evening for whatever reason, and Sam was expected to sit there and wait while his soup got cold. Sam reveled in the last moment of peace before he had to endure another dinner with the Dark Queen. He took a deep breath and slowly glanced up.

The first thing Sam saw were the boots—the sandy brown boots with a slight heel. He'd seen them so many times in a jumble by the lake. *It can't be.* He kept his gaze going, his heart beating out of his chest. He followed the soft ruffles of a deep gray skirt that was cinched at the waist by a thin brown belt. Sam thought he might pass out from the excitement. *How did she get here?* Sam didn't care the answer to the question. He leapt from his seat, tears filling his eyes, ready to embrace the woman he loved.

He wrapped his arms around her tight, afraid to let her go. "Belli, how are you here? Are you hurt?"

"No, I'm all right. Where are we?" The voice was like an angel singing in his ears.

"Somewhere dangerous. We need to get home before she finds us." He pulled Annabelle's hand, but she wouldn't budge.

"I've missed you," Annabelle said, pulling him toward her and wrapping her arms around his neck.

"I've missed you too, Belli. More than I can even say." He wrapped his arms around her waist.

Annabelle reached up and kissed Sam, pulling him in deep. Sam kissed her back, emotions exploding through his body at the realization that he had Annabelle in his arms, safe. Annabelle leaned in, her hands traveling down his body, reaching into his trousers. "Oh, Sammy," she moaned.

"Stop!" Sam pushed her off of him, panting with rage. "You never call me Sammy. Only . . ."

Sam scanned her body, only now noticing her hands decorated in jewels—a sapphire ring on her finger. He stumbled backward and fell to the floor when he met the woman's gaze. She cackled as she looked down at Sam.

Sam was horrified.

Heartbroken.

The woman standing before him looked just like his Annabelle. But it wasn't Annabelle. It was the sick monster Sam had come to know.

In an instant, the woman who looked like Annabelle disappeared, and the Dark Queen stood before him. This was her newest bit of torture—her most gut-wrenching.

"How could you? How could you do this to me?" Sam's chest sped as the anger in him boiled to the top. He stared at the Dark Queen in Annabelle's clothes. *Annabelle's clothes. Dear God, no.* "Where is she? What did you do with her!" Sam rose from the ground and charged the Dark Queen, pushing her into the wall behind her, and held her firm by her shoulders.

"Oh, Sammy, I knew you'd like the dress. But are you sure you want to do this here, where everyone can see?" She gave Sam the same look she had given Enos that night outside her chambers.

Sam pressed her shoulders harder, bringing his face within inches of the Dark Queen's. "You stop that! I will *never* be with you. Now where is Annabelle?" Sam could hardly control his breathing, and for a moment, he thought he could see fear in the Dark Queen's eyes. No, not fear. Sadness.

The look was gone as quickly as it'd come. Keres walked into the room and struggled to remove Sam from the Dark Queen. Gadriel joined in, and eventually the two were able to pull him back.

"So that's what you feel like." The Dark Queen's lips coiled upward, and a fire raged in Sam all over again. He charged, only this time he was met with the Dark Queen's hand. He stood still, tears streaming down his face, sweat dripping down his palms. His blood was hot, and he saw red. The Dark Queen opened her mouth. "Oh hush, darling. Your precious Annabelle is just fine. I had my seamstress make these. Quite remarkable in its similarities, don't you think?"

Sam wasn't sure whether or not to believe the Dark Queen. He desperately wanted to—for Annabelle to be safe. Sam thought of all the others he'd seen the Dark Queen kill, the pride she took in it. He was sure that if she had hurt Annabelle, she wouldn't be able to shut up about it.

"Why would you do this? I haven't done anything to you."

"Yes, I know, and I'm growing rather tired of that." She licked her lips.

"Stop it! You can't impersonate someone to get what you want!"

Sam's jaw dropped as the Dark Queen stood and Chaos clouded her, floating away and revealing a version of Sam. "I can do whatever I want."

Sam was speechless as he stared at his face on the Dark Queen's body, in her dress and jewels. She sounded exactly like him. This level of trickery . . . It was evil.

The Dark Queen changed back to herself and released Sam. As soon as he was free of her grasp, he started to walk out of the hall.

"Where do you think you're going?"

"Back to my room. I'm not hungry anymore."

"You will stay," the Dark Queen commanded, lifting her hand and spiraling Chaos toward Sam.

Sam's feet turned back into the room toward his chair. He sat down, picked up his spoon, and ate his cold soup.

He couldn't finish fast enough. He'd managed to go the meal without having to speak to the Dark Queen, and he wanted to keep it that way. Just one more course, and he'd be free to leave.

As soon as the cake was placed before Sam, he stuffed it down. Three giant bites later, he'd finished. He looked up to the Dark Queen, still dressed in the gray dress that buttoned up to her neck, pleading to her with his eyes to let him leave.

He felt her release his feet from the floor and rushed out of the room before she could change her mind. He made sure to walk at a brisk pace. He didn't want her following him like she'd done the last time he ran out of the hall.

Sam opened the door to his room as every emotion hit him at once. He walked into the bathroom and undressed. He stood there naked, in a haze. The Dark Queen was evil. He knew that. So why was this so hard for him to deal with? This time, it was personal. She'd tried to seduce him before, but never like this. To pretend to be Annabelle, to get him to feel joy and rip it away . . .

Sam filled the tub, only turning on the hot source. He stepped in and made his way to the seat, letting the water slowly fill the enormous tub and crawl up his body. Water lapped at his mouth, splashing up into his nose before he realized how full the tub had gotten. He reached out and stopped the flow, draining a bit out. When the water was at chin level, he leaned back, closed his eyes, and drifted off to sleep.

THE WARMTH of the bath lulled Sam deep in his sleep. The steam had cleared up his lungs, and he breathed smoother. His tears had melted into the pool, and as Sam dreamed, his anger washed away too.

He dreamed of an open meadow. Of running free with Annabelle by his side. They collapsed into a field of flowers. It was peaceful. He grabbed Annabelle, pulled her close, and kissed her passionately. Annabelle kissed his neck. She got up and circled around him, kissing his head, his back. She brought her hands to his shoulder and started kneading, like she always did after a hard day's work. It seemed so real, like she was there touching him. Then she grabbed firm to both shoulders and shook him. *Why is she shaking me?*

Sam was jolted awake by the hand on his shoulder. It took Sam a moment to realize where he was. He threw his hands over himself to cover up as best he could. "Mara, what are you doing here? I'm not decent!"

"Sorry. I was doing my nightly rounds and your door was wide open. I saw you weren't in bed, and I got worried. What are you doing sleeping in the bath?"

Sam desperately tried to keep his whole self covered, which was proving difficult after the dream of Annabelle. He needed a moment to calm down. Sam moved toward the towel he'd left on the edge of the tub. "Can I have a minute, please?"

"Oh, right. Sorry. I'll be out there. I brought you something to sleep in."

"Thanks."

Mara left, and Sam finally got out of the tub. His hands were raw, and his fingertips were rigid to the point he couldn't feel them anymore. *How long was I in there?* Sam looked to the window before remembering it was just a painting. Since he couldn't tell how late it was, he went to the chair and grabbed the clothes Mara had set out for him. Once he was dressed, he headed into his bedchambers, where Mara stood waiting.

"I didn't mean to frighten you. I was just worried." She bowed her head low.

"It's all right, Mara. I was just exhausted is all."

"Well, you should get back to sleep. Sunup is in only a few hours."

"What? Was I really in there for that long?" The deep blue, almost black window, confirmed Mara's words.

Mara walked to Sam's bed and pulled down the covers. "I guess so. Come on now." She patted the sheets.

Sam walked over and flopped onto the bed.

"Goodnight, Sam." Mara bowed.

"Wait." Sam hesitated. His pain of missing Annabelle twisted his stomach so much he could hardly breathe. He needed human connection—someone to talk to. "Do you wanna stay and talk?"

Mara grinned and hopped up on the bed. "What do you want to talk about?" She studied Sam's face. "Annabelle." She smiled.

"Is it that obvious?"

"You're a man in love—of course it is. Tell me all about how beautiful she is. No! Tell me how you met. No, no! Tell me about the moment you knew you loved her. I bet that's a great story." She crossed her legs and propped her chin up on her hands like an excited schoolgirl.

Sam chuckled. "All right." He smiled, remembering the moment as if he were living it right then and there. "We were so young, around your age, and we'd been friends for years. The day was just like any other we'd spent together—reading books and eating whatever treats we could sneak from the kitchen in our pockets. I was working on one of my first poems.

"All the other kids said I was a fool for thinking I could be anything other than a worker, but Annabelle understood me. She was the first person to tell me I should write down my stories. That day, Annabelle had found some hard chewing gum from one of the women of the house and brought us each a piece. Neither one of us had tried it before, so we had no idea what to expect."

"What's gum?" Mara interjected.

"It's this weird food that you chew but don't swallow."

"That sounds . . . useless."

Sam laughed. "That's exactly what we said. We popped it in

our mouths and started chewing. The sensation was so odd; we both looked at each other and spat them onto the floor, lost in a fit of laughter. We were so loud we caught the attention of Mildred. We heard her clamoring up the stairs, grabbed our books, and ran behind the broken, dusty old sofa that sat in the corner of the room. Mildred stood at the top of the stairs, scanning the room, and found the gum we'd spit out. She was so mad she ran back down the stairs to find who had stolen her gum. Annabelle and I collapsed on the floor in laughter." Sam paused, smiling as he relived the memory.

Mara grabbed his hand. "And then what?"

"Annabelle composed herself, and we could hear Mildred traipsing around again. I tried so hard to stop laughing but I couldn't. Annabelle put her hand over my mouth to keep me quiet, and it worked. As soon as she touched me and looked into my eyes, everything changed. I could hear my heart beating in my entire body, and my palms instantly turned damp with sweat. Annabelle left the room without a word and snuck back down so we wouldn't get caught together. The moment she was out of sight, my heart ached to be near her again."

"And that's when you knew?" Mara asked, wide-eyed.

"And that's when I knew." Sam couldn't stop smiling at the treasured memory. He needed to get back to Annabelle. The girl, now woman, who made him laugh and kept him poised yet wild at the same time.

Mara sighed, her smile turning downward. "I want that."

"And you'll get it." Sam placed his hand on Mara's shoulder. "You have plenty of time to meet someone that makes you smile and fills your life with more joy than you ever knew you could feel."

"You really think so?"

"I know it."

Mara smiled her childlike grin and jumped off the bed. "It's time to go to sleep. Goodnight, Sam."

"Goodnight, Mara." As soon as he turned over, he was asleep again, back in the meadow with Annabelle.

CHAPTER FIFTEEN

The cold morning air pricked Sam's face as he walked in line out of the castle gates and down the grand staircase. It was the first time he'd been off the grounds since his arrival, though he couldn't see much in the shadows before sunrise.

They walked in rows of two, with the Dark Queen leading the way, Keres at her side, Gadriel directly behind. Sam stood next to Mara, right in the middle of the charge. He figured they meant to keep him from running once they were clear of the bridge, though the Dark Queen's wall of fire would suffice.

The sun had not yet risen, but everyone around him looked their best. He walked slowly with the others on the dead leaves, hearing them crunch beneath his feet.

After they stepped off the bridge, the group took a sharp left, heading down a steep cobblestone path. Sam kept his head down, trying to ignore the moans of the people tied up in the air. He couldn't bear to look at their faces if there was no way of saving them.

Sam had no idea where they were going, only that he was told to get dressed and follow along. Palms sweating, heart beating slightly faster than normal, he tried to discern what could possibly be awaiting him. It had never occurred to him before how many people lived in the palace until they were all lined up in the main corridor—there must have been almost a hundred of them, though they all appeared to be servants, as their fine wears were much less lavish than those on the Dark Queen's cortege.

Only footsteps sounded around them. No crickets, no birds, nothing. He didn't know what was scarier, the castle or the dead woods in the dark. Staring out into the black abyss, Sam prayed no creature would stalk them this close to the palace. The group kept on walking until they reached a case of ascending stairs. Sam couldn't quite make out what waited at the top of the steps. There didn't appear to be any lights to show the way. The only light came from a torch the Dark Queen held, so he could only see a few paces ahead. He found it odd she would carry a torch herself.

He climbed the stairs, careful to follow the light up to the top. When he reached a breezeway, he could see the Dark Queen wasn't holding a torch at all. The fire came from her hands. Sam shuddered at the sight. All those people burned alive in their homes, she did it with her own hands. Why was he even still surprised at the horrors the Dark Queen could inflict?

Once the rest of the line had made it up the steps, the Dark Queen sent fire pouring from her hands in a river of flames, lighting the torches surrounding them. When they were all burning, Sam could make out a structure with the orange glow.

He still couldn't tell where they were, but he could see the outside clearly. Before him stood a massive structure lined with columns all around, similar to the palace. The columns were so sizeable it would have taken five large men standing hand in hand to wrap around it, and higher than Mr. Anderson's three-story manor stacked onto itself. It appeared to be much more ancient than the palace, and Sam was mesmerized by the sight.

The group stood in wait outside the structure. Many tried their hardest to get close to the flames to warm their hands. Sam didn't dare draw attention to himself in the light of the fires, so he wrapped his hands in his cloak as best he could, rubbing them together to try to fight off the bitter cold air.

"It's beautiful, isn't it?" Mara stood by Sam, seeing the amazement on his face.

Sam nodded. "What is this place?"

A couple near them shot Sam a dirty look. "Shh."

"You'll see," Mara whispered, ushering Sam up toward the front of the group.

A large cutout of stone and marble stood before Sam, covered by a white curtain. Suddenly, a head poked between the curtains, scanning the crowd. When the man locked eyes with the Dark Queen, he gave her a simple nod, then opened the curtain fully, standing to the side to hold the drapes back. The Dark Queen approached the door and disappeared inside. She was followed closely by her cortege.

Mara shoved Sam forward, urging him inside. Sam slowed his pace as he neared the opening, admiring the stone snake statues that matched the ones guarding the castle. Mara went up behind him and grabbed his arm, leading him inside.

Sam's eyes tried to adjust as the torches faded while he stepped into darkness. Only candles shone light through the temple, lining the perimeter of the room and surrounding a large figure at the end of it.

Mara kept pulling Sam up the aisle as he looked around. While this place was dark, it felt different than the gloom of the palace. It was warm—welcoming. As Sam and Mara approached the far side of the room, he made out the figure before him.

A large bronze statue of a woman. The statue stood twenty feet high, and she wore a loose dress that draped her petite figure. A crown of flowers sat atop her head. In one hand, she held a cornucopia of fruits, and in the other, a sheaf of wheat. Sam approached the woman in bewilderment. A basket of white roses sat on a table several strides before the statue; people took a flower and placed it at the base of the statue. Mara picked one up and pulled Sam to the woman.

Mara knelt before the statue and laid her flower at the woman's feet. Sam noticed an inscription just below the woman's left foot.

DEMETER

Mara offered Sam a rose, but he had already figured out where they were. They were in worship, here to praise this woman and provide offerings. Sam refused the rose. He wasn't about to praise a false idol. Sam searched around the room for a way out, but the only way was the one he'd come in through, and the Dark Queen had already made her way back there. He was stuck.

Mara and the other servants walked over to a set of cushions near one side of the altar. Each person knelt on a pillow and bowed at the statue.

Sam tried to think what to do. He wasn't going to partake, but maybe he could make this his own sort of church. He prayed his Father would forgive him for stepping into a false temple. Sam sat down, legs crossed, on a cushion facing away from the altar. He wiggled around until he found the sweet spot, then put his hands together and bowed his head.

Our Father, who art in heaven, hallowed be thy name—thy kingdom come—thy will be done . . .

Sam kept praying for hours, talking to God about all he had gone through, asking Him for help. Help to break the curse the Dark Queen had cast to kill Annabelle, help to get home safely, and he prayed desperately for time to be on his side so Annabelle was there when he returned to her. It was a lot to ask, but he'd seen many miracles in his life, and trusted fully in the Lord.

Sam continued his prayers until a soft hand grabbed his shoulder. He was the only one still praying on the cushions, and a servant he'd never seen before was there, looking at Sam with kind eyes. The man waved for Sam to follow him. Sam nodded and followed the man out of the temple, where the sun had reached its peak in the sky.

The rest of the group was at the bottom of the stairs, so Sam walked down to join them. He spotted Mara off to the side and sauntered toward her.

"What now?" Sam asked.

"Shh." More hushes from those around him.

Mara grabbed Sam's hand and led him to a table of food,

showing him a plate and motioning for him to take what he wanted. The sight of food made his stomach growl, and he filled his plate. A nice, shaded area away from the others and under a tree was the perfect place to sit and eat his meal.

Sam looked up, wondering if the Dark Queen was still around. A small tent with guards sat near the group, and Sam assumed she was eating her meal inside. One of the guards stared at him, giving him a half smile. He wasn't sure what to do, so he gazed up at a tree, pretending to be fascinated by the branches.

Mara startled Sam when she plopped down next to him. "Sorry we can't really talk. We're not supposed to on worship days," Mara whispered.

Sam whispered back, "It's fine. I just didn't know the rules."

Mara smiled and got up, walking back toward the others, but not before swiping a cookie from the table and stuffing it into her cloak pocket.

He closed his eyes to enjoy the breeze through the trees, the wind hissing as it whipped around the trunks.

As Sam finished his meal, the Dark Queen emerged from her tent. Everyone stood a bit taller and turned toward her, waiting for her next move. The Dark Queen twisted back toward the temple and ascended the stairs once again, the rest of the people following. Sam had no choice but to go back, so he took a deep breath and began the climb.

They reentered the temple, though this time it was different. There were more candles brightening the room, and the curtain was left open to allow a soft breeze in. There was also a group of young men and women standing next to the altar. They were singing a haunting song—it had no words, but Sam got the sense of it.

The servants headed back toward the cushions, but this time they sat cross-legged as Sam had before. He was about to turn away from the statue when he saw the Dark Queen making her way toward it.

The Dark Queen took something out of her cloak, which appeared to be an empty vial. Opening the lid to wave her hand over it, the vial filled with a black sparkling dust, and she closed the top before placing it at the foot of Demeter's statue. An offering of her own magic. The Dark Queen must have been a devout worshiper to offer something so valuable to her.

When the Dark Queen returned to her spot of worship and began to pray, Sam swiveled around and resumed his conversation with God. As soon as Sam closed his eyes, he knew his prayers had been answered.

Sam peeked over his shoulder at the vial of magic that sat on the altar. He recalled his conversation with the Dark Queen about her curse for Annabelle. She'd told Sam the only thing that could break the curse was her own magic, and she would never do that. But the Dark Queen didn't have to give Sam any of her magic. He could take it, and he could save Annabelle.

Sam slowly turned his head back around and bowed into his hands, returning to his prayers. *Thank you.*

Hours ticked by as Sam sat with the Lord. Once again, candles flickered the only light through the temple. The sun had set the hour before, and the worshippers were finally getting up to return to the palace. If Sam wanted to get that vial of magic, this was his chance. He waited until everyone had assembled into their line. Mara waved him over, but he held up his hand to let her know he needed one more minute.

Sam wove through the people toward the statue. There, sitting at her feet, was his chance at saving Annabelle. Sam's heart sped up with pure excitement. He had to breathe deep and focus on steadying his shaking hands, careful not to give away what he was about to do.

He walked up to the statue and knelt before it, getting as close as he could. A bead of sweat formed on his brow, and his breathing narrowed. Reaching his hand out of his cloak, he went for the vial. Just as he was about to grab it, a pair of feet appeared next to him. Out of the corner of his eyes, he made out the royal sapphire cloak that draped around the figure. It was the Dark Queen.

The queen cleared her throat, and Sam hesitantly gazed up at her, guilt written all over his face. She stared back at him blankly, and simply gestured toward the rest of the group. Sam had no choice but to join the others empty-handed.

He fell in next to Mara, and the Dark Queen made her way toward the front of the line. Sam followed the others back out through the curtain, turning back to see the vial was gone, along with his best plan for saving his love.

The assembly made their way down the steps and back toward the castle, their only light being the Dark Queen.

CHAPTER SIXTEEN

Sam sat on his bed, contemplating his next move. Now that taking the Dark Queen's magic was on the table, he was one step closer to his escape. But where had the magic gone? He needed to get back to the temple on his own so he could look around. Leaving the castle alone wouldn't be easy, but he needed to find a way. Sam lay back on the bed, letting his legs dangle over the edge.

A plan began to form in Sam's mind. No chance the Dark Queen would just let him out the front door. His only access to the outdoors was that garden. He would go when all eyes were elsewhere and find a way out through the bushes. The more Sam thought about his plan, the more excited he became. *This could work.*

It was late into the night, a perfect time to try his plan. Sam sat up, slipped on his shoes, and made his way out of the room. Poking his head out to scan the hallways, he found no one in sight. He stepped out and made his way toward the door to the garden.

The castle was silent, the only sound Sam could hear was his breathing. He rounded the last corner, ignoring the guards on either side of the exit, and reached out for the door. It wasn't until he'd pushed it open that he remembered what Keres had said. *The Dark Queen spends her evenings in the garden.*

As he saw the Dark Queen on a bench across the garden, Sam stopped dead. She held a single white rose up to her chin, enjoying its scent, lying flat on the bench, her other arm hanging over the side. He'd never seen the Dark Queen look so . . . human.

Inching his way back inside, Sam was careful to hold the door so it didn't make a sound as it closed. When he was sure the Dark Queen hadn't seen him, he turned on his heel and started the walk back to his room.

"Wait!"

Sam froze. He didn't recognize the voice. Who could possibly be calling out to him this time of night? Sam turned to see one of the guards jogging over to him.

"Hey, Sam. You dropped this." The guard held out Sam's notebook.

Sam patted his jacket, wondering how it could have fallen out. "Oh, thank you." Sam grabbed for the notebook.

"It's no problem." The guard smiled at Sam. He was a short fellow, but built muscular, as he would expect any of the Dark Queen's guards to be. Straight blackish-brown hair swept to his collarbone, and he looked at Sam with large brown eyes. Sam began to turn back toward his room. "I'm Somchai."

"Hello." He tried to turn again to leave.

"I've seen you around before," Somchai said.

"Uh-huh." Sam was confused why the guard insisted on talking to him.

Somchai gave Sam a sheepish grin. "Okay, then, have a good night. I'll see you later."

"You too." Sam turned and walked quickly back to his room, not wanting to get stuck talking again. But then a thought dawned on him, and he walked right past his chamber doors.

Sam kept going until he was staring at the Dark Queen's doors. He stood there motionless, looking for an ounce of courage. He had to do this before the Dark Queen left the gardens. He didn't have much time. Sam shook out his arms, preparing for what he needed to do.

Only one explanation remained for where the vial of magic had gone, and he stood outside its door. The Dark Queen was the last person at the altar. She saw him there, could have figured out his plans. She had to have the vial. He prayed she took it here, that it wasn't still with her. Sam's head pounded with his heartbeat. His mouth went dry. He was about to break into the Dark Queen's chambers, the last place he wanted to be in this wretched palace. Sam steadied himself and reached out. Everything went dark.

What happened? Sam's eyes flitted open. He was on the ground outside of the Dark Queen's chambers. Everything was so fuzzy; he could barely see. He couldn't remember what had happened, he could barely remember why he was there. Shouts emerged from down the hall. Sam looked in their direction, but they hadn't gone around the corner yet. He still had time to get away.

Sam pushed up against the ground, but he fell onto his face. *Get up. Hurry.* He tried again, but he kept slipping. His arms were of no use.

The shouts drew closer.

Sam rolled over and pushed as hard as he could with his legs. He scooted forward an inch on the floor. *This isn't working. Go!*

No footsteps had entered the hall, but he could hear them nearing the corner. Sam looked behind him and saw the library doors open. He rolled over and tried one last push.

Nothing.

His vision was beginning to clear up, his mind becoming less hazy. The memories flooded back to him.

What was he thinking? Breaking into the Dark Queen's chambers? Of course it would be enchanted.

Sam flopped onto his back, ready for his fate. Then he realized—he'd been rolling back and forth. Sam zeroed in on the library doors and began to move. He didn't have time to think about how foolish he looked spinning around on the floor. He needed to get away from the chamber doors.

Sam slipped inside the library and was able to kick the doors closed as shouts filled the hallway he'd just been in. Sam looked around for something to block the door. No. That would only make him seem guilty. His eyes darted around the room and stopped on a chair. He needed to get there, to pick up a book. He needed to appear innocent.

Sam struggled over to the chair. The shouts had stopped, and he knew it was only a matter of time until they came to the room closest to the Dark Queen's chambers. He lopped his arm up into the seat and pulled as hard as he could, but he got nowhere.

He heard the men outside talking, speaking the last thing he wanted. "Maybe they went into the library."

God help me.

Sam pulled, but his body still wouldn't budge. The footsteps drew nearer. Surely, there would be punishment for attempted thievery, and the Dark Queen would pull the truth out of him one way or another.

His plan was ruined.

He'd never save Annabelle.

A click sounded behind him, and Keres rushed into the room from behind a set of bookcases. Before Sam knew what was happening, Keres had his arms around Sam and hoisted his large body off the floor and into the chair. He grabbed a nearby book and opened it, putting it in front of Sam. Then he grabbed his own book and sat in another chair opposite Sam just as the guards opened the library doors. It was Somchai.

"Who's in here?"

Keres said, "Shh. It's just Sam and I." He pointed to the books.

Somchai bowed low. "Forgive me, my lord. Have you heard anything out of the ordinary? Someone tried to break into the Dark Queen's chambers."

Keres put the book down and cocked his head to the side. "No, we have been captivated by our books. Now, who would be foolish enough to do that?"

"I don't know, sir, but we will find out. Sorry for the disturbance."

"No problem at all. Good luck with your search."

Somchai bowed as he exited the room. "Bye, Sam." He smiled.

"Oh, bye."

Somchai closed the door, his footsteps disappearing down the hall along with the other guards.

Sam let out a huge breath and turned to Keres.

"Thank you. But how did you know I was in trouble?"

Keres turned to face Sam, pushing the book aside. "I heard the commotion. And like I told the guard, no one is foolish enough to try to break into the Dark Queen's chambers. No one except you."

Sam's cheeks heated.

"I knew you needed my help. My room is closer to here than where the guards were stationed. I know a shortcut"—Keres pointed to the bookcase he'd come through—"and it seems like I made it just in time. What were you trying to accomplish?"

Sam hung his head, the feeling in his limbs returning to him with a tingle. "I thought maybe the Dark Queen had some magic in a vial that I could use to break the curse. It's stupid, I know."

Keres stared at Sam. "It's brilliant."

Sam looked up. "Really?"

"Yes! Of course the Dark Queen would keep her precious magic close to her. But her room is always sealed. Except . . ."

"Except when?"

Keres looked apprehensive, twisting the ring on his finger. "When she's inside."

Sam shook his head. "No. That's out of the question."

"You're probably right. But what's the alternative?"

Sam thought. "She left her magic at the altar during temple."

Keres looked surprised. "She did?"

"Mhmm. So, when is the next worship? In a few days? Next week? If I can figure out a way to be alone with—"

"Sixty days."

"What? No, that can't be right." Sam lost his breath from the gut punch. "I can't wait that long."

Keres brought his hand to his chin, thinking. "We'll figure something out. But for now, I need to leave. We can't risk being seen out in the open, talking like this." Keres stood and walked toward the main doors of the library.

"Wait. Why not? The guard just saw us together."

"Something I had wished to avoid, but you gave me no choice. You can't keep walking around here being foolish. The Dark Queen's patience does not run deep."

Sam sighed. "Yeah, I've noticed."

"Then we're in agreement. We must stay away from each other to avoid the Dark Queen's suspicions and wrath."

Sam nodded.

"Stay safe. Stay smart," Keres said as he walked out.

"I will." Sam yawned, exhaustion hitting him. Sunrise would be coming soon, and he needed his rest.

Once Keres was out of earshot, Sam looked down at the book still open in front of him. He began to close the book when something on the page caught his eye. A map of the palace. He scoured the pages. Each page showed a different section of the castle, and with the size of the palace, the map took up a large chunk of the book. Sam already knew what most pages showed: the chambers, the main halls, the garden.

But one room stood out among the rest. Too big to be a

bedchamber, but not as large as the other main halls. The room sat tucked away in a far corner of the upper level of the castle, which perplexed Sam. He grabbed the magnifying glass nearest him and stared at the label on the corner of the page. A cluster of words spoke to him.

Treasury

Treasury? A treasury of what? Sam kept reading.

Athens

Sam had read all about Athens in an old history book he'd found at the orphanage. Suddenly, it dawned on him. DEMETER. That's why it sounded so familiar. He'd read about her in a mythology book. She was the goddess of . . . something. He tried to think back to the statue in the temple. She was holding a cornucopia and wheat. Sam wracked his brain: *that's it!* The goddess of harvest. He hadn't realized anyone still worshipped the mythological goddess. Why would they worship her? He turned his attention back to the page.

London

He'd heard all about London from Annabelle. One of the girls in her home had lived there for several years before moving across the ocean with her younger sister. She'd told Annabelle tales of London and how wonderful it was. Annabelle always thought it would be fantastic to visit someday, though they both knew they would never have the money to travel across the seas. Sam looked back to the page and continued on.

Varanasi

Kinshasa

He'd never heard of these places before but assumed they must have been from Earth as well, though far from anywhere he knew. When Sam looked at the last word, his stomach dropped.

Savannah

Sam rubbed his face and looked again to make sure his tired eyes weren't deceiving him. Savannah was only a few days' journey from Charleston—one Mr. Anderson took quite often for business.

Sam scanned the map again to locate the room in the palace. He had to get in that room. He stood from the table, but his legs gave out. The spell from the Dark Queen's chambers had not yet worn off, and it drained him; he wouldn't make it that far. The search would have to wait until morning. In the meantime, he put the book back onto the shelf, then headed back toward his chambers. In the morning, he'd find that room, and hoped to find an answer for how to get home.

SAM AWOKE FEELING MORE RESTED than he had since arriving in Taegaia. The Dark Queen's spell had taken a toll on him and knocked him out all night. At least something good came from it. Not only was he energized enough to search for the room, but he found the room because of his stupid mistake. Sam made a vow to be more careful when it came to finding an escape. Another slip-up like the night before, and he might never make it home to Annabelle.

He took out his notebook. *Tick.* Thirteen. Sam found the hole in his jacket the notebook had slipped through the night before, reminding him he needed to fix the rip as he put the notebook in another pocket.

After Sam washed and dressed, he headed out into the hallway. He tried his best to remember the way to the room, but everything looked so different actually walking through the palace halls. Nothing looked familiar, so he made his best guess.

He wound up a staircase, tiptoeing to conceal his footsteps hitting the cold stone steps. When he climbed up to the top floor and stepped off the landing, he had to stop and catch his breath. Exhaustion didn't usually hit so quickly, but since he hadn't been working his body, he could tell the impact it had on him. His stomach started to soften up, something he'd never experienced before. Sam made a mental note to work out every morning so he would be back to his normal vigor.

The hallway was silent and drafty, almost forgotten. The other halls in the palace were lit with small torches that always burned, but there was no light here except for the slight rays pouring through the small windows.

Sam headed straight for the end of the hall. One detail he remembered clearly: the room sat secluded in a far corner.

The other doors in the palace were all a black wood with iron details, this one was made entirely of stained glass. Sam had to take a step back to get a full view of the image.

The picture depicted three women joining hands. He recognized one of them as Demeter but had no idea who the other two were. Behind them, a door floated in the air. But it was not a regular door—it had a sheen across the front that looked like waves of an ocean. At the women's feet lay mounds of goods. White roses, which did not surprise Sam one bit, seashells, and a pile of glittering dust that looked like what the Dark Queen had vialed. Only instead of black, this had blue specks flickering in white. Sam had no idea what the image meant, but he had to get into that room. He stepped forward and pushed.

Sam hadn't known what he had expected to find, so he wasn't sure why the sight surprised him. In each corner of the room sat piles of trinkets, with a lone pile in the center, each labeled on the wall with a symbol. Sam quickly realized each pile must represent each location he'd read on the castle map.

He immediately searched for the one connected with Savannah. It seemed like the symbols on the wall were in hieroglyphics of some sort, which was no help to Sam. He contemplated for a moment before he realized the problem was actually quite easy. Sam looked down at the stacks and deduced each seemed to be separate themes.

There was a set with clothing in a fashion he'd only seen as a resemblance of clothes the Dark Queen had made him wear. Another had elements that mirrored the temple outside the castle. A third pile was full of mostly weaponry ranging from small daggers to arrows to rifles. The fourth pile caught Sam's eye as the most familiar, and he thought his heart might burst through his chest.

Sam tiptoed toward the stack he knew was from his part of the world, a distant memory crawling its way forward as he stared at the bridle and whip, and he dropped to his knees as tears filled his eyes.

He almost didn't see the figure come out from the back of the pile and jumped around to see who was there, quickly wiping away his tears.

A woman walked toward a stack across the room, her back turned to Sam. Nestled under her arms, a scroll sat close to her chest, and she fidgeted with something in her hands. She didn't acknowledge Sam at all, instead walking toward the stack closest to the door. Leaving the room now would only get him spotted.

When Sam had composed himself, he called out to the woman. "Excuse me." The woman didn't flinch. Clearing his throat, Sam tried again. "Ma'am?"

Again, the woman didn't stop, seemingly oblivious to Sam's presence.

Unsure why she continued to ignore him, Sam headed for the door to be on his way. As he passed by the woman, he looked her in the eyes, and that's when she finally saw him. The woman gasped and jumped, holding her hand up to her chest and dropping what she had been holding.

An orange rolled over to Sam and stopped at his feet. He picked it up and took it to the woman. "I'm so sorry. I called out to you."

The woman took the orange and bowed her head at Sam. When she stood straight, her thick black hair fell back and revealed a pair of long, pointed ears. *Another elf.*

Her hair fell in tresses down her back. Small in both height and frame, she only went up to the base of Sam's chest. The woman looked at Sam with large, angular brown eyes. A hint of rose could be seen on her cheeks beneath her beige skin. This woman seemed sweet, and Sam felt terrible for startling her.

"What exactly is this place?" Sam looked at the scroll she was carrying. "Do you keep track of everything in here?" The woman stared at Sam, who awkwardly adjusted his stance. Why was this woman not talking to him? Had he done something wrong? The woman tucked away her belongings into her pocket and lifted her hands.

She moved them in a beautiful pattern Sam had never seen before, then pointed to her ears while shaking her head. *Huh?* Sam didn't want to be rude, but he wasn't sure what the woman was getting at.

"Can you understand me?"

The young woman gave a slight nod and continued to wave her hands in front of her and gestured to Sam's lips, then back to her ears, shaking her head again.

Oh! He felt like an idiot for not realizing sooner. That's why she had ignored him and wasn't answering—she couldn't hear him. "I'm sorry, I didn't realize."

The woman waved it off, giving him a kind smile.

"I'm Sam."

The woman again moved her hands about, and pointed at Sam.

"Me?" Sam held his hand to his chest.

The woman nodded, gesturing again, and grabbed Sam's hands. She helped him move his hands in the same pattern she had, then placed her hand on his chest.

"Does this mean 'Sam'?"

The woman nodded.

"Wow, thank you," Sam said. "What's your name?"

The young woman swiped her thumbs across her fingertips. Sparks flickered from her fingers, and Sam almost stepped back before she lifted her hands and again moved them through the air. Only this time, words appeared before Sam's eyes.

My name is Ju. What are you doing here? Sam watched the words in amazement as they disappeared, leaving a wisp of smoke in their place before dissolving completely.

"Hi, Ju. I was just wandering around and found this place. Is it okay that I'm here?"

Ju nodded, relief washing over Sam. She put her hand on her chest and gestured toward the door. Ju grabbed his arm and motioned for him to follow her out of the room. Sam went along, unsure where they were going. When they reached the hallway, Ju pulled out a key and locked the door. Her words filled the air once more.

I have somewhere to be. I can't leave you alone in there.

"Oh, all right. Well, it was nice to meet you."

Ju smiled and gave Sam a bow of her head, then scurried off down the hall. Sam stayed where he was, glancing back at the door, contemplating its meaning.

CHAPTER SEVENTEEN

Several days had passed since he'd found the room of earthly items, yet Sam was no closer to finding his way out. He'd been trying to figure out a way to get a vial of the Dark Queen's magic without breaking into her room with her inside but had no luck coming up with anything. He tried talking with Keres about what to do next, but Keres wouldn't talk to him about it anymore. He saw it as too big of a risk—the Dark Queen had ears everywhere. Sam was on his own.

At least he'd gotten the hole in his jacket mended. He'd asked Mara for some supplies to fix it, but when he returned from dinner one night, it had already been repaired.

He sat in the library, combing through the book that had led him to the treasury. He stared at each map, hoping to find an answer somewhere among the pages. He knew Keres had found a hidden passage after he'd saved Sam in the library, but when Sam opened it up, it just led back around to the hallway on the other side. So, he kept scouring.

Sam was about to give up on the book when a thought occurred to him. He'd read a novel back home on royalty and secret tunnels. The maps had hidden the tunnels with a sort of special ink. It was a long shot, but maybe that was happening here as well. After all, almost all books he'd read on castles and palaces had a mention of secret passageways. But how did they find the ink again? Sam picked up his teacup and lifted it to his lips for a sip when the orange slice caught his attention. A memory flooded back to him. One could use citrus, a lemon, to write hidden messages on paper, and all it required to reveal the message was . . . was . . . *heat!*

He blew hot air on the pages, but nothing happened. He wracked his brain, trying to recall the elements he was missing. His breath wasn't hot enough. Scanning the room, he found a roaring fireplace and a lamp lit by candle. The fireplace seemed too risky, so he tried his luck with the lamp.

Sam lifted page after page over the lamp until they were hot to the touch. Nothing seemed to be happening until a section appeared overlaid with ink of a different color. Sam's heart skipped a beat as something finally seemed to be going in his favor.

There was a tunnel directly over the map he'd been looking at, near the garden entrance. Sam stared at the page, trying to find the entrance. When he put the edge of the page up to the lantern, a golden mark appeared.

He frantically grabbed a magnifying glass and looked at the mark. It was on the wall at the end of the tunnel, and it appeared to be a door. Sam's body filled with excitement. Even if there was nothing to be found, perhaps he could use it as a place to talk things over with Keres. Sam didn't know enough about this land yet; he needed an ally.

Ready to go exploring, Sam closed the book and shelved it, cleaning up the ring the tea had made on the table with a cloth from his breakfast tray. He cracked the doors open and peered into the hall. All clear. Sam stepped out and headed toward the garden, trying to keep his nerves in check.

When he got to the entrance, he looked around for the area the hidden door should have been. He pressed on the wall, thinking maybe a stone pushed in to reveal the entrance to the tunnel. When Sam had pressed all along the wall without success, he stepped back to look it over. Transfixed on the wall, he hadn't heard the footsteps approaching until they were right next to him.

Gadriel studied him.

"What do you want?" Sam said.

"I'm just passing through, getting all the arrangements in order for tonight's feast." Gadriel's face was smug.

"Hmph." Sam let out a laugh through his nose.

"That is my duty. Though I will say, I wasn't expecting you to be standing here like an imbecile just staring at a wall. That's a new one for you."

"Why don't you just keep moving along and leave me alone?" Sam was over talking to Gadriel every time the conversation began.

"Maybe I'll stand here a while. Whatever you're staring at seems to be fascinating, perhaps I'll give it a go."

"Whatever." Sam turned and began the walk back to his chambers. He couldn't search for anything with Gadriel watching over his shoulder.

"Lovely to see you again, Sam," Gadriel called after him.

A WARM BATH provided the perfect sanctuary to think about everything he still needed to accomplish and come up with a plan to hurry things along. It had been almost two weeks in this new world, and that could be much longer in his own—months, years, even decades. Sam pushed the thought from his mind. The focus needed to stay on getting home, not worrying that there may be no home to get back to.

His mind kept going back to the same conclusion: he couldn't wait until the next temple day to try to get the vial of magic. No. He'd have to go into *her* room while she slept. The thought made Sam sick.

While he'd considered himself safer than the rest of those in the palace because the Dark Queen needed him, this could get him killed if he were caught. How long would the Dark Queen tolerate the insubordination? But he had no choice. Without the magic, even if he did manage to find a way home, Annabelle would die. He had to do this for Annabelle. Tonight.

ATTEMPTS TO AVOID the Dark Queen's gaze had gotten him through more than one meal, and she never said anything about it. Fine by him. He welcomed the silence at the table. Sam tried to finish his meal as fast as possible to get back to planning. The race against time pressed on him hard, and though he may have already lost that battle, he would escape this prison at any cost.

But this evening, as Sam rose from the table, the Dark Queen stopped him.

"I will send my seamstress to your room in the morning for you to be fitted for proper attire."

Sam grew used to the Dark Queen giving him lavish clothing to wear. "Fine." He tried to leave again, but she continued.

"I want you looking your best for our wedding day."

Sam choked on his breath. "What?" He finally looked to the Dark Queen, meeting her sneering gaze.

"How else did you think I would attain power from your love? You need to give your love to me willingly."

"I will never love you!" Sam kept trying to leave, but his feet were stuck in place. She wasn't about to let him leave this conversation.

"Oh, but you will. Otherwise, I'll have no choice but to kill your precious Annabelle myself, if she isn't already dead."

"You wouldn't dare!"

"Sam, I thought you knew me better than that. I would do it without a second thought. If you want her to live, you will bond to me, and me alone."

"Forcing someone isn't them 'willing.' Taking away all my choices won't make me love you."

The Dark Queen waved her hand without a care. "Semantics."

Sam looked to Keres, who kept his gaze forward and void of all emotion. Keres couldn't defy his queen, not at this moment anyway. He needed to find the tunnel to meet with Keres and figure a way out of this. He had to leave, and it had to be soon. There was no way he would marry this madwoman.

"Why now? Why have you kept me here so long to do this now?"

The Dark Queen chortled. "It was more fun this way." With that, the Dark Queen rose from her chair and left the dining hall, leaving Sam stuck to the floor with his mouth hung open.

SAM PACED his room in a panic; sweat dripped down his back and he was hardly able to breathe. Anxiety sank in with the creeping reminder that he hadn't yet found his way out. Time moved too slow as he waited for the palace to settle for the night. This needed to work.

When he was sure it was late enough into the night, Sam opened his door, stepped into the hall, and walked toward the Dark Queen's chamber. Sam heard his heartbeat pounding in his ears as he stood outside her doors. Sweat dripped onto the ground from his palms, and he wiped it away on his pants.

Pull it together. You have no choice. You can do this.

Sam took a deep breath, put his hand on the door, closed his eyes, and pushed.

The room was not as eerie as Sam had imagined it would be. Yes, there was a certain darkness about it, with torn paintings along the walls, but the rest of the room was in pristine condition, everything in its place. He stared at the Dark Queen sleeping soundly in her bed—Enos asleep beside her—looking more peaceful than he'd ever seen her. She almost looked human instead of pure evil.

Sam looked around the room and immediately searched behind curtains and under rugs. Anything that wouldn't make noise. There was nothing to find, not even dust. He kept moving, praying to find the magic fast so he could get out before the Dark Queen sensed his presence. Every time Sam thought he may have found a spot for the magic, it turned out to be nothing.

Something moved on the table beside the window. Sam rushed to see what it was, but it was gone. The only things there were the Dark Queen's jewels—her silvery snake armlet lay in the middle of various other gems and trinkets.

Out of the corner of his eye, Sam spotted a large wooden chest. He approached the box and attempted to lift the lid, only to find that it was locked. *This must be it.* He scanned the room in search of a key.

He looked at her neck, hoping to see a key, but with no luck. The only jewelry she wore was the sapphire ring still on her finger. If he wanted to hide a key, he'd do it in books. *Darn.* No books in sight. Then he thought of what Annabelle would do.

Annabelle's most precious possession was the photo of her parents that abandoned her. He wasn't sure why she held it so dear when they had left her, maybe she thought she could find them and reunite a happy family. The one time he asked her, she shut him out. Annabelle never shut Sam out, so he knew he needed to leave it alone until she was ready to tell him. But that photo she always kept close. So Sam used that. He turned to the portrait that hung above the Dark Queen's bed—a family portrait with the faces slashed out. He had to see behind it, but how?

Sam crept over to the bed, looking for a way to the torn portrait. Sam found it odd that a heartless queen would keep such a thing so close to her. He grabbed for it, but it was just out of his reach. He needed to get closer, so he put a knee on the bed and reached for the painting.

He froze as the Dark Queen grumbled in her sleep, but she only turned over, and Sam continued.

Just a bit farther . . . got it!

Sam slowly brought the painting toward him. Stomach dropping, a scream threatened to pass his lips as he caught a glimpse of the Dark Queen in his periphery, and both eyes stared at him. He turned to try to explain himself, if he even could, but instead met the closed eyes of a sleeping queen.

Had he just imagined the entire thing?

Sam thought he'd lost his mind from his nerves and took a deep breath before continuing. He flipped the painting over, where a silver key lay taped to the back of the portrait. Sam grabbed it and set the portrait against the wall, doing his best to stay silent. He was sure the Dark Queen could hear his heartbeat thumping through his chest, but he kept going.

Sam inserted the key into the chest and turned it.

Clink.

It had worked! Sam gently opened the chest to find an array of items. He dug through them, desperately searching for a vial of magic. He picked up several items. Branding iron? No. Locket? No. *Here it is!* Sam picked up a vial with black dust and shimmering blue flakes and shoved it into his pocket.

A thump sounded in the hallway, and Enos groaned. Sam closed the lid and locked the chest back up, racing back to the portrait to put the key away. As he placed the photograph onto the wall, he stared at the sleeping queen, and the thought of killing her there crossed his mind. It would solve all his problems, and the rest of this world's. But when it came down to it, he wasn't sure he could take another life, no matter how evil and necessary.

Scurrying back to the door, he poked his head out—the hall was empty. He took the opportunity to run back to his room and closed the door behind him, diving into his bed and throwing the covers over his head. His stomach threatened to erupt.

Sam leapt up and ran to the bathroom, barely making it as the vomit spewed from his lips.

He'd done it. Sam took the vial from his pocket and looked it over. He held the Dark Queen's magic in his hands—he needed to put it somewhere safe. As he looked around the room, his eyes settled on his clothes from back home.

He opened the jacket and reached into the inner pocket. A small rip in the back of the pocket opened just wide enough to slip the vial inside without being detectable. Even Sam couldn't tell anything out of the ordinary as the tiny bottle sat seamlessly behind a button—the perfect hiding spot. Hanging the coat back with his other clothes, Sam headed to bed. It would be the first night since arriving in Taegaia he could sleep with a smile on his face, knowing he'd gotten himself one step closer to home. One step closer to Annabelle.

CHAPTER EIGHTEEN

The scent of roses comforted Dorthea. Her garden was the one place she felt anything other than rage. She pressed the petals against her nose, escaping into its delicate fragrance. Dorthea's mind drifted to a time long ago, when the sense of wholeness and freedom veiled her life.

Dorthea giggled as she ran down the palace hall, peeking over her shoulder to make sure she wasn't being followed. She rounded the corner and stopped for a rest. She panted as she tried to calm her breathing, peering around the hall. A thud sounded behind her, and she ran off again. On the next corner, she bumped into her father. Little Dorthea stared up at him.

The king stared back at Dorthea with a blank face, then held up his hands and growled. Dorthea squealed with joy and ran back the way she'd come. Her father chased her down the hallway, easily catching her. He lifted her in his arms and tickled her tummy as she kicked and laughed, trying to break free as his beard tickled her cheek.

"There you are," a woman's voice called out.

"Big Bear, you found me!" Dorthea ran to the elf as her father set her on the ground.

"Yes, Little Lion. You are quite loud for such a small one." The elf laughed as she planted her hands on her hips.

Dorthea ran up and hugged the young elf, almost knocking her over. Dorthea giggled. "I'm almost as big as you!"

"Yes, you are. But I'm still in charge, and we need to get you to bed."

"Aww, but, Big Bear—"

"Dorthea, you do as your nursemaid says," the king cut in.

"Yes, Daddy." Dorthea ran to her father to tell him goodnight. "I love you."

"I love you too, Dorthea. Your mother will be in shortly for your story."

The elf grabbed Dorthea and took her back to her room to wash up for bed.

Dorthea hopped into bed as the queen entered her room. "Ready for a story?" The queen swept her long, brown ringlets to one side.

"Yes, Mama!" Dorthea jumped up and down.

"Calm yourself first, sweetheart."

The elf started to walk out of the room.

"Goodnight, Big Bear! I love you!"

The young elf looked back at Dorthea with her bright fuchsia eyes. "I love you too, Little Lion."

Dorthea fell asleep listening to the sound of her mother's voice.

The peace and freedom fell away, replaced by anguish and disdain. As Dorthea wiped a tear from her eyes, someone cleared their throat behind her.

"Your Majesty, it is almost time to receive the villagers," Gadriel said.

"Thank you, Gadriel. Tell Sam I expect him to be there." Dorthea twisted the rose between her fingers.

Gadriel bowed low. "Of course, my queen." He went back into the castle, leaving Dorthea alone once more.

Dorthea turned back to look at the roses, closed her eyes, and let her mind wander again.

CHAPTER NINETEEN

Gadriel gave Sam a nasty look, gesturing to his foot. Sam stopped tapping. His nerves had started to get the better of him as he stood in the Great Hall, the same room where he'd met the Dark Queen his first time in the palace. Only this time, he stood with the Dark Queen's cortege. Gadriel stood at his side, Ju on the other side of Gadriel.

He hadn't realized Ju was so important in the castle—this being only the second time he'd ever seen her. The nervous man that had replaced Ilia stood in front of the Dark Queen as she sat on her throne of roses and thorns.

It surprised him Keres had managed to get out of this. Somchai stood guard by the door, and when Sam looked his way, Somchai gave him a wink. Sam returned a half smile, then continued with his worry, running through all the ideas in his mind, trying to figure out a way to open the hidden tunnel.

For days, he'd been to the entrance, tracing his hands along the wall to find some sort of concealed key or knob. He'd been on his way to the wall again that morning when he was stopped by Gadriel and escorted to the Great Hall.

They had been standing there for almost an hour before the Dark Queen arrived, not caring that she'd been keeping them waiting. Sam had no idea what to expect, but he was sure he wouldn't like whatever was to come.

"Das," the Dark Queen spoke at last, "begin."

The nervous man, apparently named Das, bowed low to the Dark Queen, then scurried to the main door. He poked his head out, and Sam could hear whispers just outside the room. Das stepped back and ushered in an old man carrying a large box, who, despite his age, walked with the vigor of a man in his twenties. Sam had never seen an elderly man so spry.

Das walked in front of the man toward the Dark Queen, who sat unphased.

"John Grower, head eragat of the Grower land." Das introduced the old man to the Dark Queen, then backed away to a table with parchment, readying himself to take notes.

"I know my own castle's food eragat, you idiot," the Dark Queen spat at Das.

The old man, John, set the large box down in front of the Dark Queen.

"What do you want?" The Dark Queen spoke so indifferently, twisting in her seat like a bored child sitting in a school chair before regaining her composure.

"Your Majesty, I come again to ask for Harmony."

Harmony. Sam recalled the word from a book in the library. It was the magic the Dark Queen had abandoned for Chaos.

John continued, "Without it"—the old man opened the box

—"we get this." The man tilted the box and poured out fruits and vegetables black and bruised, covered in dust.

The Dark Queen laughed. "You've gotten quite terrible at working your land. Perhaps you are unable to manage it any longer." She still did not give John her full attention.

John turned red. "You know our world runs off of Harmony. Our land is dying without it. *You* did this, not me."

The Dark Queen looked the man in the eyes for the first time. "Excuse me?"

Sam cringed. This was not going to end well.

"Our soil is dead. Your people are dying."

The Dark Queen stared daggers into the man. She looked like a statue on her throne, thinking of what to say next. "Gadriel!"

Gadriel stepped forward. "Yes, my queen?"

"Send Octavia to the Grower land." Someone let out a small gasp near him. "If they cannot manage to grow food, she will."

"Thank you, my queen." John bowed to the Dark Queen. Sam's nerves grew as he waited for the Dark Queen's wrath.

A door behind Sam closed, and he heard footsteps approaching. Keres fell in line next to Sam, who gave him a wink. "Forgive my delay, dear queen." Keres gave a slight bow.

"No matter." The Dark Queen waved Keres off and turned back to address John. "You are relieved of your post."

"You can't—" John froze, terror crossing his face.

Sam looked up at the Dark Queen, his body turning numb. The queen took off her arm cuff and held it in her hands. The silver cuff spun, growing as it slithered between her fingers. Within moments, it was several feet long. It seemed as if she were molding some sort of weapon. But as it grew, the truth revealed itself to be much more horrifying.

The silver was now over six feet long, wrapping around the Dark Queen's body and sliding toward her feet. The hiss confirmed Sam's fear—it was turning into a silver snake. Once the snake left the Dark's Queen's body, it grew another fifteen feet. Its eyes were sapphires, and its tongue sharp swords. The snake continued growing until it reached over fifty feet, curling around itself in a ball.

"Persephone," the queen commanded as the snaked twisted to face her.

This is Persephone? Oh, dear God . . .

The snake swam to its master, letting the Dark Queen stroke her skull. The queen locked eyes with John, who shook his head and backed away slowly.

"Mother got you a treat."

Persephone coiled around, her eyes stopping on John. He attempted to turn and run, but Persephone reached him before he could spin all the way around. She snapped herself across the room with such force, a hum rang through the air. Persephone latched on to John and curled herself around him. She curled tighter and tighter; John's face turning purple as he struggled for air. A crack cut through the air as Persephone snapped his body and inhaled the lump of flesh that remained.

Sam closed his eyes tight. He couldn't bear to watch the horror of Persephone devouring another victim of the Dark Queen's wrath. Someone nudged Sam—Keres. Scanning the room, Persephone was nowhere to be found. He looked at the Dark Queen, whose arm cuff was back where it belonged.

Sam said a silent prayer for John's family.

Das was again at the door, ushering in the next visitor.

One after another, villagers from across the land came to ask for the Dark Queen's help. Each time, the Dark Queen listened half-heartedly, uncaring about the suffering and death throughout her kingdom. She gave nothing to anyone else but the farmers that provided food to the palace.

Somehow, thankfully, there was only one death by the end of the day.

What was he becoming if he considered any death a victory . . .?

THE HEAT from the bath water soothed Sam's aching muscles. It'd been too long since he'd done physical labor, the workout that afternoon made him extra sore. He grew thankful for the immediate availability of hot water. Back home if he wanted a hot bath, his only option was to boil water over the fire and wait, and the heat didn't last this long. It was the only time in his life he felt wealthy, sitting in this bathtub.

Sam continued to toss ideas around, quietly thinking out loud to himself. "How do I get in the tunnel? The wall has no key, no opening . . . Or do I even need the tunnel? How do I get out of here?" As helpful as it would be, he didn't know how much more time he could waste trying to find a way in. Maybe he needed a new plan for getting home. He could go back to the treasury. No, he'd already been there several times and couldn't find anything useful.

Keres had made it clear they weren't to talk out in the open anymore, and he couldn't risk asking anyone else for help.

What he needed was a new perspective on the matter—some fresh air would do him good. Sam got out of the bath and dressed, then headed out toward the gardens.

The cool air was a drastic change from the bath, and he welcomed it. He needed to change things up if he was going to figure this out. The bench beckoned him over, and he sat, staring at the rosebushes.

Only a moment passed before he heard a noise coming from the work shed. Sam turned his attention toward it and listened. It sounded like Octavia's voice, though he couldn't quite make out what she was saying. There was a groan and a large thud, followed by a crashing sound and more groans.

"Octavia," Sam said to himself as he popped off the bench and sprinted to the shed. He pressed his ear against the door, but the noises had stopped.

He tapped quietly on the door, hoping Octavia was all right. There was no reply. Sam's mouth went dry. What if someone from John's village heard about her taking over the land and intended to hurt her? Or worse, kill her.

Sam pressed the door open as gently as he could to not spook anyone who might be inside. He realized right away that this was no work shed, but a small house. There were tables and chairs set around the room, personal items along the walls, and a door he could only assume led into a bedroom. Sam stepped inside, slowly closing the door behind him. Then the noises started again. He could hear Octavia groaning behind the door.

She's in pain!

Sam dashed across the house to the door and threw it open, frantically searching for the woman who needed his help. When he found Octavia, his stomach dropped.

She was completely naked, and her legs were up in the air. A hand caressed her breast, and a head moved between her legs. Octavia's moans grew louder.

Oh my Lord. Oh my Lord. Get out of here!

Sam turned to leave, but ran into a table, knocking a vase of flowers to the ground.

The crash caught Octavia's attention, and she looked at Sam. "What are you doing here?" She grabbed the blanket nearest her and covered herself.

The head between her legs popped up, and a fully naked Ju stood from the bedside.

"I—I, uh, umm—I am so sorry. I thought you were hurt . . . Bye." Sam sprinted from the room and out the front door as fast as he could manage. Sweat poured from everywhere on his body, and Sam thought he might be sick.

Stupid. So stupid! Why did you go in there?

As he ran toward the palace door, it began to open. Not wanting to find out who was on the other side, Sam darted behind the nearest bush. Covering his mouth, he tried to control his breathing as someone walked past him. When the person went back into the palace and closed the door, he let out a huge sigh and relaxed.

He started to stand to head back into the castle when something shimmering caught his eye. On the wall in front of him, he noticed a gold mark like the one from the map. Sam looked around, making sure no one was near, and stepped closer to the wall. The mark disappeared, and then reappeared as Sam stepped back to where he was.

Why is this here? What does it mean? Then it dawned on him. Of course! A wall has two sides, and he was looking on the wrong one. Why hadn't that occurred to him earlier? He hadn't guessed the tunnel could be outside. He needed to stop making these stupid mistakes, or he would never make it home to Annabelle.

Sam looked the wall up and down, searching for more clues. Nothing. As he walked closer, staring at the wall, it disappeared. He stuck his hand out and touched where the mark had been on the wall. It felt different from the rest of the stones. Sam closed his eyes and prayed as he pushed the spot. A set of steps descending into a dark tunnel appeared at his feet, leading deep beneath the palace. As Sam fully entered the tunnel, the door above him closed, and he was surrounded by complete darkness.

Sam continued down the steps, feeling around the wall to help guide him. He stopped when his hand hit something metal against the wall. He pushed on it, and the entire tunnel lit up with torches on either side, calling to Sam to continue his journey. He heard nothing but his own footsteps and his breath as he continued under the palace. The tunnel wound again and again, bringing Sam farther into seclusion.

When the steps stopped, Sam stood outside a nearly empty room. The stone room wasn't large—a square no more than five strides. The only items in the room being a small bookshelf with a single, giant book laid on top. As soon as he entered the room, a shiver crawled up his spine, and the room became ice cold. Sam rubbed his hands together, trying desperately to get warm. He sauntered over to the book, and as soon as he grabbed it, the room returned to a warmer temperature.

As Sam opened the book, the light in the room disappeared. Sam stumbled around looking for the torches to light again. He staggered around for several minutes before a thought dawned on him—it was nearly dinnertime, and he needed to get back to change. Sam left the book where he'd found it and sprinted back up the stairs. He pushed on the door, which opened back up.

He poked his head out of the hole like a groundhog, making sure he was still alone, then exited the tunnel. He was back in the castle as the tunnel door sealed shut.

DINNERS with the Dark Queen seemed to drag on longer and longer each night. Of all the places he wanted to be tonight, this was certainly the last. He'd finally found something to get him closer to home, yet here he sat, stuck at the table, listening to the Dark Queen boast about what a remarkable ruler she was for allowing the "filth" into her palace to beg for her greatness. Sam rolled his eyes. She was no ruler.

Sam propped his elbows on the table, chin in his palms, and stared into the tank. He hadn't seen Zael for several days. Sam hoped he'd escaped somehow, but doubted it. He continued looking into the tank until the Dark Queen cleared her throat.

"Hoping for a show, were you?"

"No, I'm just tired is all."

"Then let's wake you up." The Dark Queen snapped her fingers, and the water began to swirl.

Sam went wide-eyed. "No, stop. I'm fine."

The Dark Queen ignored him.

The whirling water came to a stop, and Zael appeared. He

looked thinner. His ribs were starting to show, and his skin seemed paler.

Sam glared at the Dark Queen.

"He's hungry," Sam said. "Look at him, he's weak."

"Perfect." The Dark Queen smirked.

Sam turned back to the merman, praying he could help him. Then the water began to move again. But this time, not in a whirl. Sam looked to the top of the tank. It was quickly draining. Sam's eyes widened in horror.

"You're going to kill him!" Sam pleaded with the Dark Queen to stop. She ignored him.

Sam watched as the last of the water left the tank, and Zael sat at the bottom in the sand. Sam started to look away, not wanting to watch as yet another person died before his eyes, but stopped when a white and blue dust encircled Zael. When the dust cleared, Zael was fully human, and stood on two legs.

Zael turned and ran toward the back of the tank. Before he could make it two full strides, the tank instantly filled again with water. Sam watched as Zael choked on the water, his limbs flailing. Just as before, a shimmering dust surrounded Zael, and his legs turned back to fins.

The moment his fins were revealed, the Dark Queen took the water again. Zael lay on the ocean floor gasping for air until his magic transformed him back into a human. He turned over and coughed up water, barely able to breathe. His magic was not as fast as the Dark Queen's.

"Stop!" Sam felt his mouth forced closed, and his feet glued to the floor. Her grim entertainment was never ending.

Zael stared forward, his gaze dead. Sam hoped to catch Zael's eye, to let him know he wasn't alone. But Zael didn't look at Sam. He just looked . . . broken. With a wave of her hand, the Dark Queen sent Zael away.

Sam felt himself be released but continued to stare at the glass. His knees quivered, and his stomach was queasy. Sam wasn't sure how much more of the Dark Queen's torture he could handle. She needed to be stopped.

"Dinner is served," the chef announced.

The idea of sitting at the table with the Dark Queen was something Sam couldn't handle. He stood there, staring into the glass cage she'd built for her prisoner. Zael needed out of the palace, and Sam came to realize now more than ever, he couldn't do anything to help.

It was just like when his mother needed his help—Sam was powerless yet again to protect the innocent from the monsters of the world. The look on Zael's face mirrored his mother's. The face that told the world they had given up. Once again, the echoes of his mother's screams rang in Sam's ears. A horrid vision flashed before his eyes. The crack of the whip was like lightning, bringing a constant storm down upon his mother. The blood and screams chilled Sam to his bones. He sat behind the bush with his mouth covered, holding tightly to David's hand—showing their faces would mean certain death for them both. Sam pleaded with David to stay, but his big brother couldn't leave his mother like that. David sprinted over to help her. Sam closed his eyes and covered his ears as he rocked back and forth, praying for it to stop. When he opened his eyes again, all was quiet. It was the last time Sam saw either of them.

"Join me, Sam," the Dark Queen said.

"No," Sam whispered. Following the Dark Queen's orders

exhausted him. It was all too much. He was a man now. He should be able to help these people.

"Persephone, help Sam to the table, won't you?"

Sam put a hand on the glass, staring into the abyss of water that stretched out into blackness. He almost didn't notice the strength of the snake lifting him off the ground and placing him at the table.

"ALMOST THERE," Sam said as he led Keres through the blackened tunnel. Sam slid his hand along the wall, searching from memory. "Got it!" Sam grabbed the button and the tunnel lit up with torches.

Keres yawned from behind him. "Tell me again why we're here so early?"

"Because," Sam said, "the Dark Queen is in her garden at night, and I don't want anyone else knowing where I am. Early morning is the only time everyone is asleep."

"Mhmm," Keres mumbled groggily.

Sam smiled to himself. He hadn't taken Keres for someone who hated early mornings. But when Keres had opened his door that morning when Sam knocked, he was surprised to see there was still nothing out of sorts. His silk pajama suit had no wrinkles, and even his hair was perfectly in place.

The tunnel was especially cold in the early hours of the day. Sam wished he'd thought to bring his coat when he saw the empty room at the end of the staircase. "Here!"

Keres rubbed his eyes and glanced around the room. "Well done, Sam. This is perfect. The Dark Queen doesn't know about any hidden chambers . . . at least, she's never said anything about one, and she tells me everything, even when I don't want to know." Keres grimaced, then continued, "I can barely believe this castle has one."

Sam grew impatient. "So, what are we going to do? I can't stay here, but I still haven't come up with a way to escape. Is there anything you can tell me?"

"Well, I might have something, but I don't know if it's even possible. Not without magic . . ." Keres's voice trailed off as he met Sam's gaze.

"Tell me, maybe we can figure it out."

"All right. In our land, the main way people used to travel, before the Dark Queen gave in to Chaos, was by fading."

"Huh?" Sam raised his brows.

"You might call it . . . teleportation. We had stations set up all across the land. Simple to use, efficient. But the stations do not reach everywhere, and sometimes, when lines were full for them, people would use a device passed down through their family, if they were lucky enough to have one."

"Uh-huh . . . but how does that help me?"

"It's an object enchanted with magic that, when touched, will take you anywhere you need to go. I've heard rumors that if the magic is powerful enough, it can take you between worlds. It may even be how the Dark Queen brought you here in the first place."

Sam's eyes lit up as he began to understand what Keres was saying to him. "Let's do that! Where can we find one of these objects?"

"It's not that simple anymore. The Dark Queen has taken all these relics and subdued magic throughout the land."

"How?" Sam said.

"Well, as you know, the only ones in our realm who yield magic naturally are those of royal descent. She got rid of them."

"What? She got rid of everyone in her own bloodline?"

"No. The Dark Queen is the last in her bloodline," Keres answered.

"So, who did she kill?"

"The other royals."

"There's other royals?" Sam was stunned.

"Why of course, Sam. This world has three kingdoms, and you have only seen the Dark Queen's. There are also the merfolk of the Triti Sea and the magical creatures in the Ecaté Forest. We passed through it quickly on your way to the Dark Queen, but only the outskirts of the kingdom."

"Wow, so the only way to use magic is by creating it or stealing it from the Dark Queen?"

"Precisely," Keres said.

"But what about Octavia? And Ju? And Gadriel? I've seen all of them use magic."

"That's because it flows through them. It's not Harmony or Chaos or Alchemy. Their magic comes from something else."

"From what?"

Keres shook his head. "Does it matter?"

Sam sighed. "I reckon not. But why didn't you tell me about this before?"

Keres shook his head. "I don't have Harmony. I'm really not versed in all this magic stuff. So even if we could find one of the objects, we don't have any magic to activate it."

"And you don't know how to get any?"

Keres contemplated. "I'm afraid not. I'm sorry."

Sam dropped his head. "Well, at least I have somewhere to start, I guess. I'll go back to the library and see what I can find. Thanks."

"You're welcome."

Sam grabbed Keres's arm. "No, really, I couldn't have done any of this without you. You are risking everything for me, and I can't even repay you."

Keres clasped Sam's hand and looked into his eyes before he gave Sam a smile, then released him.

Both men chuckled as they turned back to leave the tunnels. "We should probably meet back here every couple of days to strategize."

Keres agreed, "Excellent plan."

As the two ascended the stairs back into the palace, Sam let himself believe something he hadn't in a long time. There was a way home.

CHAPTER TWENTY

Pages of books fell to the ground as Sam flipped through them forcefully, tossing them aside as they disappointed him. He had no need for tales of grandeur or the life expectancy of a harpy. Hands shaking, Sam grabbed the next book. Someone walked into the library to find Sam on the floor. Keres must have followed him in. They quietly cleared their throat, but Sam was too focused to even notice them until they stepped in front of Sam, stopping him where he crawled. "Move. I need to figure this out."

"That's why I'm here."

Sam's head snapped up when he heard the soft voice. "Mara, I'm so sorry. I didn't mean to be so rude. It's just . . ."

"I know." Mara smiled, grabbing a seat at the table and reading through a stack that Sam must have already been through twice.

"It's no use, there's nothing here." Sam's head slunk down as the surge of defeat enveloped him.

"Hmm," Mara started. "If there's nothing here, then where could something be?"

Sam looked at Mara in astonishment as a thought hit him. "Mara, you're a genius!" He hopped up and ran for the door, then turned back to give Mara a hug. One book remained in the palace he had not yet read. "Thank you."

Mara looked confused. "Glad I could help."

Sam dashed out of the library and toward the garden, taking care to slow around the corners before sprinting each hallway to avoid being stopped by the Dark Queen or anyone else. He hated how well he knew the halls—the shortcuts, which ones to avoid at certain times of the day. It was a sense of familiarity he wished he didn't have.

He calmed himself as he took the last turn, trying to steady his breath before exiting to the gardens. At this time of day, it was impossible to know who might be outside enjoying the crisp air among the roses. Sam approached the door and cracked it open. Someone faced away from him, but he couldn't quite tell who it was. All he could make out was long white hair. Sam inched the door open a bit more to try to get a better look —Gadriel.

Sam closed the door and turned around, heading toward his room. He wasn't about to walk out there and possibly face Gadriel when something so important was on the line. He only made it a few steps before someone yelled after him.

"Sam," Keres called out. He walked up to Sam and raised his brows at the defeated look on his face. "What's wrong?"

Sam dropped his voice to a whisper. "I need . . . outside, but Gadriel is in the gardens."

"Sam, we were just there. Why do you need to go back?" Keres looked over his shoulder, ensuring no one was listening.

"There's something down there I need to look at. A book I haven't read yet."

Keres nodded in understanding. "I could go distract him, but—"

"But what?"

Keres paused. "Gadriel is too good at sensing when someone is lying, and I'm a terrible liar. He'd know something was up and go running to the Dark Queen. He's been after my position since before even I had it."

Sam sighed. "So, I go back later." The words barely came out.

"I know this is difficult, I'm sorry." Keres put a hand on Sam's shoulder.

"Thank you. I just . . . I can't keep doing this. Who knows how much time has gone by for Annabelle. Every moment I'm here . . ."

"I know," Keres contemplated. "The garden should be empty just before lunch, as Gadriel and most of the staff will be busy. I'll meet you then."

Sam forced a smile onto his face, then walked back to his room to wait.

It hadn't been longer than five minutes before there was a knock at the door. Sam rushed to open it, thinking Keres had come to tell him that Gadriel was gone, and the plan could move forward early.

As Sam threw the door open, he was met only with disappointment. Gadriel stood before Sam, wearing a long silver tunic detailed with gold swirls that looked like fire. His hands were crossed in front of him as he waited for Sam. His manner almost came across as a patient man, aside from the smug look that always painted his face.

Sam rolled his eyes. "What do you want?" He turned back to the room and left the door open, making his way toward the sitting chair under the far window.

Gadriel muttered something too quiet for Sam to hear. "I am here on official business. The Dark Queen wishes you to accompany me on my rounds today."

Sam turned around, eyebrow raised. "Why?"

"Well, Sam, it was brought to the Dark Queen's attention that you have not done much to contribute to our great palace or kingdom, and she would like to remedy that. When you marry the Dark Queen, you will have responsibilities, and she wishes your training to start now." Gadriel's smile grew even wider. "It's a shame you won't have time for whatever it is you do all day."

Sam's stomach dropped. "What? No, that's not going to happen. I'm not helping with anything."

"You know, Sam, I didn't think you were a complete simpleton."

"What are you talking about?" Sam rolled his eyes again. He couldn't help it anytime he had to interact with Gadriel.

"You don't think, do you?" Gadriel narrowed his gaze, the shift in his demeanor somehow making him look taller. "You go around here saying whatever you want, and the Dark Queen lets it slide. And do you know why? Because she needs you. But what do you think happens after the bonding ceremony, when you no longer provide any value to her? You really think you'll be so lucky? We have a dungeon, you know. You staying here"—

Gadriel motioned around the room—"is a gift. Once the Dark Queen gets what she wants from you, there's no telling what she'll do."

Sam's eyes widened in horror. The thought of him failing had never even occurred to him, let alone what he'd be expected to do following the wedding. If he had nothing to offer, the Dark Queen would dispose of him just like everyone else who crossed her. Though he wasn't sure why Gadriel cared —he'd probably get exactly what he wanted. Sam would undoubtably be killed once the Dark Queen got her power and continue the royal line with Enos. But still, playing along would buy him more time.

Sam bit his tongue, trying his hardest to keep his next words from leaving his lips, but he knew he had no choice. "All right, I'll come."

Gadriel smirked at Sam, reveling in his victory of breaking Sam just one more bit. "You can't wear those. Change." Gadriel stood his ground as Sam made his way to the washroom to put on the outfit Mara had left out for him that morning, the one he'd ignored so he could wear his own clothes as usual.

Sam stripped down to his drawers and grabbed the loose-fitting pants. The clothes here still made no sense to him. They were like nothing he'd seen back home, and the styles always seemed to be changing. Annabelle would probably be able to make sense of it all. She was always making clothing and keeping up with any changing fashions.

He pulled the thick evergreen tunic over his head and fashioned the sash around his waist. He looked in the mirror and hated what was staring back at him, but at least he got to wear his favorite color. It reminded him of the trees surrounding his and Annabelle's lake. Sam let out a sigh and made his way back to Gadriel.

"Let's get this over with." Sam followed Gadriel out to the hall, closing the door behind him.

Gadriel led Sam to the kitchen. They watched over the staff as they cleaned up from breakfast and began preparations for lunch. They stood mostly in silence, with the occasional break for Gadriel to reprimand a staffer for not being perfect. The Dark Queen demanded perfection, and Gadriel wouldn't allow anything less in the kitchen. When the menu was set and everyone started on their tasks, Gadriel took Sam out of the kitchen. "Chef can take it from here. We'll be back for final inspection before the meal is served." Sam nodded his understanding.

The pair made their way from room to room, checking in with the maids and guards, and making a list of all the duties that needed done by the end of the day. Gadriel kept everyone in running order, and Sam could see the respect, or maybe it was fear, from everyone they encountered. No one wanted to let him down.

As the two began to make their way to the next duty, tussling sounded from behind them. Sam turned to see two of the guards shoving each other, then one punch the other in the stomach. Gadriel was between them before Sam even had a chance to blink.

Gadriel had both men pinned against the wall by their sternums. The two attempted to calm themselves before a punishment could be made, but Sam could tell by the look on Gadriel's face that it was too late for apologies. One of the guards was massive, and Sam was sure Gadriel wouldn't have been able to hold him back without his inhuman strength. The guard was almost twice as tall as Gadriel, the muscles on his arms the size of Gadriel's torso.

Sam's stomach tightened as he saw the other guard was Somchai. Though Sam didn't know him that well, he'd been kind when he didn't have to be. Gadriel smirked at the two men, then called out to the other guards standing by. "Guards, assemble the palace, and tell the Dark Queen that today there will be a match."

The guards saluted Gadriel and ran to do as he commanded. Somchai looked horrified, but the other guard just smiled. Gadriel handled the men and twisted their arms behind their backs, guiding them through the palace. Sam wasn't sure what to do, so he followed.

"Sam!"

"Yes, Gadriel?"

"Go to the kitchens. Tell the staff that lunch is canceled, and to prepare assortments for today's match."

Sam hesitated.

"Now!"

Sam took off toward the kitchen to deliver the message. When he reached the staff, their eyes widened, and they whispered among themselves.

"What is it? What's a match?" Sam was beyond confused.

One of the staff spoke up. "It's a fight to the death."

"What!" Sam's head became cloudy. "Can we stop it?"

"Not unless you want to enter the match yourself."

Sam shook his head. "I won't go."

The staff member grabbed Sam's hand. "You must. No one

may miss it, or you are automatically entered to fight the winner."

In a daze, Sam walked toward the door when he caught sight of a familiar face.

"Ilia?" Sam rubbed his eyes in disbelief. The timid man who'd introduced him to the Dark Queen, who he thought to be dead, stood in the corner of the kitchen. "Ilia, what are you doing here?"

Ilia did not move as he stared ahead, back against the wall.

"Are you okay?" Sam walked to Ilia and placed a hand on his shoulder.

Ilia recoiled hard, slamming his head into the marble wall, and drawing blood.

Sam grabbed a nearby towel and offered it to Ilia, who seemed unphased by the injury. "You're bleeding. Take this." Sam put the towel in Ilia's hand, who withdrew his arm and charged Sam, screaming incoherent noises.

"That's enough, Ilia!" the chef ordered as Ilia scurried back into the depths of the kitchen.

Sam attempted to follow.

"Leave him," the chef said as he continued his work with the vegetables.

"But I upset him. I didn't mean to."

The chef shook his head. "It's not you. He's like that now, after his time down in the dungeons."

"He was in the dungeon? I thought the Dark Queen killed him."

The chef stopped working and sighed. "That would have been a far better fate." He retreated into the kitchen, leaving Sam alone.

Sam stumbled out of the room, not sure what to think. Gadriel came up behind Sam and dragged him down the hall.

"Stop!" Sam pushed off of Gadriel.

"Then hurry up. The match will start soon, and anyone not in their seat will pay the price. Even you."

Sam wasn't going to risk it and followed Gadriel out the front doors to the top of the grand staircase. Instead of walking down, Gadriel turned left, passing the massive columns and making his way to a side staircase Sam hadn't noticed before. They walked down to an open area of cobbled stone. It looked as if this place had been used for events and markets, but now lay deserted, as empty as the Dark Queen's heart.

The two headed on toward the arena Sam had seen once before in the watch tower, the day Keres had given him a tour of the palace. Now that he stared at the arena head-on, it stood far grander than he'd thought before.

Though not nearly as tall as the palace, that did not take away from its magnitude. Full circle, with columns lining all around, and intricate stonework hidden among the pillars. White marble encased the structure, hand-painted with small red roses that danced along the curvature. Sam stood in awe of its beauty, forgetting the horrors about to happen inside, as Gadriel huffed at him again.

Sam followed Gadriel through the gates, which led into a hallway of stairs going up. The elf turned right to ascend the first set of stairs, and as Sam began to trail him, Gadriel held up a hand. "That's far enough. This area is for the Dark Queen and her cortege. As the Dark Queen did not specifically request your presence here, I will make the executive decision." Gadriel made a sweeping motion with his hands and gestured to the center of the arena. "Seating for the commoners is through there." Gadriel gave Sam a smug grin and turned back to continue his ascent.

Sam crossed his arms and snorted before realizing he preferred it Gadriel's way anyhow. The hall began to fill with other palace dwellers. He followed the crowd through until the hall opened up into the arena, every bit as beautiful inside as out. Seating surrounded the central ground of dirt and stones, and Sam made his way up a set of stairs to where a group of maids sat. He spotted Mara and made his way to her.

"I can't believe this is happening," Sam said.

"It doesn't happen often, but the others, they get really into it." Mara lowered her voice. "Don't speak out against it, most won't agree with you."

"What?" Sam was baffled. "I can't believe it." He looked out to the crowd as more spectators poured in. "Who is Somchai fighting?"

"I'm not sure. I just heard it's one of the guards."

"Yes, the really big one."

"Ah. That's Titan." Mara's eyes turned somber.

"His name is *Titan*?" Sam said.

"I heard he ripped through his mother when he was born and killed her. He came out as big as a child. I think his father was part giant."

"What? There's no way that's real."

"You've seen him," Mara said.

Sam thought back to the beast of a man. He made even Sam look small. Titan was a fitting name.

"This isn't his first match, you know." Mara looked up at Sam. "He's been in dozens of them. He doesn't lose."

"So Somchai doesn't stand a chance."

Mara didn't answer.

"Why would she let them fight when Titan is at a clear advantage?" Sam could not comprehend the logic in this.

"She doesn't care about the outcome. All she wants is a good show."

Sam's jaw dropped. "I shouldn't even be surprised anymore." He sighed. "So, what are the rules?"

Mara shrugged. "There are none."

A horn blared out, and everyone took their seats. The arena was filled to capacity. *Where did all these people come from?* The Dark Queen's cortege emerged from the far side of the arena, making their way to a balcony, where the Dark Queen herself emerged. When she had taken her place at the front of the balcony, she looked at her people. She stared in silence, scanning the arena until she locked eyes on Sam. "Fight."

CHAPTER TWENTY-ONE

Two cage doors rattled open at the base of the arena. The crowd roared as two guards stepped out. The men had been stripped from their armor down to a simple chiton and sandals—nothing to fight or protect themselves with.

Somchai wore white, Titan gray.

As Titan's legs were taller than his opponent's entire body, Somchai entered at a severe disadvantage. It baffled Sam as to why Somchai had picked a fight with him in the first place.

The crowd chanted in chorus. "Fight! Fight! Fight!"

Titan sprinted at Somchai, who turned and ran back toward the gate he'd come out of. Before he could reach the opening, a wall of fire erupted, blocking his path. Sam looked up—the Dark Queen twirled her hands to the motions of the roaring fire.

Somchai turned and sprinted around the perimeter, leaving

Titan in his dust. At least he was faster, but who knew how long that would save him.

After several minutes of playing cat and mouse, a vine ripped out of the ground and caught Somchai by the foot. He tripped over the vine and slammed into the stone wall before rolling onto the ground. Titan closed in.

Somchai searched around him for anything to defend himself. There was nothing but dirt and stone. Titan reached his prey and lifted him by his clothes. He punched Somchai square in the face, and blood poured down, pooling at his feet. As Titan pinned him against the wall, Somchai's body went limp, his face so bloodied Sam could hardly see his skin through the red. His head slunk, and Sam thought he might already be dead. There was no way Somchai would survive another hit from the brute.

Titan reared his fist back for another blow, but Somchai's head whipped up, and at the last moment he used the wall to his advantage and kicked off, leaving Titan surprised and stumbling around. It was just enough to distance himself from his attacker.

Sam internally rejoiced, fearful to show any emotion as those around him booed. A basket of bread dropped into Sam's lap. Looking around, he watched as baskets of food passed among the rows. Sam couldn't imagine eating at a time like this, as his stomach knotted itself up tight, so he pocketed a piece of bread and passed the basket to Mara, returning his focus to the match.

As the chase continued, the Dark Queen threw obstacles at the men of fire and vines. The crowd cheered as the men scrambled, dodging what they could and occasionally getting sliced by the thorns. Somchai seemed to be tiring, and Titan closed the distance between them.

"Caco! Caco! Caco!" the crowd bellowed in unison.

"Who's Caco?" Sam asked.

"This isn't good," Mara whispered as she kept her gaze forward. "They're bringing out the Mother of Shadows."

The stadium rumbled as an enormous gate opened beneath the bleachers where Sam stood. Titan and Somchai stopped running and faced the opened cage. A roar unlike anything Sam had ever heard thundered in the arena. Sam gasped as a giant beast emerged from its cage and circled the arena floor.

The beast exceeded the size of ten large men—even Titan paled in comparison. Her head was shaped like an alligator, scaly and long with rows of gigantic sharp teeth. Black tufts of fur covered her neck, resembling a lion's mane. The beast's body was muscular, perfectly sculpted to bring death and suffering wherever its tracks may roam. The hiss and roar the creature made sent everyone in the crowd jumping back at the sheer power before they cheered her on again.

She continued her walk around the arena floor, stalking her prey. Only it wasn't clear to Sam which victim she had chosen —Titan, Somchai, or both. Somchai sprinted from the beast, and both she and Titan chased after him. The three tripped over vines and ran through fire like they weren't even there.

The creature jumped for the wall, balancing along the edge like a cat strutting atop a fence. Her eyes narrowed on the two men scrambling in the arena. The shadow beast lowered its body, preparing to pounce. She lurched forward, horrifying the horde as she whipped her head back and grabbed a member of the crowd in the front row. She carried the man into the arena with her, the screams of a man in a beast's jaw echoing along the walls.

The shrieks were cut short as the beast clamped down and viciously shook her head from side to side. Blood sprayed over the dirt and rocks. Satisfied with her kill, Caco tossed it aside and sprinted for Somchai.

Somchai scurried away, but collapsed at the edge of the arena, and the crowd cheered. He was surrounded by vines and had nowhere to run as Titan stepped in front of him. Caco leapt into the air, ready to devour her next meal, as a cloud of sparkling dust stopped her mid-air. The Dark Queen blocked the attack, allowing Titan to finish the job.

Just as Titan reached out to claim his victory, Somchai grabbed a vine from behind him and kicked off the ground to run up the side wall, wrapping the vine around Titan's throat as he went. The crowd thundered in cheers as Titan was brought to his knees, Somchai choking the life from him.

Sam found it hard to contain himself, and let out a scream for Somchai, then quickly snapped his lips shut. Just as Sam thought it was all over, a member of the crowd ran forward and leaned over the wall, throwing a dagger to Titan. In one swift movement, he caught the dagger and spun around, thrusting the weapon into Somchai's side. His white robe turned red, and he collapsed.

Titan stood and faced the audience, pumping his arms up and down as he let out a scream. The crowd erupted once more, and the fires and vines receded, clearing a path for Titan to exit the arena.

Sam sat in stunned silence. There really were no rules in the death match. He almost didn't hear the scream coming from below.

The crowd let out a collective gasp as Somchai stood and yanked the dagger from his ribs. He stumbled a bit, leaning on the wall for support, then stood on his own. Titan didn't look back, too caught up in his apparent victory. Somchai raced to Titan, kicking off the ground hard and landing on Titan's back, Somchai's legs wrapped around his waist.

The crowd erupted in laughter as Titan attempted to pull Somchai off but couldn't reach his arms around. Titan tried to grab Somchai's arms at his waist, but his bulging biceps wouldn't let him. Somchai crawled up Titan's body and wrapped his legs around Titan's chest. Titan reached up to throw Somchai off but wasn't fast enough. Somchai grabbed the dagger and stabbed Titan through his skull.

Titan stood still for a moment before he slowly tipped over. Somchai leapt off of his back as he hit the ground, causing a reverberating thud through the arena.

Everyone was silent.

All at once, the crowd exploded in applause at the newest victor.

Somchai staggered as the adrenaline wore off, and he collapsed. Sam bolted up to help, but Ju already made her way out to him. She pulled several vials out of her pockets and poured them over Somchai's wound. Almost instantly, Somchai rose from the ground, and walked out of the arena like nothing had ever happened.

Caco sauntered back to her cage, guided by a cloud of Chaos, snarling as she stared back at the fresh meat of Titan's body.

No one bothered to move Titan's body from the ground as the crowd exited the stands.

Sam didn't dare move.

A pat on the back from Mara brought little comfort as she walked back to the palace to return to her day's duties. Moments later, Gadriel found Sam and motioned for him to follow.

The two walked up to the Dark Queen's balcony. Waiting at the steps as instructed by Gadriel, Sam watched Gadriel approach the Dark Queen. She whispered in his ear and handed him a scroll that he tucked into his pocket. The Dark Queen made her way back to the palace, not once looking at Sam. Good. He couldn't stand the thought of talking to her then anyway.

"Back to work," Gadriel said.

"Just like that?" His head was still spinning from the shock of it all.

"Yes. Now, be quiet and follow me, there is still much to be done."

Sam sighed, pulling the bread out of his pocket to eat on the way now that his nerves were calmed. As they left the arena, Sam looked back at the body that was still lying in a pool of blood.

Sam followed Gadriel down a hallway he'd never been before, chewing on the last bit of his food. They headed deep into the castle, descending stairs every once in a while. They must have been underground by that point, as there were no windows to let in the light of day. The only light was a bright glow emanating from the ceiling. As they continued their trek, Sam began to hear loud grunts and clanks.

"Where are we going? What's down here?" Sam got nervous as they neared a door at the end of the hall.

"You'll see." Gadriel yanked the doors open and ushered Sam inside.

Sam was in awe as he looked around the room. Hundreds upon hundreds of men in full sets of Gladiator-style armor dueled in what appeared to be training sessions. The men were in groups spanning the length and width of the enormous chamber. Sam could barely even make out the back wall from where he stood. There were groups of men with nothing but a sword, some with spears and shields, and others with rifles and handguns. *How odd.*

Gadriel made his way to the far right of the room, and Sam followed closely behind. A man broke away from his group as soon as he saw Gadriel and walked over, bowing low. Gadriel gave the man a slight bow of his head before speaking. "Updates, Supreme Commander?"

The man gestured toward several large groups. "The new recruits are learning fast, even with the drop in forces. We expect them to be fully trained up in no time."

"Excellent. And the former general and her legion, still no sign of them?"

"No, my lord. We had to call off the search in order to train our officers with the new weaponry. They are all being marked as casualties of combat."

"Mhmm." Gadriel assessed his surroundings. "I will report your progress and findings to the Dark Queen. This is for your eyes only, Supreme Commander." Gadriel grabbed the scroll the Dark Queen had given him out of his tunic and handed it to the commander, who tucked it under his chest plate. "That is all for today."

Gadriel bowed his head, and the commander bowed low again.

As Gadriel led Sam back to the doorway, Sam couldn't help but watch the men. They were intimidating in size even to Sam, though none quite as large as Titan. Each man looked like a weapon in his own right. Their armor resembled those of long-gone empires but with the latest weaponry. With all this, plus the Dark Queen's magic on their side, they were an unstoppable force. Sam shuddered as the door closed behind him, and Gadriel took them back to the main corridor of the palace.

"Why does the Dark Queen need all those troops? Isn't her magic enough?" Sam asked.

"And why would I tell you that?"

Sam thought. "Because if I'm supposed to marry the Dark Queen and learn about her palace, it seems I should know about all its working parts."

Gadriel scoffed. "So now you want to learn?"

"Aren't you the one who said I was supposed to?" Sam couldn't help his taunting tone.

"Fine. As powerful as our queen is, Chaos has its . . . limitations . . ."

Not that I've seen.

". . . and the Dark Queen fancies herself ready for anything."

Sam thought about the conversation between Gadriel and the supreme commander. "What happened to the former general?"

"She and her troops disappeared in the middle of the night during a training exercise in the mountains. The initial belief was an avalanche or cave-in. No bodies have been found, which suggests the creature of that area was responsible."

Sam gulped. A creature that could take out a general and an entire legion skulking on the same mountain he was on now? He tried to push the thought from his mind. "What kind of creature?"

Gadriel ignored the question.

"Now what? More chores?" Sam's feet hurt in the formal shoes the Dark Queen made him wear.

"Dinner preparations. Then I have an important mission you are to follow me on. I'm sorry, but you will be missing your dinner with the Dark Queen tonight."

Sam couldn't help the smile that appeared on his face. "Where are we going?"

"I am to check on the food supplies and ensure the transition of power has gone smoothly."

"We're going to the Grower land?" Sam recalled the man the Dark Queen had so mercilessly killed when he asked for her help to grow the kingdom's food.

"Yes. You have thirty minutes to pack enough supplies for the next three days."

"Three days?" Sam panicked, thinking of the book below his feet he hadn't yet gotten to read.

"Is that a problem?" Gadriel stopped and looked at Sam, challenging him.

Sam stammered as a lump appeared in his throat. "Not at all."

"Good, then you better get packing. And don't forget to go to the kitchen for provisions." Gadriel turned down a hall that led away from Sam's room, leaving him on his own.

Three days? Everything about the plan was becoming impossible. He needed to figure out how to get back to Annabelle yet had no choice but to follow Gadriel to the Grower land. If he could just find Keres, maybe he could help. Sam raced to his room to find a bag already packed.

Mara.

A smile crossed his face in gratitude. He grabbed the bag and headed for the kitchen, poking his head down each corridor in hopes of spying Keres. When Sam rounded the last hallway, Keres walked in his direction.

"Keres!" He approached him quickly, while they were still alone.

"What is it?"

"The Dark Queen is sending me away for three days. I need your help."

Keres shook his head. "I wish I could, Sam, but she is sending me away as well, for even longer."

His stomach turned over. "No. This can't be happening."

"It'll be all right, friend. Just do what you have to. And don't make any trouble, understand?"

Sam nodded.

"You best get going, then. I'll see you when I get back."

"I'll see you then." Sam waved goodbye to Keres and continued on to the kitchen. If nothing else, at least he was able to avoid the Dark Queen for the next few days.

Sam wrapped up enough food and filled a canteen with water for the journey, then made his way to the front of the palace. Gadriel was waiting with his bag. He said nothing as Sam approached, simply turned toward the castle's entrance.

Gadriel pushed the doors open; Sam slipped through just

before they closed. The two walked in silence over the blackness of the bridge. A shiver crawled up Sam's spine at the tortured souls that awaited, and the fence of fire barricading them in. When they reached the end of the bridge, Gadriel grabbed a lamp, and stepped through the wall of fire, letting its flames light the torch.

Sam's stomach lurched, keeping him from following.

Gadriel stared back at Sam. "Oh, come on."

Sam swallowed the lump in his throat and followed him through the fire. The two headed off into the night.

CHAPTER TWENTY-TWO

Chills from the cold night air stung Sam's cheeks as he and Gadriel wove their way down the charred path. The glow of the torch kissed the trees surrounding them, and the hairs on Sam's back rose every time there was a noise beyond the light he couldn't identify.

After his first journey through the woods with Keres, Sam couldn't believe Gadriel would take him out at night. Anyone, or anything, could be waiting for them in the dark, and Sam would be at the disadvantage. It was the only time being around Gadriel gave him some form of comfort over repulsion.

The exhaustion from the day hit Sam hard. He'd been up before sunrise searching for answers, then traipsing the palace all day with Gadriel, and not to mention the emotional toll of the match. Gadriel didn't look tired at all; he was still going strong and not losing pace as the hours went by. Sam hoped they would rest soon.

Sam rifled through his bag, searching for something warm.

A cloak nestled in deep, and he took it out, throwing it over his shoulders and fastening the button around his neck. It wasn't warm, but at least it helped block the cold air from weaving its way through his clothes.

The violet moon shone bright as they made their way out of the ashy woods. Sam reached his hand out to touch a tree branch that smelled of pine. He closed his eyes and let the scent wash over him, wishing to be back by the lake with Annabelle in his arms.

Sam jumped at the chattering that emerged in the distance. He opened his eyes to the glow of a fire just up ahead. Sam let out a sigh of relief, the aching in his feet intensifying as he knew they would get to rest soon.

Sam followed Gadriel in continued silence through an archway that led up to a farmhouse.

The two went around back to find a group of workers covered in dirt and sweat, sitting down to their evening meal after a long day's work. Though the dinner wasn't quite as festive as in the town his first night in Taegaia, it was much livelier than what he'd become used to in the palace. People laughed and smiled as they enjoyed each other's company. As Sam and Gadriel neared the group, people started to notice them, and Sam spotted a familiar face.

Recalling the last time he'd seen Octavia sent heat to his cheeks. He never had a chance to make things right with her; to properly apologize for his tactlessness. As he cautiously walked to her table, Octavia met his gaze and instantly popped up, skipping over to him with a giant smile on her face, and wrapped her arms around him.

"Oh!" Sam casually put one arm around her. "Hey, Octavia. How are you?" Sam still squirmed in his skin.

"Wonderful, Samuel. Thank you for asking." Octavia kept on smiling, seeming to forget their last encounter entirely.

Sam whispered in Octavia's ear. "I'm really sorry about what happened. I thought . . . Well, that doesn't matter. I'm sorry."

"No apologies necessary. It was an accident."

Sam stood awkwardly, relieved he was forgiven, but still not sure how to act. "So, you and Ju, huh?"

Octavia blushed. "Yes," she continued in a whisper, "but let's keep that between us, please." Octavia motioned toward Gadriel with her eyes.

"Ah, of course."

"You must be starving. Come, eat!" Octavia turned and waltzed back to the table. She was so childlike from behind, with her bouncing dresses and the way she was always barefoot, which would have hurt another person, but for Octavia the earth beneath turned lush and green with each step cushioning her elegant feet.

Sam walked to the table and joined Octavia and the rest of the group. Octavia placed a full plate of food before Sam. "Samuel, I want you to meet everyone. This is Billy, and Nikki, and Thomas, and . . ." Everyone's names went by so quickly he could hardly keep up, so he politely nodded as he picked at the food on his plate.

He was beyond thrilled to be having his evening meal without the Dark Queen. Sam almost forgot about Gadriel and glanced up to find him at the end of the table, standing with his arms crossed and the same sour look on his face that he always had. He wondered why Gadriel was always so stiff, so unrelenting. He'd probably never know why.

Gadriel continued to stare at the table and appeared to be assessing them, as he'd done with the palace staff all day.

Tired of the relentless stare, Sam turned his attention back to his food and the people around him. One of the men across from him—*Henry?*—had just finished a joke, and everyone else laughed uncontrollably. Sam smiled to seem like he'd been listening but kept looking at his surroundings out of the corners of his eyes. He couldn't see everything clearly in the night but could make out a couple of quaint houses spread apart and a large field in the middle that connected them all together. He squinted to make out what was in the field when someone tapped on his shoulder.

"Tired?" Octavia stared at Sam with a sympathetic look on her face.

Sam nodded. "Yes, I think I am."

"Then let's get you to a room." Octavia rose and walked toward the closest house, waving Sam on to follow.

Sam took one last sip of water from his glass and followed Octavia, trying his best to avoid Gadriel's gaze as he passed. Octavia was already bounding up the stairs and opening the front door when Sam made his way over. He walked in just in time to see Octavia slip into a bedroom on the far side of the house.

Sam called out. "Are you sure it's all right for me to stay here?"

Octavia poked her head out of the room. "Of course, Samuel, now come here! You look absolutely exhausted."

Sam couldn't argue with her there and walked to the bedroom.

The room was significantly smaller than the one he had in the palace, but it at least had a proper bed, which suited him just fine. Octavia pulled the blanket back on the bed and fluffed his pillow.

"Oh, you don't have to do that," Sam insisted.

"It's no bother." Octavia tiptoed back to let Sam have room to get in bed.

"Thanks?" Sam slid off his shoes and sat in bed, leaning against the wall behind him. "I hope you don't mind me asking, but what are you? I noticed you have magic, and your purple eyes . . ."

Octavia giggled. "I'm a nymph."

"A nymph?"

"Of course! Haven't you ever seen one before?"

"I don't think so," Sam said. "We don't have them where I'm from. I've only heard of them in legends, and you don't look like what they describe at all."

"Oh! Well, none of us look the same. I'm a forest nymph, a dryad, but I don't live in the forest. They're much more treelike there." Octavia smiled.

"What about water nymphs? Are they real?"

"Hydriads? Yes, but I've never met one."

"Hmm." Sam nodded, not knowing what to say next. "Have you ever seen a match at the palace?"

Octavia looked stunned. "Yes. Why?"

"There was one today. It was horrible."

Octavia covered her mouth. "Who lost?" Worry flashed behind her eyes.

"Titan. He lost to Somchai."

She put her hand to her chest, letting out a long sigh. "Oh, dear. I've always liked Somchai. But poor Titan."

Sam crumpled his brows. "Yeah. It was horrifying to watch them forced into battle like that. The Dark Queen . . . she's beyond evil. She's barbaric."

Octavia sat on the edge of the bed. "She's lost her way."

"Lost her way? Really? She's lost her mind. She's mad!" Sam couldn't understand how Octavia could keep defending her.

"Dorthea is a woman full of love and passion. Somewhere along the way, things got turned around for her, but I know she's still in there."

"How?"

Octavia smiled. "Because I know Dorthea."

Sam shook his head. Octavia was more naive than he'd thought. A person couldn't possibly come back from all the unspeakable horrors the Dark Queen had inflicted upon her world. If Dorthea was in there, it didn't matter. "I should sleep. I don't know what Gadriel has planned for me tomorrow."

"Yes, Samuel. I'll let you sleep. Goodnight."

"Goodnight, Octavia. Thanks for everything." Sam removed his tunic and scooted down into the sheets, turning out the light beside him. He sank deep into his pillow and closed his eyes, desperate for some rest. The door closed, and Sam drifted off to sleep.

Morning came too soon, the bustle of people outside his door waking him as they moved about the house. Sam turned over toward the back wall, hoping for even a minute more of peace, when there was a knock at the door.

"Yeah?" Sam grumbled. He turned back to the door to see Gadriel walk into the room.

"I think you've had enough sleep. Let's go, we've got work to do."

Sam mumbled. "Fine. Just give me a minute."

Gadriel stood still, refusing to leave as Sam slowly sat up and stretched. "Hurry along."

"I'm coming." Sam rolled his eyes. "How are you not tired?"

Gadriel scoffed. "I have no need for such things as rest."

Sam raised his brow. "You mean you don't sleep?" Sam swung his legs over the bed and grabbed his bag off the floor, looking for something to wear.

"Sometimes. But that's no concern of yours. Let's go." Gadriel turned on his heel and closed the door to allow Sam to dress in private.

Sam looked in the bag at all the ridiculously lavish items. He was about to pick a dark silk tunic when he noticed his own clothes tucked deep in the bottom of the bag. Sam smiled. *Thanks, Mara.*

As soon as Sam was dressed, he pulled his notebook from his pocket once again. *Tick.* Twenty.

Sam made his way outside, where Gadriel stood waiting. He looked Sam up and down, shaking his head. "Today we are to observe the efficiency of this land to determine its productivity, and report back to the Dark Queen our findings on whether or not this is a suitable parcel to continue the yield of crops or if she should find another property that can do the job."

"And if this place isn't running to her standards?" Sam asked.

"Then it serves no purpose to our realm, and the Dark Queen will deal with that as she sees fit."

Sam swallowed the lump in his throat. He hoped Octavia had had enough time to turn this place around, that her magic was strong enough to save this farm and its people.

The rest of the household came outside then, quieting as they saw Gadriel. They walked to the field while Gadriel grabbed out a bit of parchment and followed them. Octavia was last out of the house, so Sam walked with her as he went. The homes around the ground looked similar to the one he'd stayed in the night before, and each one had a group of people walking out, all seeming to meet in a central spot. When they were all together, Gadriel spoke.

"You all know why I am here today. If you impress me, you can go about your business as usual. If not . . ." Gadriel trailed off, and Octavia stepped forward.

"Don't worry, dear Gadriel. These folks are some of the best eragats I have ever worked with. They won't let you down." Octavia smiled to those around her, trying to give them encouragement, but it didn't seem to alleviate their worries. The crowd dispersed, each person going to their own area to work a plot of land.

Sam scanned the field, and most everything was dead or dying. Octavia went from group to group, using her magic to give life to the earth, but by the time she got to the next group, the land had already decayed from the last. These people were struggling to keep anything alive, and Octavia's magic wasn't enough.

Gadriel scowled as he scribbled on the bit of parchment he had. "Well, this is no good."

Sam scrambled to think of something, watching the fields bloom and decay in a matter of moments. What they were doing was not working, and they would pay for it with their lives. Once again, he was powerless to stop the Dark Queen from destroying families and their homes.

I wonder . . .

"Gadriel!" Sam ran up to Gadriel, standing closer than he'd ever dared before.

"Yes?" Gadriel answered, annoyed.

"How long are we here for?" The wheels in Sam's mind turned faster and faster.

"We are set to leave in two days, but I must say, with results like these, I have half a mind to leave right now."

"Don't!" Sam tried to contain himself. "I mean, what if I could help?"

"Ha! You? Help? I'd love to see that."

Sam glared at Gadriel.

"Fine, if you can somehow fix this situation, I will stay until sunset," Gadriel said.

"Thank you." Sam turned to the field and jogged over to where Octavia was. "Octavia!" Sam could see the look of worry in her eyes as she struggled to get the earth to produce anything. "Octavia, I have an idea."

"Please, Samuel, anything."

"Have you only ever used magic to grow these lands?"

Octavia looked puzzled. "Yes. Magic has run through these grounds since this world was created."

Sam smiled. "What if we did it without magic?"

"No magic?" Octavia seemed baffled by the suggestion.

"Yes. What if we brought the soil back to life without working magic against magic?"

Octavia slowly nodded. "That might work. But, Samuel, these people don't know how to farm without magic. No one does."

Sam rolled up his sleeves and grabbed a nearby shovel. "I do."

Octavia called over the eragats, and Sam told them his plan. They were mostly skeptical but willing to try anything. He had them grab shovels and wheelbarrows and followed one group to the nearest barn. He sent another group to collect the food scraps from the week before, while a third he sent to the tree line to collect leaves.

Sam smiled at the animals as they entered the barn—they were much more normal than he had expected. There were cows, pigs, and goats all roaming free in designated sections of the barn.

"Now what?" one of the men asked.

"Start shoveling." Sam began to shovel the waste into the wheelbarrows. Some of the crowd cringed, then all reluctantly joined him. When the wheelbarrows were full, the group went back out to the field to join the two other groups that had collected the food scraps and leaves.

"How is this going to grow our food?" a woman called out.

"Yeah! These are all the worst parts . . . we can't grow anything with these," another said.

"I have been farming most of my life." Sam jumped in. "Trust me, I know what I'm doing. Your soil is dead. This will fix it."

There was chatter among the group, and some nodded their heads in compliance.

"Tell us what to do."

Sam gave everyone a job, from shoveling muck out of the wheelbarrows to mixing the ingredients. While the eragats worked and dug into the soil, Sam went to the field. He worked from one side to the other, breaking apart the earth and adding in the freshly made manure. The labor dragged sweat from Sam, and he was glad for once to have the sapphire orb shining in the sky over the sweltering Carolina sun.

Other men had joined Sam in cultivating the field. The eragats were shoveling, mixing, and digging. *This is going to work.*

The hours rolled on, and they finally neared the end of the field. Sam kept shoveling, kept mixing the soils, until he reached the last part of the ground. Looking up, he expected to see Mr. Anderson, but was startled by Gadriel. He'd forgotten where he was with the work that he was all but used to doing day in and day out. Gadriel seemed less than impressed, but Sam wasn't going to stop there.

He turned back to the people to discuss the next part of the plan, sending one group to collect water, and another to get the existing food from their homes. Octavia stood in amazement as she watched the eragats water the land and prepare the seeds. Sam chuckled at the look on her face. He imagined it was the same look he'd had the first time he saw magic.

The eragats continued their hard work as the sun began to set. When the light dimmed, Gadriel approached Sam and the group. "Time's up. I don't see any food."

"It takes time. In just a few weeks, you'll be able to see some begin to grow. I've already told everyone how to care for each crop, and they will work hard to keep them growing. They did an incredible job."

Gadriel walked the field, closely examining the soil. "Well, it's not dead. Perhaps you're right."

"I am," Sam said. "These crops will grow, I promise." Sam looked at the people's faces as they waited in anticipation for Gadriel's verdict.

"Very well. I will return in four cycles to check the progress of the crops."

The groups shouted in a collective triumph. Sam had bought them time, and he knew this land would yield crops enough for the palace and nearby villages. Octavia and several others ran to Sam and embraced him.

"Thank you so much."

"We can never repay you."

"You are our savior."

Sam blushed. "You're welcome." He welled up inside, filling with a sense of pride that had long since gone. For just a moment, he thought he saw the scowl on Gadriel's face turn into a subtle smile.

"We must celebrate!" Octavia shouted. The rest of the people joined in, ushering Sam and Gadriel back for a celebration.

"We best be going," Gadriel said sternly.

Octavia's lip dropped into a pout. "Oh, Gadriel, always so serious. Samuel worked hard today. Let him have a break."

Gadriel looked Sam over. "Fine," he sighed.

"Yes!" Octavia squealed, pulling Sam's arm and then skipping off toward the main house.

Sam was relieved Gadriel had changed his mind. Otherwise, these people didn't have a chance. A weight lifted off his shoulders knowing they would be safe as he watched them celebrate.

Dinner was much more festive the second night with Octavia and the eragats. Someone brought wine, and another even brought out an instrument to play music. Sam enjoyed himself until Gadriel insisted they head back to the palace. Once everyone had thanked Sam one last time for his heroism, the two headed back toward the castle, Octavia waving them off.

When Sam and Gadriel entered the tree line and could no longer see the glow of the fire from the farm, Sam spoke. "Thank you."

Gadriel kept his gaze forward. "For what?"

"Giving me the day. Giving them a chance."

"My orders were clear. They simply met expectations . . . this time a least." Gadriel hesitated. "Good work today. It turns out you aren't completely useless."

Sam smirked. Gadriel didn't have to give him the time. And a compliment? Maybe Sam was wrong about him.

"Why are you always so . . . surly?" Sam asked.

"Excuse me?"

"You know what I mean. I've never seen you relax. Or smile."

"I don't have anything to smile about anymore." Gadriel's voice trailed off.

Sam contemplated what he meant. "Did you used to?"

Gadriel paused. "Yes." His voice croaked.

"Oh." Sam wasn't sure what to say next. They continued their walk in silence, and Sam watched the last bit of daylight slip behind the mountain.

Gadriel grabbed a torch from his satchel and lit it. The shadows from the trees danced across the path, becoming thinner as they walked. Before long, barren and charred trees appeared as a reminder to Sam that they'd arrived back at the palace grounds. The castle came into view, and Sam's stomach once again felt hollow. The walk across the bridge was too short, and he closed his eyes as Gadriel pushed the doors open. The echoes of footsteps bounding off the walls was all too familiar as he made his way back to his chambers. A child ran toward them, arms out wide.

"Gadie! You're back."

Sam stood in disbelief as Gadriel dropped to a knee and embraced the young boy. "I am. But shouldn't you be in bed?"

The boy looked down and half smiled. "Maybe."

Sam smiled at the young boy. He had big apple cheeks, and stood just knee high to a grasshopper.

Gadriel let out a laugh. "Off to bed, little one. I'll see you tomorrow."

The boy hugged Gadriel once more, then scampered back down the hallway.

Sam was stunned. "Gadie?"

"Shut up." Gadriel's tone was back to its normal self.

"Was that your—"

"No," Gadriel said.

"Then who was it?"

Gadriel sighed, rolling his eyes. "If you must know, I give my time to the young ones in the children's wing. Most are orphaned but still too young to work."

"Wow," Sam said. "I had no idea."

"That's because it's really none of your business. Now, I have things to do. Go back to your chambers." Gadriel stalked off, leaving Sam speechless as he made his way to his room.

He sat on his bed, feeling emptier than he had since his arrival. The day made him feel like he was back home, and the realization that he wasn't even close tore him apart all over again. Sam waited until he knew the Dark Queen would have long left her gardens and retreated to her chambers, then snuck out into the hall. He wouldn't waste one more second not reading that book.

CHAPTER TWENTY-THREE

The black binding and intricate red and gold lettering were nothing like the books in the library. He hadn't taken the time before to appreciate its elegant beauty, but now it entranced him. Sam struggled to lift the tome off of the shelf because of its enormity. He'd never seen one so large. He prayed the size of the book would mean he'd learn something to help get him out of this wretched kingdom. Sam wrapped his arms around it and heaved the book off the shelf, dropping it onto the floor faceup.

He examined the spine, but no title indicated what it was about. Peeling back the cover, he stared at blank pages. Sam turned every page, each blank. Butterflies encircled his stomach. *Why would someone make a magical book with nothing inside? They had to have written something in it . . . Wait!*

Sam wracked his brain to remember what Mara had told him about objects hidden in magic. It reminded him of the room where he could smell the tea and feel the roar of the fire, but everything remained hidden from him until Mara did her spell. Perhaps this book was the same. He said a quick prayer before placing his palm on the cover, tracing the patterns Mara had shown him.

Images and letters swirled around each other until a clear message appeared.

Bonds: Blood and Power

"Huh?" Sam stared at the cover, trying to figure out why the words seemed so familiar to him. *Bonds . . . bonds . . .* "That's it!" His stomach fluttered as he recalled what the Dark Queen had said about him. She was going to *bond* with him. Surely this could help in some way.

Sam flipped the book open, rifling through the pages, but found only blank paper staring back at him. *No, there has to be something here!* Sam's stomach churned as he neared the final pages of the book. At last, a page with words appeared. The last page in the book.

Sam put his finger to the page and scanned it. He found a section called *Power* and started there. The Dark Queen had said their bond would give her power.

Bonds

The two bonds are that of power and blood. One soul may create a multitude of bonds, though this becomes dangerous if those bonded have hidden or dissimilar intents. Going against a bond means certain death . . .

Power

The bonds of love are a powerful weapon. When love in one's heart is true and pure, the bond will create a spark of magic. This powerful magic can be used in Harmony to strengthen the lives of those bonded, or in Chaos to bend to one's will. Bonds cannot be broken and must be fully sanctioned to stand the test of time.

The section went on, but Sam got the gist. The Dark Queen really would become more powerful creating a bond with Sam. *Bonds cannot be broken.* Sam couldn't let that happen. If he bonded to the Dark Queen, he could never be with Annabelle. Sam continued.

Blood

Blood bonds are used among family, friends, and allies. They go beyond even the strongest magic. Those who share blood may not harm one another or go against the bond. This effect can be created through Alchemy—instructions to follow.

Sam skimmed through the ingredients and instructions for performing the blood bond. They were all things he'd never before dreamed to be real—blood from a dragon, scale of a mermaid, feather of a winged horse. The items became more and more obscure as the list went on, so Sam skipped ahead to the rest of the section.

When performed properly, a blood bond can create a speck of magic.

A smile appeared on Sam's face. *This is something.* He may not have all the answers yet, but Sam was halfway there. Magic was needed for the fading tokens, and if Keres didn't have any, then they could make some. It would also be helpful in giving Keres the power he needed to defy the Dark Queen and lie to others, especially Gadriel, when he needed to most. As much as he trusted Keres, it would be nice to have assurances that nothing could spoil their plan.

Sam read the ingredient list over again, looking for something he could find on his own. Just one, maybe. He'd have to wait until Keres came back to the castle for the rest, whenever that would be. But once Keres did return, they could move much more quickly with Keres's freedom to defy the Dark Queen.

Sam laughed as he let out a sigh. He would beat the Dark Queen at her own game.

IT HAD BEEN TWO DAYS, and Keres still hadn't returned. Why did he and Gadriel have to return early? The Grower land at least kept his mind off things here in the castle while waiting for Keres.

Sam continually filled with anxiety, sure the Dark Queen could read the plan all over his face. He'd become much shorter with everyone due to the nerves and was hardly able to stomach anything more than a bite at each meal. He tried his best to go about business as usual, but it was proving to be an impossible task. He needed Keres to return now.

The Dark Queen seemed pleased with his work on the

Grower land. Since his return, she'd been almost tolerable. Almost. Perhaps it was another trick to try to get him to stay. It wouldn't work.

Sam still hadn't acquired the one ingredient he had a shot at getting on his own—the mermaid scale. Sam had only ever met one merperson, and he wouldn't exactly call Zael a close friend, but he did have a deep-seated hatred toward the Dark Queen, which Sam could hopefully use to his advantage.

Sam paced back and forth in front of the glass wall, searching for Zael. He'd come early each morning, but Zael hadn't shown. Perhaps the Dark Queen decided she'd had her fun with him. *No.* Sam shook his head to keep the thought from his mind. He knocked as loudly as he dared on the glass, praying it caught no one's attention but the merman. The waters were still. Sam hung his head in defeat and turned to walk back to his room when a voice sounded in his head.

"Leave me be."

"Zael! Where have you been? I was worried about you." Sam spun around to greet the merman, but no one was there. "Where are you?"

"Don't concern yourself with me. Just leave me alone," Zael said.

"I need your help. I—"

"I know why you are here, Sam. I can't help you. It is a lost cause, and I would only be killing myself if I help you. The Dark Queen would boil these waters if she figured out I had aided you. Or worse."

Sam contemplated his next words. "Is there anyone else that can help me?"

Silence.

"Zael?" Sam's voice quivered with hopelessness.

"Everyone who would help you is dead. The Dark Queen made sure of that."

"That's not true." Sam chimed in. "There are people who the Dark Queen has not yet gotten to. There's still hope."

Zael laughed. *"There is no hope. What you want is impossible."*

"No, it ain't." Sam huffed, crossing his arms. How could this man not have hope? "I will get home to my love."

"Love?" Zael seemed intrigued by the word.

"Yes. Annabelle, she's waiting for me back home. I need to get back to her. And there are people here who will help. You're wrong." Sam thought of Annabelle, saw her smile dance in front of him. He thought of Mara, the young girl who lost everything but still made him smile even in the worst of places. Octavia, the confident woman who did what was right, who somehow saw humanity in the Dark Queen. Ju, the sweet woman who cared for others, even in impossible situations. He thought of Gadriel, a man he may have misjudged, who was hurting perhaps just as much as everyone else in the Dark Queen's kingdom. And Keres, the one who would help him get home.

A drop of water hit Sam's shoulder. He looked up to see something falling from above. He reached out his hands and caught the object—a fish scale. No, a mermaid scale. Sam smiled to himself. "What made you change your mind?"

"I know what it is to have loved another soul beyond comprehension and to have it taken away forever. No one deserves that."

"Thank you." Sam turned to leave, stopped again by Zael's voice.

"Sam?"

"Yes, Zael?"

"Be careful who you trust. No one in this castle is what they seem."

Sam raised a brow in confusion. "I will." He put the scale in his pocket and walked back to his room, turning the last words Zael had said over in his mind.

Sam was making his way back to his room when he bumped into someone in the hall. "Oof! I'm sorry." Sam looked at the figure. "Ju! Oh, I'm so, so sorry." He was apologizing for more than just the run-in.

Ju smiled, waving her hand like Sam had nothing to apologize for.

Sam looked down at the pile of scrolls Ju had been carrying. "Oh, here, let me get those." Sam picked up the pile. "Where to?"

Ju raised her brow.

"I'm not going to run into you and then not help. It was my fault for not looking."

Ju smiled and walked down the hall, Sam following close behind. She made her way up the stairs, back to the room Sam had first met her in, then unlocked the door and walked inside. She motioned to a small table, and Sam dropped the scrolls onto it. He was about to leave when he noticed the look on Ju's face.

"Is something wrong?"

Ju nodded, holding her hand to her heart.

"Are you in pain?"

Ju shook her head.

Sam thought. "Is it about Octavia?"

She nodded, looking worried.

"She's okay. I was just with her. She's at the farm helping them grow food. She's doing a great job." Sam hated that he knew exactly how Ju felt—separated from the one he loved and fearing for her life.

Seeming calmed by Sam's words, Ju tidied up the scrolls. She looked Sam in the eyes and lifted her hand to his heart, pointing at him.

The sentiment was clear—she sensed the connection as well. "Her name is Annabelle. She is the best person I've ever known, and I have no idea if I'll ever see her again." Sam bit his lip. "I just want her back."

Ju nodded with understanding, then grabbed Sam's hands and kissed them, and somehow it comforted him—having someone to share in the pain with. Ju turned back to her work, and Sam let her be, heading back down to his chambers.

While winding around the corners, he did his best to keep his hand off his pants pocket. He couldn't draw attention to the fact that he had a priceless item to help him get back home. If anyone found the scale, he'd have no explanation for it. *Just breathe. Keep walking. No, don't touch it!*

Sam almost jumped out of his skin when someone tapped him on the shoulder. He spun around to see who it was. "Somchai!" The guard didn't have a mark on him, and he stood like he'd not been stabbed only a few days prior. "How do you look so normal? Titan beat on you pretty hard."

Somchai laughed. "Ju is quite the miracle worker. Best healer in the land."

So that's what Ju does. A healer and a records keeper. Interesting.

"I saw you at the match. It looked like you were worried about me." Somchai gave a shy smile.

"Of course I was. Titan was a beast. Why would you fight

him on purpose in the hall? He could have killed you with one punch."

Somchai's cheeks turned red. "He said something about you."

"Me? He barely even knew me. And why would you care?" Sam didn't think he'd ever understand Somchai.

"It wasn't very nice. And you are nice—you're wonderful." Somchai's breaths shallowed.

"Uh, thanks. You're nice yourself, but you didn't have to do that for me. Titan was just a bully. Mara said it wasn't even his first match."

"Not by a long shot. He loved those matches. Made any excuse to enter one. I guess I just fell for it."

"Well, I'm glad it was you that made it out. Titan always scared me."

Somchai laughed. "He scared everyone. He was the Dark Queen's favorite guard. I thought she would punish me for beating him, but she respects the outcomes of the match."

"I'm surprised."

Somchai shrugged. "Do you . . ." His voice trailed off.

"What's that?" Sam leaned in, and Somchai's entire face went red.

"Do you want to hang out sometime? I have a couple games in my room if you ever need a distraction." Somchai bit his bottom lip.

"Sure, that sounds great. Thanks." *Why does Somchai want to spend time with me?* "Well, I best be going."

"Okay. Let me know if you ever need anything. I'm here to serve the royal family, and soon that will be you." Somchai winked at Sam, then bowed low, turning to walk back the way he'd come.

What an odd fellow.

SAM MADE his way down into the tunnel. It was a meeting day for him and Keres, and though he knew it was pointless, he had nothing better to do. He still had the mermaid scale in his pocket and needed a safe place to hide it. Perhaps he would find a hidden compartment in the tunnel that would fit the task.

Sam paused as footsteps entered the room, his heart rate rising and palms sweating. He looked back up the steps, and contemplated running. With a deep breath, he prayed Keres was back; that he'd somehow missed his return. He peeked his head around the corner and was relieved when he saw Keres pacing the room.

"You scared me," Sam called to Keres.

Keres faced Sam with a smile. "Sorry, dear friend. I hoped you'd still show. I just returned this morning."

"Finally. I've been going crazy waiting for you." Sam couldn't wait to tell Keres all he'd uncovered. "Where have you been?"

"I told you, I was sent away on duty. Miss me that much, huh?" Keres laughed.

"I found something that I think will help." The excitement burst out of Sam.

"Oh?" Keres gave Sam a quizzical look.

Sam pulled the mermaid scale out of his pocket.

"What could you possibly need that for?" Keres asked.

"A spell. Or ceremony. I don't know what you call it." Sam walked toward the book that he'd left on the floor to show Keres.

"Have you been practicing magic since I left?"

"No," Sam started, "I found this book all about bonds. It talks about how to make a blood bond, about what it means for the people that make it. There's what seems to be a love bond, like husband and wife, and then an alliance or friendship bond."

"Whoa, Sam. That's some powerful magic you're talking about there." Keres took a step back.

"I know. But I think it can help solve our problems. You said you don't have magic, right?"

Keres shook his head.

"Well, this is a way we could make some. And then you can do what needs to be done to see this through. Even lie."

"Hmm." Keres put his thumb and forefinger to his chin. "So, if it came down to you or the Dark Queen's magic, this bond would allow me to choose you over her?"

"Exactly!"

"I don't know, Sam. It sounds dangerous. How do you even know it'll work? The bond is something long forgotten to our people, until the Dark Queen came across its power."

Sam opened the book. "Look here."

Keres scanned the page, eyes widening the further he read. "You're right. This is perfect." Keres looked at Sam's hand. "And that explains the scale. How'd you get it?"

"I have my ways." Sam smiled.

"Very resourceful." Keres looked the ingredients over again. "These are complex ingredients. They will take time to procure. I would say . . . five days to avoid suspicion."

"Five days! No, that's too long. Can't you move faster?"

"I wish I could, but most of these ingredients are not in the castle, and I'm not even positive they all exist." Keres sighed. "I will do my best."

Sam gave a half smile. "All right, if you say so."

"Don't worry, my friend. We will get you to your love." Keres put a hand on Sam's shoulder.

"Thank you."

"Now, we best go. I will gather the ingredients and meet you here in five days. In the meantime, try to act as normal as possible. Can you do that?"

Sam nodded. "I think so."

"Very well, then. I'll see you soon, friend." Keres walked out of the room and back up the tunnel, disappearing into the blackness.

CHAPTER TWENTY-FOUR

The next five days proved a challenge to keep his mind occupied and his hands busy. Keres had never failed Sam before, but creating magic was far more complicated than anything they'd ever done. Sam couldn't sneak back into the Dark Queen's chambers for more. Even if he hadn't almost been caught, there were no other vials of magic in the chest. This was his only other option.

He passed the time the first day by following Mara around the palace. He used what Gadriel had said about training as an excuse to openly spend the day with his friend as she worked. The two laughed the day away with jokes and silliness. Mara was always able to bring out his inner child. They had slid down several banisters, raced down the halls, and threw rocks over the garden hedges. They'd only been caught once by another maid, and the two giggled uncontrollably after she had left. Sam went to bed that night forgetting about his anxieties.

The second day was far less fun. After finishing breakfast,

Sam had been given a task by the Dark Queen, commanded to him on a scroll by Das. Sam was surprised Das was still alive, the nervous old fool. Sam sighed as he opened the scroll to see that the Dark Queen expected him to sit at a table all day writing down all he could about his world.

She wanted details on technology, weaponry, politics, religion, and failings. Sam thought about resisting the request but figured it could do no harm and at least keep him busy. The task took Sam two full days to complete, as he had a lot to say about the failings of his world. He also added information the Dark Queen did not ask for, like art, books, and music. He figured these things were as important as everything else he wrote about. If nothing else, at least he was writing again.

Day four dragged on the longest. Sam tried to keep himself busy by hunkering down in the library and reading adventure books, but his mind kept wandering. He tried walking the gardens, the halls, and even taking a nap. But he couldn't calm his nerves. Just one more day, and he'd have another piece of the puzzle.

Sam jumped at the knock on his door. He opened it to find a small old woman he'd never seen before. Her arms were full of fabrics and sewing tools. Sam recognized them from all the times he'd seen Annabelle wield a needle. The woman looked up at Sam and sheepishly cleared her throat.

"The Dark Queen . . . to . . . for you, sir." The woman spoke in a delicate, raspy whisper, and Sam could hardly make out the words. Perhaps her age made her voice too soft for the ears. Her white skin wrinkled more than anyone he'd ever seen.

"Excuse me?"

"I'm Thilda. I . . . clothes for you . . . wedding . . ."

Sam's eyes widened. "You're here to make my clothes for the wedding ceremony?"

The woman nodded, seeming annoyed that Sam was having a hard time understanding her. As he moved aside, the woman zipped into the room, putting the materials on a table and pulling a stool out of the wardrobe. She looked at him and patted the seat. Sam walked over and stepped up onto the stool. The woman violently shook her head.

"No . . . clothes are . . ."

"Huh?" He leaned in. "I'm sorry, I missed that." Why wouldn't she just speak up?

Thilda huffed and motioned at Sam's body. "No clothes . . ."

"Oh!" Sam removed his tunic and pants and stood on the stool in his drawers. "Sorry." This moment couldn't be over fast enough. He was already nervous and could hardly stomach *uncomfortable*.

The woman grabbed a ribbon and measured different parts of his body.

"I don't mean to be rude," Sam said, "but someone has already gotten my measurements. Can't you just use— Ow!" Sam recoiled as the woman slapped his arm.

The old woman continued measuring, and Sam stood in silence. She then grabbed different bits of fabric she had brought and held them against Sam's skin. "Black is a good base."

Sam's cheeks flushed. Unsure if that was supposed to be a compliment or not, he said nothing. Dozens of combinations grazed his skin before finding the two that satisfied her—a deep black satin underlay with a delicate shimmering gold over top. Not quite his taste, but he wasn't about to tell this woman that. And he assumed he didn't have much say in the matter anyhow.

Mara walked into the room for its daily cleaning, not saying a word as she got straight to work. It had only been a few moments when he heard something break. When he turned around, Mara stood over a broken vase of flowers, scrambling to clean up. "I'm so sorry."

Thilda marched over to Mara and slapped her across the face. "Stupid girl!" The old woman finally raised her voice.

"Hey!" Sam rushed to Mara, putting himself between her and Thilda. "Do not touch her!"

Thilda mumbled under her breath and made her way back to her station. "Stupid, stupid girl."

Sam turned to help Mara clean up, but she had already cleared the mess and was slipping out of the room. Sam walked back over to the mirror.

"Don't ever do that again," Sam threatened.

Thilda ignored him. "You will try on . . . days . . . wedding," she said.

"How long until I can try it on?" Sam braced for the swat.

"Two days . . . wedding."

"The wedding is in two days!" Sam's stomach dropped.

"No!"

Sam sighed in relief.

"Two days until . . . clothes are ready . . . just in time." The woman quickly gathered her materials.

"What do you mean just in time?" Sam asked.

The woman turned around and rolled her eyes. "Clothes . . . night before the wedding."

"Wait, the clothes will be done the night before the wedding?"

The woman nodded and left the room, not bothering to close the door behind her. Sam stood on the stool still in his drawers, stunned at what had just happened.

DINNER THAT NIGHT WAS TORTURE. Sam sat at the table, glaring down the Dark Queen. She sat in her chair eating, not seeming to notice Sam seething.

"I must say, Sam, I am actually looking forward to the bonding that is fast approaching. The ceremony might even be fun." The Dark Queen didn't look up from her meal.

Sam clenched his jaw, the heat in his body beginning to rise.

"I hope Thilda found you something suitable to wear. My last seamstress's work was atrocious, so I had to let her go."

Sam's interest was piqued. "You let her go. Like, leave the palace?"

"Yes, Sammy, she's outside of the palace." The Dark Queen snickered. "Right out front, in fact."

Sam's eyes widened in horror. "You can't do that to her!"

"I can do whatever I want! She pricked me one too many times with her needle. Now she gets to know how it feels."

Sam's stomach gurgled. No one deserved those horrific contraptions.

"I expect you to look your absolute best for my big day."

Sam shook his head. "I'm sure you'll see to that."

"Speaking of Thilda"—the Dark Queen motioned to Das,

who led Thilda and Mara into the room—"I hear my servant girl has been breaking palace property. *My* property."

Das escorted the women to stand in front of Keres and Gadriel, who stood at their usual post during dinners.

"What?" Sam's whole body went numb.

Thilda stepped forward. "Stupid girl . . . broke a vase."

"Well, we can't have that, now, can we? Mara, step forward for your punishment."

"What punishment?" Sam asked, his stomach knotting up tight.

The Dark Queen laughed. "Oh, Sammy, you should know me better than that by now."

Sam's mind raced. *Not Mara. Oh, please, not Mara.*

The Dark Queen lifted her fingers, ready to snap.

"I did it!"

The Dark Queen narrowed her eyes at Sam. "Excuse me?" Her hand was still raised.

"I did it. I broke the vase. Mara was just cleaning it up." Sam looked at Mara, who shook.

"Are you telling me Thilda lied?"

Sam looked at Thilda, then back to Mara, knowing the consequences.

"Yes," he choked out.

"Very well, then." The Dark Queen snapped her fingers, and Thilda went up in flames. Anguished, pleading screams filled the room as her body hit the floor.

Sam looked away, trying to hold back from being sick as the scent of burning flesh choked him.

"Mara, go back to work. I best not hear a rumor with your name again."

"Yes, my queen," Mara said, then scurried out of the hall.

The Dark Queen sneered. "I'm bored. Das!" The Dark Queen called over her aide. "Fetch Enos. I want to have some fun tonight. I only have a few days left with my toy." The Dark Queen winked at Sam.

"Of course, Your Majesty." Das bowed and then scurried off to find Enos.

The Dark Queen rose from her chair and strutted out of the room.

Sam sat in his chair, wondering what the queen could have possibly meant, as he was sure she'd keep her favorite lover. His thoughts whirled together with the lingering smell of charred flesh and burned-up hair, gagging him, before he finally vomited on the floor.

As soon as the sun rose, Sam got dressed and made his way to the tunnel. When Sam pushed the palace door open to the garden, he saw Mara walking down the hall, wearing a lavender dress with gold accents. She wore her hair in a long braid over her shoulder.

"Mara, are you okay?" Sam made his way to her.

"I am, thanks to you. Why did you do that? She could have killed both of us if she had seen through your lie."

"I couldn't risk it. You shouldn't have to die for that."

"What about Thilda? She didn't deserve that." Mara was so calm.

"Of course she didn't. It was an impossible situation." Sam had trouble coming up with the right words.

"I know, I'm sorry. I don't mean to sound ungrateful. The Dark Queen did this, not you." Mara smiled. "Thank you." She offered her hand to Sam, who took it and gently kissed her knuckles.

"You're welcome."

"Mara!" Gadriel's voice boomed down the hall.

"I need to go," Mara whispered. She pinched up her skirt and hurried to Gadriel.

Sam watched the two until Gadriel glared at Sam. Opening the door to the garden, he didn't walk through until he was certain Gadriel had left the hall and he wouldn't be followed. He walked to the tunnel's entrance and pushed on the stone, making his way into the darkness.

He ran down the steps into the room, but it was empty aside from the book and hidden scale. Sam paced as he waited for Keres to show with the ingredients. Time passed, and Keres still wasn't there. He was late.

Horrible visions of the Dark Queen torturing and killing Keres flooded Sam's mind. Sam's breathing became heavy as he tried to figure a way out of there without Keres, but he couldn't. Sam's stomach dropped as he heard footsteps enter the room and looked up to see Keres with nothing in his hands.

Keres held up his hand. "I know. I'm sorry I am late. I had to figure out a way to sneak in the ingredients without raising alarm." The removal of his coat revealed items strapped to his body, completely hidden from anyone he might have come across in the palace halls. Sam scurried to help Keres gently remove the items and place them on the floor. His eyes widened as he scanned the ingredients and looked to Keres.

"I know. I couldn't find a drop of dragon's blood. They are a rumor from ages ago." Keres reached into his shirt pocket and pulled out a small vial with a glimmering liquid. "But I was able to get a drop of blood from a unicorn, one of the creatures that possess the most magical bloodline in our world. It will have to do. I'm not sure of the side effects, but it should still work, my friend. Don't be discouraged."

Sam nodded. This was as good as it could get, so he would have to go along. He didn't have time to waste tracking down more ingredients that didn't even exist. The plan had to go forward. He only prayed the bond would take, and that between the two of them, they could find a way to get Sam out of there before the wedding ceremony, before the Dark Queen could keep him there forever.

As Sam watched Keres prepare the ingredients for the bond, a wave of nerves washed over him, and a question nagged in his mind. "Keres?"

"Yes?" Keres continued working over the items.

"Why are you helping me?"

Keres stopped and faced Sam. "What?"

"When you first brought me to the Dark Queen, you told me you were loyal to her. And so much of what you've done has been in allegiance to her. So why are you helping me?"

Keres set the items on the ground and walked over to Sam. "Did you know that most people who work in this castle were born for that position?"

Sam shook his head.

"Some make their way up in the ranks, but no outsiders take those positions. You must be born into it. The eragats have no chance at a life in this castle. Now, it's not always a bad life out there, before this time of Chaos, but the riches and fine clothing and large baths and so much more are not an option outside of this palace. So many eragats dream to live in this castle, but it will never happen for them. Though, a few in the palace were brought in after the Dark Queen turned to Chaos."

"Like Mara," Sam jumped in.

"Yes, like Mara. But that's because the Dark Queen has killed too many bloodlines in this palace. She needed more servants."

"Why are you telling me all this?"

"Because, Sam, I want you to understand what an honor it was that I . . . that I was not born into this life, and I was here long before the Dark Queen took to Chaos."

"You were an eragat?"

"Yes. I was born a bastard, and my mother took to wine and booze. At first it was to relieve the stress of raising a boy alone, but then she began drinking almost as often as she breathed. She put hands on me, and when I was old enough, she . . . she sold my body to the desperate souls of my village just to make extra coin."

Sam gasped. "Keres, I'm so sorry."

Keres shook his head and continued, "Through all of it, I would look at this palace as some sort of hope that I could one day escape my mother and live a better life. Children here are expected to take care of their parents until the end. My dream was nothing more than that, but it kept me going. Then one day, I awoke and found my mother still asleep in bed, which wasn't odd. I went to wake her, but she did not wake. I buried her that day.

"I looked around at our house and felt nothing. So, I came to the palace and begged for a position. Anything. A guard was sending me away when Dorthea came around a corner and heard me. She was just a girl then, but she saved my life. She got me a position in the stables, and I worked my way from there to her advisor. I owe her everything. But what she's doing to you —forcing herself into your heart and destroying our world . . . I was wrong before when I stood by her no matter what. Perhaps if I had stepped in sooner, I could have stopped—" Keres choked on tears.

Sam reached out and brought Keres in for a hug. "I don't know what to say."

Keres composed himself and stepped back from Sam. "I'm sorry for all she has done to you. For what I've done to you."

Sam put a hand on Keres's shoulder. "You're making up for it now. Thank you."

The two sighed, looking at the ingredients on the floor and silently acknowledging the need to get back to work.

Keres crouched onto the floor and began arranging the items. To give Keres the space he needed, Sam stood and watched Keres carefully consider the location of each item in the room. Once Keres was satisfied and had checked the paper he had written the spell on one last time, he turned to Sam. "Hold out your hand."

Sam did as he was told, and Keres sliced through Sam's palm with a knife. Instinct pulled his hand away in a wince, but Keres kept hold of him, doing the same to his own hand. When their blood hit the floor, the ground beneath their feet rumbled. The two men joined hands and walked among the objects in a strange movement, ending in the center of the room. Keres chanted, beckoning Sam to join him.

"We are two, becoming one. With lifelong promise, the bond is done. We are two, becoming one. With lifelong promise, the bond is done. We are two . . ." A glow appeared beneath their hands where blood pooled, and the walls shook around them. Sam continued to chant but winced as stones fell toward them. All at once, the room was filled with a bright yellow glow, and Sam closed his eyes. A hum buzzed through his veins. It was like he could feel his blood rushing around—like it was alive. When he opened his eyes, the room looked as it had before, and the quakes had stopped. The sensation in his body was gone.

"Did it work?" Sam faced Keres, who smiled as he held a ball of glowing, glittery dust in his palms.

"Quick, grab the vial."

Sam rushed to the vial and opened it so Keres could pour the dust into it.

"It worked, Sam. It actually worked." Keres's smile was bigger than Sam had ever seen, and Keres began to laugh uncontrollably. Sam joined in the laughter, relieved that it had worked, that he had a friend that would do everything he could to help Sam escape, and he had the magic required to leave this world. Keres no longer had to listen to the Dark Queen if it interfered with their plan.

Sam was in a trance as he walked back to his room, and when he lay in bed, he looked to his sketch of Annabelle. "I'm almost there, Belli. Hold on just a little longer."

CHAPTER TWENTY-FIVE

Sam awoke the next morning a nervous wreck. He stared at his notebook. *Twenty-eight.* He couldn't believe it. While he and Keres had been successful in performing the blood bond, time continued to work against him at a faster pace. The wedding was to take place the following day, and Sam still hadn't figured out how to get home. He was so close. Bonding to the Dark Queen would keep him from Annabelle forever.

He lay still in bed when he heard a tap on the door. "Come in." Sam didn't get out of bed.

"Good morning, Sam." Keres strolled into the room.

"Is it?" Sam sat up.

"Well . . ." Keres trailed off, not looking Sam in the eyes.

Sam's stomach churned, and his face dropped. "Oh, no. It's impossible, isn't it? I'm never going home. I—"

"Sam, no. I have mixed news, but I can get you home."

"Really?" Sam jumped out of bed. "Tell me!" His excitement took over.

"Well, the spell worked, and we have enough magic to get you home."

Sam's face lit up.

"It's not that easy, though. To cross realms and worlds, the token must be sacred to our people and blessed by royalty in an official ceremony to create the kind of power we would need."

"I don't understand. Is that how the Dark Queen brought me here?"

"No, no. She used Chaos, and that is not an option."

Sam shook his head. "Of course not. We aren't evil like *her*." Sam thought of what Keres said. "You said the Dark Queen killed all the royals, so how are we going to get her to bless an object? She'd never do that."

Keres bit his bottom lip and looked away. "Not on purpose. This is the part you won't like."

Sam scoffed. "Was I supposed to like the other part?"

"There are no official ceremonies in the near future . . . except for one."

Sam's eyes widened. "No. I can't marry her! I'll be bonded to her, and she'll get her power, and I'll never get home." Sam's head was getting hazy. "What if we went back the way I came, out in the desert?"

Keres shook his head. "Even if you somehow managed to make it past her wall of fire, the Dark Queen closed all doors between our world and yours. No one can come in or out without her approval."

Sam put his head in his hands, knowing Keres was right.

Keres continued, "There are certain objects the Dark Queen

must bless during the ceremony to make the bond official. If I can get to one before her, I can rig the object to send you home."

Sam paused, filling with dread. "How do you know all this? I thought you didn't know anything about magic."

Keres pulled a piece of parchment out of his inner jacket pocket. "I went back into the tunnel this morning and flipped through the book again. I found this."

Sam grabbed the paper from Keres's hands and read it over. Everything Keres was saying was written there. Sam shook his head. "I checked that whole book; this page wasn't in there."

Keres shrugged. "I don't know, Sam. Maybe it shows everyone something different. It's the only page I saw when I looked."

Sam sighed. He stared down at the scar on his hand, wiping his thumb across it. "What about you? She'll kill you if she finds out you helped me. And I imagine it would be the worst torture she can think of."

"You're right. That's why I want to come with you."

"To my world?" Sam was surprised. "Won't she just pull us both back?"

Keres turned the page over. "Look, the artifact will provide a magical shield around us. She won't be able to find us."

"This is just what I need. But—"

"I know. But the marriage won't be real. You won't finish the ceremony. You'll be free to be with Annabelle." Keres tried his best to reassure Sam.

"This is what I've been looking for. I just hate how close I'm cutting it." Sam looked into Keres's eyes. "Thank you."

Keres gave Sam a half smile back.

Sam looked down at the floor.

"Is there something else, Sam?"

"No . . . yeah. What if someone"—Sam dropped his voice as low as he could—"eliminated the problem?"

Keres shook his head. "No, Sam. That would never work. Her magic senses danger. You'd never get close."

"But I'll be standing right—"

"No!" Anger sat behind Keres's eyes, something Sam had never seen before.

Sam snapped his lips shut.

"I'm sorry, I didn't mean to yell. It's not worth the risk."

Sam nodded. "All right."

Keres put a hand on Sam's shoulder, then tucked the parchment back into his pocket and left.

Sam spent the rest of the morning running over the plan in his head. Keres would mark an object to be blessed with the magic, and once it touched Sam, the two would join hands, and he'd be home.

He thought of everyone who had helped him in this castle of thorns, and what he would be leaving behind. The Dark Queen not getting her way would not go over well. He couldn't bear to think of the trouble he'd be imposing on everyone.

The door creaked open, and Mara entered. *Mara.* She was the closest to him in the palace. What if the Dark Queen took all her anger out on her? Maybe Sam could get her out too.

Mara began dusting the room as Sam tried to find the words to say.

"Good morning." Mara smiled.

"Mara, we need to talk."

"Oh?" Mara stopped working. "Go on, then."

Sam shook his head. "Not here." He walked out the door and peered down the hallway. It was clear, so he motioned for Mara to follow. He walked as quickly as he could to the gardens. When Sam opened the hidden door and stepped into the tunnel, Mara gasped. The two remained silent as they descended the staircase. Once they were safe inside the room at the end of the tunnel, Mara spoke.

"You did it, didn't you?" She wore a wide grin.

Sam nodded. "How'd you know what I was doing?"

"From the way you talk about Annabelle. It's true love. No way you would just leave her behind."

Sam smiled. "All the pieces are falling into place, but I want to talk to you about something."

Mara threw her hands around Sam. "I knew you'd figure it out. I'm so happy for you."

Sam returned the hug. "Thank you, but I want to ask you something." Sam searched for the right words. "You won't be safe when I leave."

Mara put her hand on her hip. "I'm not safe now."

Sam sighed. "I know. But once I leave, I'm worried the Dark Queen will take it out on you. I can't let that happen."

Mara raised a brow.

"I want you to come with me."

Mara's jaw dropped. "What? No, I can't do that."

"You have to," Sam pleaded with Mara. "She'll kill you. Torture you."

Mara shook her head. "Sam, I haven't been able to tell you, but I'm leaving."

Sam was taken aback. "You are? Where? How?"

Mara crossed her arms. "You and I aren't the only ones fed

up with the Dark Queen. I've heard rumors of renouncers somewhere deep in the forest. I was going to leave tonight, once everyone had gone to bed. The Dark Queen will be distracted by the bonding ceremony, so by the time she notices I'm missing, I'll be long gone."

Sam couldn't believe it. "There's an uprising?"

Mara nodded. "So, how did you figure it out? How are you going to get out of here?"

Sam told Mara everything: about the magic he stole from the Dark Queen, about the magic book that told Keres about fading between worlds, and about the wedding ceremony.

"Are you sure it's safe?" Mara asked.

"I think so. It's my only plan; I get one shot. If the bonding between the Dark Queen and I is completed, I can never escape her."

Mara crossed her arms. "It sounds risky. I've never heard of that sort of magic. Fading within our world, yes, but never across worlds. Just when the Dark Queen brought you over with Chaos."

"I know it sounds impossible, believe me, but this is my only chance. I have to do this. I have to get back to Annabelle." Saying her name felt different. He was so close, her name no longer felt like a dream.

Mara sniffled.

"What's wrong?" Sam asked.

"I just realized; I'll never get to see you again." Her eyes welled with tears, but none fell.

"Oh, Mara." Sam wrapped his arms around her and hugged tight. "I'm going to miss you, too." Sam's eyes began to fill as well. He wasn't sure when it happened, but at some point, he began to care about this place, and he hated that he was going to miss it.

"Is this goodbye? I'm not ready." Mara squeezed tighter.

"I know." The two stepped apart from each other. "I guess this is goodbye. You're leaving soon, I suppose?"

Mara nodded. "Yes. I should ready my things now and leave at dark."

Sam took a deep breath. "Then goodbye, my friend. I will miss you deeply."

Mara smiled, lip quivering. "Goodbye, Sam. I love you." She hugged Sam again, and this time, the tears streamed down his cheeks.

"I love you, too."

The two made their way out of the tunnel and back into the palace. As soon as Sam opened the door, he bumped into someone. "Keres. Hi."

"Good afternoon, Sam." He looked around Sam. "And Miss Mara." Mara gave a slight curtsy. "Enjoy the rest of your day." Keres gave Sam a nod and wink, then headed into the garden to continue his duties as advisor.

Sam filled with content as he watched Keres leave and looked at Mara as she turned to her chambers. With the plan set and Keres's success, at this time tomorrow, he would have Annabelle back in his arms. Everything was going to be all right.

CHAPTER TWENTY-SIX

She couldn't believe her ears. It was bad enough when she'd overheard Sam and Keres talking about escaping, but a rebellion was certainly a problem. *Why is Keres helping Sam? How has he even found the time? He barely leaves my side.* Dorthea wasn't sure how to deal with her advisor, but she would come up with something for both him and Sam—a punishment suitable for each. But that would be after the ceremony. Her plan to bring balance back to her world would still work.

Keres walked into the Dark Queen's chambers. "Your Magnanimousness," he said with a grand bow.

Dorthea quickly buried the thoughts deep in her mind, keeping them hidden from herself, as to not lead Keres into suspicion. Keres stood there like an idiot, twisting his ring back and forth. How did none of them think that she, the Dark Queen, would know all the enigmas of her own palace? Fools.

Absolute fools. She'd kill them all. Rage built inside the Dark Queen as she looked upon Keres's face. She would wait and take complete pleasure in the downfall of each of them.

The Dark Queen smirked at Keres. "What do you want?" She said the words with such a sharp tongue she nearly spat on him from across the chambers.

"My queen, I am here only to serve you. In fact, I bring good news. Sam has agreed to the marriage bond. Your plan is working perfectly."

Dorthea fought to keep all thoughts of what she knew out of her mind. He had a way of reading people, and this was not a time Dorthea wanted Keres to know a thing. She put on her best surprised face. "Well, that is good news. It makes me feel all warm in my little heart. I want this bonding ceremony to be grander than anything in our world's history. Understood?"

Keres bowed his head. "Of course, my queen. You will have all that you desire and more. The staff has already begun plans to make it a splendid event."

"I hope so. You know how I hate to be disappointed. You have not failed me yet, that is the only reason I keep a pathetic excuse for a man like you breathing at all. If one thing falters during the ceremony, it will be your head."

"Naturally, Your Majesty." Keres bowed low.

Unsure as to how Keres had found a way to solidify his plans, the Dark Queen grew suspicious of the traitor before her, who looked rather unworried. *Put it away. Do not lead him on.* "I have changes to the ceremony I want made. I will make my list and send it along with Gadriel. Have him here before dinner to look over the changes."

"I will, Your Majesty. This will be a day that lives on in your heart forever." With that, Keres turned on his heel and left the Dark Queen's chambers.

CHAPTER TWENTY-SEVEN

Panic woke Sam the day of the ceremony. Everything was in place, but Sam had a bad feeling in his gut. He could barely swallow as the lump in his throat grew, taking deep breaths to calm the jitters. He tried to reassure himself that the plan would work, that Keres did what needed to be done, but his nerves were still getting the better of him.

Sam got out of bed and went into the washroom, walking right past the wedding attire Gadriel had made him try on the night before. Running himself a hot bath, Sam slid in, hoping to alleviate some of his worries.

The water soothed his skin. Sam grabbed different oils to smell but decided to forego any scents. After washing up, he got out of the tub, not feeling any better. Naked, he stared at the ensemble he was expected to wear to the ceremony. He had to admit he looked good in it, but he could hardly stomach staring at it now. Sam didn't want to go home as anyone but himself, so he walked past the clothing again and grabbed his own. After putting on his jacket, he patted the pocket, hoping to coax his nerves. He grabbed his notebook out of his pocket and flipped to the last page full of tallies—too many tally marks—and made the last tick: twenty-nine. Looking at himself in the mirror, he almost chuckled at the sight of himself barefoot. That was how he'd come to this world, and that's how he was going to leave it.

Sam went over the plan for the millionth time in his head. All he had to do was go along with the ceremony. Keres had explained the procedures to him the night before. As long as he wasn't marked for royalty, the bond wouldn't be complete. Before that happened, Keres would run up, grab Sam's hand, and touch the enchanted object.

It was so close, Sam's stomach bubbled with anticipation. His mind began to wander, going through scenarios if the plan didn't work. He had no backup plan. If they were bonded, he would be stuck forever.

The room spun as Sam thought about the plan failing. He had to have a plan in case things fell through. He wouldn't be the Dark Queen's prisoner forever. He couldn't live like that.

Sam made his way to the kitchens, where the staff ran around preoccupied with wedding preparations. He scanned the room to find what he had come for. Right in front of him was a large knife, and no one was near it. Sam slid toward the knife and attempted to grab it when someone grabbed his wrist.

"Now, what could you need this for?" Gadriel glared at Sam.

Sam had no retort.

"Get out." Gadriel shoved Sam out of the kitchen, ruining his plans.

Sam thought of where else he could find a weapon in the palace that the Dark Queen wouldn't have locked up tight. A thought sprang to mind, and Sam sprinted up the stairs. He could hardly keep up with his feet as they carried him to the mysterious room of earthly objects. Sam halted in front of the stained glass door. He reached out and turned the knob, but it was locked. With the hope Ju might be inside, Sam began pounding on the door before realizing how foolish that was. Ju wouldn't be able to hear him.

Backing up to the opposite wall, Sam prepared to bust through the stained glass. He took off at full speed when he caught Ju in his periphery, and veered off course last second, slamming into the wall. "Ah!"

Ju ran to Sam, bewilderment on her face as her wide eyes questioned Sam.

"I know that was stupid, but I need inside, and it's locked. When I saw you, I tried to stop myself." Sam rubbed his aching shoulder.

Ju sighed, shaking her head. She grabbed Sam and helped pull him up, then opened the door and ushered him inside, motioning for him to sit in the chair at Ju's table. She put up her hand to him, and he stayed while she went to the back to get something.

Sam waited for her to disappear behind a pile and used the opportunity to get what he came for. He ran to the pile of weaponry and found a knife he could easily conceal on his body. Once it was tucked away, he ran back to the chair, sitting down right as Ju came back into view.

She held a box of vials of different shapes and colors, then pulled out several and mixed them together. Ju rubbed the concoction over Sam's shoulder—his pain instantly disappeared.

"Wow, you really are the best healer." Sam rotated his shoulder, and still no pain.

Ju shook her head, averting her eyes before looking him in the face.

"How not? My pain is totally gone." Sam held up his hand, and she grabbed it. "What's wrong?" Ju snatched another vial and poured it over the cut Sam had gotten from the blood-bonding ceremony. The scar faded to nothing. "You are definitely the best."

Ju smiled but insisted she wasn't.

"All right, whatever you say," Sam teased.

Ju laughed and put her ingredients away. She lifted her hands and wrote through the air. "I'm sorry about today."

Sam became somber. "Thank you."

"Shouldn't you get changed?"

Sam shook his head. "I'm done pretending to be anyone but me."

Ju smiled and placed a hand on Sam's shoulder. "Good luck."

"And to you, too. I hope Octavia comes back soon." Sam saw the glimmer behind Ju's eyes as she nodded her thanks.

Sam stood from the chair, returning the bow Ju offered, and headed toward the door. He glanced back once more to see Ju bury her face in her hands and cry; he left her to be alone.

Sam put his hand over the knife inside his pocket. He had it. He had his backup plan. Now to head back to his room to wait for Gadriel to take him to the ceremony, a feeling of slight calm over him.

As Sam paced the room, his stomach bubbled and churned

in anticipation of being escorted to the ceremony. Sam scanned the room one last time to ensure he hadn't forgotten anything. He had his notebook, his clothing, the vial, and the knife tucked away in his pocket.

When he heard a faint knock at the door, his mouth went dry. "Come in." He was surprised when Mara stepped into the room.

Sam bolted toward her. "What are you doing here? I thought you would be gone by now."

Mara shrugged. "I thought so too, but the Dark Queen had us on special duties last night for wedding preparations, and I couldn't go. But I can slip out the back once the ceremony begins. I'm sure the Dark Queen will be too focused on you and her new powers to worry about where I am. Gadriel sent me to get you."

Sam nodded in agreement. "Let's go."

The two walked silently down the corridors toward the rose garden. Mara grabbed his hand, and it comforted him more than he could ever put into words.

When they opened the door, Sam became speechless. A hedge had been removed to reveal the edge of their world in all its swirling colors. Columns wrapped in twinkling lights continued throughout the garden, and the bushes were adorned with more roses than he'd ever seen. Palace members sat in chairs on either side of an aisle that was laid with a deep blue cloth and lined with rose petals.

Sam winced at the Dark Queen waiting for him at the edge of the garden, stunned by her attire. The white gown covered her from neck to toe, form-fitted on top and in her sleeves. Gold embroidery embellished her bust, and a large gold belt accented her waist, where the rest of her dress flowed away from her body and draped on the ground. Her usual crown had been replaced with a simple golden tiara. The only other jewelry she wore was her sapphire ring. Beauty, in a way he'd never seen from her before, radiated from the Dark Queen. For once, she let her own beauty shine through, rather than speaking it with her body. She looked remarkable, and Sam hated her for it. This was supposed to be him and Annabelle.

He closed his eyes and pictured Annabelle. This was all for her. If he wanted to get back, he had no other choice. Inhaling a deep breath, he quietly whispered on the exhale, "I can do all things . . ."

Sam walked toward the Dark Queen, catching Mara in the corner of his eye as she stepped away from him into the background, and prayed for her.

Partially up the pathway, a bustle broke out from the crowd, and shouting ensued from several attendants. He scrambled for an explanation until he saw a figure being dragged toward the Dark Queen, a look on her face as evil as he'd ever seen. His mind raced, coming up empty as he opened his mouth to speak. The Dark Queen bellowed above them all.

"I know we are here for my glorious day, but I have some business to see to first. We have a traitor among us."

Sam thought he might be sick. She'd figured him out. Keres was somehow caught.

"My own servant girl."

No. No!

Mara was thrown to her knees before the Dark Queen, looking at Sam pleadingly. Sam began to run to her but was grabbed by several guards around him. He threw a punch and hit a man straight in his jaw, knocking him to the ground. He elbowed another in the back of the head, and as he lifted his fist for a third time, the pain of someone kicking the back of his legs dropped him to his knees. He tried to heave himself up, but he was outnumbered. With his hands held behind him, he struggled to think of what to do. Hoping to give himself just one moment of surprise against his captor, he stopped fighting.

Sam pushed off the ground and jumped up, catching the guard holding him by surprise, and wriggled himself free. He plunged his hand into his pocket and grabbed out the knife, keeping the guard an arm's length away by swinging it back and forth.

His eyes locked with the Dark Queen's, and she stared at him blank-faced. Sam only had one thought run through his mind. He turned the blade toward himself, pointing it at his throat. "Let her go, or you lose me." Sam could hardly control his breathing as he waited for the Dark Queen to listen to his demand, praying his plan would somehow work.

The Dark Queen scowled and laughed. Sam closed his eyes. *I'm sorry, Annabelle. I will always love you.* He pulled on the knife, but just as it touched his skin, it disappeared from his hand. When Sam opened his eyes, he stared at the Dark Queen, who now held the dagger, mocking Sam.

Guards tackled him to the ground before he could make a move. The full weight of the men pressed down on top of him, his face pushed into the dirt. He couldn't move anything but his eyes; he could only watch in horror as the Dark Queen grabbed Mara by the hair, lifted her blade, and slashed.

CHAPTER TWENTY-EIGHT

Sam froze in place. He couldn't move, couldn't breathe, couldn't think. The only thing his body would let him do was stare at the river of blood now flowing toward him, pouring from Mara's throat. No. How could she be dead? She had a plan to leave and help the renouncers against the evil in the kingdom. Sam stared at Mara's face. Her eyes, once so full of hope and joy, now a void as they pointed directly at Sam. Her mouth hung open, though he never heard the scream. Bright red hair sprawled around her, joining the pool of blood on its journey down the pathway.

Sam wriggled his arms free and reached for Mara. The trickling blood coated his hands and trailed up his arms.

Tingling coursed through his body, which built to fear, and landed on rage. He should have killed the Dark Queen while she slept in her bed, while he had the chance. Then Mara would still be alive. If he'd looked harder, he could have figured out another way home.

He'd failed his friend.

All at once, Sam's body shook with the heaves of his tears as he mourned his dear friend, his sister. *Mara. Mara.* Sam didn't know what to do, so he curled up as the guards got off of him. The Dark Queen did not allow Sam to stay in his grief and demanded he rise to continue with the ceremony. Sam didn't move. His ears rang as his anger grew.

Mara is dead. Mara.

Nothing made sense to Sam anymore, if something so pure and innocent could meet such a horrific end. He had just seen her. Hopeful—about to leave her life of pain behind and start anew with those like her in the forest. But she would never get there. Mara was dead. It was all his fault.

All he could think about was the young girl who so selflessly helped a stranger in his time of need. This was the consequence. Sam choked back his tears and wiped the snot from his face to look back at Mara, hoping it wasn't true. But as he looked up, he only saw Mara's lifeless body being dragged away by the guard Sam had elbowed in the back of the head. He watched helplessly as he pulled Mara's body farther from Sam's reach.

Not that he could do anything for her now.

When Sam saw where the man planned to take Mara, he leapt to his feet without a second thought. He tried to run to her, to save her, but stayed in his place thanks to the Dark Queen's magic.

"No! No! You can't do that to her!"

The Dark Queen scoffed. "I can do whatever I want with the traitor. And what does it matter to you what I do with her? She's dead."

Hearing the words aloud was a punch to Sam's chest. He stood as the man heaved Mara's frail corpse over his shoulder and tossed her into oblivion, where she would be lost forever.

More tears flooded Sam's eyes as he watched Mara's body float out as if on water, distancing her from Taegaia. It took only a moment until she was too far to see.

"I'm sorry, Mara. Goodbye."

He would never be able to have a proper goodbye for this young soul, a girl so deserving of a grand sendoff that only received the treatment of taking out the garbage. He could not bury her as she deserved, so he said his final goodbye and turned his attention back to the Dark Queen. "How—" Sam choked on his words and cleared his throat. "How could you? She did nothing wrong!"

The Dark Queen simply shrugged. "You really think anything goes on in my castle without my knowledge?"

Sam dropped his head. She must have known about the tunnel underneath her palace. How had he been so stupid? She'd overheard everything. Wait. She'd overheard everything. *Oh no.* Sam frantically searched for Keres among the crowd. He looked to the Dark Queen's side, back at the entrance, and even near the edge. Keres was nowhere to be seen. "What did you do to him?"

"I couldn't have him ruining my special day, now, could I?" The Dark Queen nodded to a guard near her, who stood and walked toward the Dark Queen, carrying chains in his hands. Heartache overcame him as Sam watched another friend dragged to the Dark Queen and dropped before her. *No. Please, God, no!*

This couldn't happen again—he wouldn't let it. With all his

strength, Sam charged the Dark Queen. He hurled himself toward her but stopped midair, as if slamming into an invisible wall. "No!" Sam fought with all he had, but it was no use. The Dark Queen put a stop to him with no effort and had Sam moved across the path from her. Sam looked down at Keres, his heart ripping out of his chest at the thought of losing another friend.

"Don't worry, Sam. I won't kill him yet. A traitor of this level requires something special. He will witness the power you give me through our bond, and then he will be my first kill with my new power. What an honor for you, Keres." The Dark Queen motioned for the man behind them to begin the ceremony.

Persephone slithered down the Dark Queen's arm and grew, wrapping herself around Keres tightly as he cried out in pain, his face turning purple.

A band near the front plucked away at their instruments, creating a shaky melody of fear and panic. As the song ended, Sam's head was turned to look upon the Dark Queen.

The man she had motioned to spoke. "We are here today to bond our beloved Dark Queen, Dorthea Emagine Rayzel, to her chosen and willful suitor, Samuel Ellis Jones, who just yesterday morning gave his unwavering consent for today's events."

Why did I do that? Why did I agree to this? They're all going to die. I'm going to die. Annabelle . . . Sam's knees shook at the realization he would never again see Annabelle. She would never know what happened to him; she would think he abandoned her. The thought killed him. These last moments of his life would be pure torture, having to think about his failure, knowing he would not have one last look upon Annabelle's beautiful face.

"You have invited friends from across the land to mark this joyous day in our history . . ."

Sam choked at the sound. *Joyous day.* This was the worst day of his life. The loss of his mother and brother held that slot for so many years, but watching Mara's life leave her body—it was like reliving that moment of horror all over again.

". . . creating a bond that cannot be broken between two lovers. You two will share your lives as one, bringing forth heirs to our kingdom to serve nobly as those who have come before, and those who serve now."

"What?" Sam couldn't have heard that correctly. *Heirs?* Surely the Dark Queen would kill him following the ceremony —after killing Keres.

"Of course. While I gain power from you, I also must bear your children for my queendom to continue long after me. We will raise them to rule as I have. No mercy." The Dark Queen turned back to the man. "Please, continue."

Sam's chest lifted faster and heavier as he realized how much worse this was. Keres would be dead; he would have no friends and no help in escaping this land. The Dark Queen would force herself on him to produce heirs to her evil kingdom. What could he do? His only choice would be to take the Dark Queen's life, or his own.

"Now that we have gathered before the Blessed Iris in ceremony, we shall mark Samuel as a ruler of our kingdom and solidify the bond."

"What? No!" Sam panicked as his arm was pulled from his side toward the Dark Queen. He tried to fight, but it was no use. Her magic was too powerful. "Please don't." She was going in the wrong order. She was going to bond with him before he could leave. Even if he made it home, the bond would be too powerful for the cloak of the fading charm to hide him.

Another man walked up the path, rolling a large iron vat toward them. As he got closer, Sam could see something that made every bone in his body shake. There was a branding iron soaking in the fire.

Mark. Oh God, he said mark. "What are you doing?" Sam tried to retract his arm as the man pulled the iron from the vat, revealing a glowing rod in a shape that matched the Dark Queen's tattoo—three roses.

The Dark Queen snickered. "All royals are marked, Sam." She pointed to the roses on her chest. "And everyone will know you are mine, wherever you are."

Sam struggled, but only internally, as his body did not budge. It wasn't until that moment he too wished for magic as he stared into the Dark Queen's eyes, the man rolling back his sleeve as the iron rod hovered above his arm. If he could, he would send daggers from his eyes to hers. He shrieked as a splatter grasped his skin.

Sam looked to his friend, probably for the last time, just before the brand was thrust onto him. Keres went wide-eyed as the rod scorched Sam's forearm, and it was the last thing he saw before a flash appeared. His ears rang loud, and his nostrils filled with the scent of soap and pine trees.

CHAPTER TWENTY-NINE

Annabelle jumped as Sam sprang from his trance-like slumber. He'd been asleep for an hour, and when he awoke, he was hysterical. Sam frantically looked around, Annabelle grabbing his hands to calm him.

"Shh, Sam, I'm right here," Annabelle spoke in soothing tones. "It's all right now."

Sam locked eyes with Annabelle and pulled her close, refusing to let go. "I made it. I can't believe I made it."

Annabelle could feel Sam's heart pounding through his chest. Though she was confused, she held him tight. "You made it. You're here with me."

Sam released Annabelle and looked at her face, then pulled her in for a kiss. Annabelle returned it, realizing after a moment that they were out in the open in the middle of the day, showing affection. Annabelle instinctively pulled away and looked around her, but her friends only smiled back. She had nothing to fear here—she looked back at Sam and kissed him again.

When the two pulled their lips apart, they sat on the forest floor, staring into each other's eyes. Annabelle wanted so badly to know what Sam had been through, to understand everything. "Sam, my love, what happened?"

The joy turned into agony.

She'd never seen Sam like this before. He had always been so strong, holding her up when she needed him. She wrapped her arms around him as he curled up and sobbed, stroking Sam's back, trying her best to comfort him.

Ace walked to them and dropped on his knees, letting his presence be known. He sat quietly with a still face.

All Annabelle could hear was Sam's heartache, the sound she'd made when she thought she had lost him at the jailhouse. Sam slowly calmed himself and looked at Annabelle again. She prepared herself for what he was about to say, the knot in her stomach tightening in anticipation.

"I'm sorry, Annabelle."

"For what? You didn't do anything wrong."

Sam hung his head. "I didn't want to. She made me. It was the only way I could get back."

Annabelle lifted Sam's chin with her finger. "Sam, just tell me what's going on."

Sam sighed before speaking, barely taking a breath as he tried to get the words out as fast as he could. All the things Sam said sent her head spinning. He talked about a desert of black sand, of trees so tall they touched the clouds. He told her of the creatures he'd seen with wings and pointed ears and bright-colored skin. He told her all about the people he'd met, the friends he'd made. He stuttered, seeming to skip a detail he couldn't yet share. His secrecy sent a knot into her stomach.

Then he told her about the Dark Queen and why she'd taken him. About how she wanted to marry him, how she tortured and killed so many innocents. Annabelle didn't know what to think. It was all too much. Aside from stories, she'd never heard Sam talk like this. Sam's voice dropped low, and he told Annabelle about how he'd gotten back to her, about the wedding. Annabelle gasped—she didn't think she was ready for what came next.

"Belli, I had no choice. It was my only way home." His eyes were glued to the ground.

Annabelle contemplated what to say next. Her head spun as she tried to make sense of everything Sam had said. She looked at Sam. He seemed smaller somehow. "Sam, I love you."

Sam gazed up at Annabelle, looking unsure. "You forgive me?"

"There's nothing to forgive. You came home to me."

The two embraced again, and she could feel a weight released as he collapsed into her.

"Mara . . . Mara . . ." Sam kept repeating the name over and over.

"Who's Mara?"

Sam told Annabelle about his young friend, who'd taken care of him, given him hope, and helped him feel free in his prison. Annabelle was in tears as Sam ended his recount of the girl floating off into nothing.

"Sam, my friend," Ace finally spoke, and Sam turned to face him, Annabelle holding his hand tight. "Do you know how much time passed since we were banished?"

Annabelle watched Sam search for an answer. "No, but I don't think long. I never heard your names mentioned, but the Dark Queen seemed to have recently become . . . that."

Ace nodded, a hint of a smile still on his face. Then Ace looked to the oracle. "Is there any way we can get back? There may still be hope our family is there, alive."

The oracle shook her head. "I'm sorry, but without a piece of the Dark Queen's magic, there is nothing I can do."

Sam went wide-eyed and jumped to his feet.

"What is it? What's wrong?" Annabelle asked.

"Where's my jacket!" Sam frantically rifled through the bags until he pulled out the tattered remnants of what used to be a jacket. "Oh, no, please." He reached in and dug around, pausing abruptly before slowly pulling his hand out of the jacket. Annabelle couldn't tell what Sam was thinking as he held up his hand and opened it.

A small vial with what looked like shimmering black sand sat upon Sam's palm. Ace gasped and ran over to Sam. "Where did you get this?"

Sam shrugged. "I took it." Elroy made his way over then, his eyes wide in disbelief.

Annabelle looked at everyone's excited faces. "What is that?"

Sam looked at Annabelle, and his face instantly turned sour.

"What's wrong?" Ace asked.

Sam kept his eyes locked on Annabelle's. "This is a vial of the Dark Queen's magic."

Annabelle smiled. "Well, that's good news, isn't it? Now they can go home."

Sam shook his head. "I brought it back for you."

Annabelle was confused. "For me? Why?"

The oracle approached Annabelle and grabbed her hand. Her eyes turned white as she squeezed tighter. After several moments, the oracle gasped and dropped Annabelle's hand. "I don't know how I missed this before."

Annabelle looked back at Sam, her heart pounding. "Sam, tell me, what's going on?"

Sam cleared his throat. "Belli, I was never in danger. My curse . . . the curse was for you. You're going to die."

Annabelle couldn't believe what he said. "What? No, I feel fine." She looked at her friends, whose faces had turned somber.

"Sam?" Annabelle's voice quivered.

"I'm so sorry. Without this magic, you'll die. It's the only way to break the curse."

"Actually," the oracle chimed in, "there is another way."

The group looked to the oracle. "How?" Elroy asked. His voice was strained.

"You can stop a curse at the source."

Annabelle had never been so confused. "What does that mean? What's even going on?"

Sam walked over to Annabelle and grabbed her hands. "The Dark Queen is worse than you could imagine. She uses power and fear to get what she wants, and tortures anyone who stands in her way. She cursed you to force my hand. My only way back to you, to save you . . . she manipulated it all. I only got back because Keres thought one step ahead of her. But this is what will save you."

Annabelle dropped her voice to a whisper and saw her friends out of the corner of her eye. "But what about them? They'll never get home."

"I can't risk this, Belli. You will die. I can't let that happen."

Annabelle turned to the oracle. "Tell us more."

The oracle gave a slight bow of her head. "If the one who cast the curse is destroyed, so is the curse."

Annabelle looked into Sam's eyes. She could see him struggle with what to do. "Sam, you know we have to do this. These are our friends, and there's a whole world that is suffering."

Sam swallowed hard. "I know." Sam stroked Annabelle's cheek with his thumb. "I know. But it's not that simple. Belli, we might not ever come home. And if we do, everything we know could be gone. By hundreds of years."

Annabelle contemplated. "Would that really be the worst thing? Right now, there's nothing for us here. Even a life out west . . . it's not guaranteed for us."

Sam nodded and gave her a half smile. "I hate how you're always right." He leaned in and kissed her cheek.

The two turned toward Ace and Elroy, who stood looking down at their feet. Sam spoke. "Your world is real. It ain't something to be left to the Dark Queen, or for you to never see your families again. We can get you home and still save Annabelle."

The brother's faces lit up.

"Are you sure?" Elroy asked.

"Absolutely," Annabelle said.

Sam walked over to the oracle and handed her the vial. "We're going back to Taegaia."

The oracle took the vial and smiled, pouring out the magic into her palm and lifting her hand. "Ready?"

The group nodded. The oracle waved her hand around until a shimmering wall appeared in front of them. Annabelle shook as the four joined hands and approached the door. Just as they were about to step through the Rip, the oracle called out, "Remember—kill the queen, break the curse, save Taegaia."

Annabelle gazed up at Sam, and met a roaring sense of determination in his eyes—of hate. It was a look that didn't belong to her Sam.

"Kill the queen," Sam whispered.

Sam tugged Annabelle's arm. As she went through the shimmer, everything went black.

THE ADVENTURE CONTINUES ...

SEA OF CHAOS

BOOK TWO

COMING SOON

ABOUT THE AUTHOR

Raised in the picturesque Puget Sound, Megan Aldridge attended Pacific Lutheran University, where she earned her degree in Communications with a minor in Music on the trombone. At the age of nine, Megan knew she wanted to be a writer—and a professional baseball player . . . and an FBI agent—and as she grew up, her love and passion for stories never left. Considering her childhood obsession with dragons, it was only natural she broke into the Fantasy genre. Megan currently lives in Southern Georgia with the love of her life and their adorable dog. *Queendom of Chaos* is her first novel.

www.meganaldridge.com

instagram.com/megan_aldridge1
youtube.com/MeganAldridgeAuthor
facebook.com/387293725726392

CPSIA information can be obtained
at www.ICGtesting.com
Printed in the USA
BVHW081943050622
638965BV00005B/116